Charlie Card

TARA HOWE

DEDICATION

*Written in loving memory of my grandmother,
Eleanor J. Travis, for all the ways she
touched the lives of others.*

"The past is our definition. We may strive, with good reason, to escape it, or to escape what is bad in it, but we will escape it only by adding something better to it."

~Wendell Berry

ACKNOWLEDGMENTS

I want to thank all of the family and friends who helped make this dream a reality. Thank you for the editorial support, and for the overwhelming encouragement over the years. I also want to acknowledge the homeless boy and girl who inspired this novel. Wherever you are today, I hope you're safe and warm, and living out your happy ending together.

CHAPTER 1

"So, how much do we have?" I ask, while Liam counts our change. I shoot him a weary look and rub my hands together as we make our way down Boylston Street.

"Not feckin' much," he replies. "But it's enough."

We pass the nameless man in his usual spot, pressed against the entrance to Copley Station, in front of the Boston Public Library. He's a black man in his late-sixties, with iron-gray hair that looks like straw. Liam says he's "not the full shilling," which is Irish-speak for crazy, but I'm not so sure. The only thing I know is that he likes to keep to himself, and I certainly can't fault him for that.

I nod and he nods back. His equally ancient dog, a black and brown mutt, perks his ears at the sound of our footsteps crunching by in the snow. He starts to cough like an old man.

"This is brutal." Liam remarks, ignoring the old man and his dog as we pass. "Everyone's on holiday, and there's no way to make any money." He jingles the coins around in his pocket. "It's effin cold."

"Now there's the Christmas spirit," I say as I shove my hands in my coat pockets. He laughs.

At a brisk walk, we pass storefronts decked out for Christmas, playing the muffled songs of Burl Ives and Nat King Cole. "BK for dinner?" I ask, as we approach the brightly lit Burger King sign.

"Where else would we go?" Liam answers, as he jumps in

1

front of me and opens the door. The heat and greasy smell of fried food closes over me like a tidal wave. I shut my eyes and breathe it in.

We go inside and stand in line. I blow hot air into my hands and wait for them to thaw. Liam nudges me and points at the boy in front of us. He's watching me curiously, with his chin on his mother's shoulder. He smiles at me and I smile back.

"Fuzzy," he says, pointing at my beard. I scratch my chin and laugh. His mother turns around and eyes me skeptically. She pulls him to her chest.

"I'm not gonna steal your kid," I mutter under my breath. The woman takes her toddler to the next register.

"I can help whoever's next," the cashier with the crazy hair calls out. Her expression changes when she sees us. Her smile says 'how can I help you', but her eyes say 'here we go again'. Apparently, she can tell we're homeless.

Liam steps up to the counter and empties his pockets, revealing a small mound of change. "Two whopper juniors and two small fries," he orders.

"And two waters please." I add. The attendant pulls our money to the edge of the counter and ignores me as she counts it. "We usually get it from the fountain machine, we just need the cups," I explain as I point to the stack behind her.

"I know where the cups are," she says as she punches something into the register. "And water on the machine is broken today. I'll have to get it from the tap." She sighs loudly.

"Oh, I don't know if I can drink unfiltered water," I respond jokingly. She rolls her eyes.

When she returns with the water, she doesn't make eye contact with either one of us. She just slides our food across the counter and moves on to the next person in line.

"She was a right eejit, wasn't she?" Liam poses as we settle into one of the bland vanilla booths. I unwrap my burger and dump my fries onto the white paper.

"Something like that." I respond, smiling at his choice of

words. I bite off half my burger and swallow it much too quickly to enjoy. My stomach reacts like a pulse, pumping it through my digestive system like blood through the ventricles of a heart. It only ignites my hunger.

I pop the last of the burger in my mouth and reach for my water. I watch the cup fall, in slow motion, onto its side and then pour over the ledge of the table. My throat burns with thirst. This is exactly why I take the glass half-empty approach to life. That way, when the cup spills over you're not as upset.

"Ye can have some of mine," Liam offers, sliding his cup across the table.

"Thanks buddy." I take a sizeable gulp of his water while I watch him attack his fries. He eats like they're going to wander off his plate. He chews quickly, smiling at me out of the corner of his eye. I smile back sadly.

Liam's like a brother to me. I found him by the river one night, getting the shit kicked out of him by a piece of trash named Kain. It was by no means a fair fight. Liam's skinnier than a chicken bone, and Kain's a dirty fighter. I eye the unsightly evidence over his left eye. The scar stretches halfway down his cheek.

It's no surprise Liam's a target of ridicule. He's as Irish as a leprechaun, with freckles and pointy ears, and an accent as odd as his face. I don't know why, but I liked Liam instantly. I look across the table at the tall, gangly goof with fiery orange hair. Maybe it's because he's broken like I am.

We linger over our empty wrappers until the first closing announcement at 10:45. "I could eat about another six of those," I say as we walk reluctantly to the door. A hard-edged wind welcomes us home, blowing sand and newspapers and taking my breath away as it whips through the black night. Steam seeps from the grates in the sidewalk. I zip my jacket and glance up at the John Hancock Tower, glowing with the light of a thousand offices. Workaholics burning the midnight oil. What I'd give to be one of them right now.

Growing up, my parents were on welfare. We lived in a trailer and had a constant supply of food stamps and free school lunches. That doesn't mean we had heat, or electricity, or even food in the refrigerator most days. My father liked to trade the food stamps for alcohol. My mother used what little we had left to buy junk food. She fueled the obesity she faulted me for.

I needed an escape back then. My job at McDonalds provided that for me. It meant a hot meal before school, money to buy clothes that fit, and the social interaction made me feel like I had friends. I only had that briefly, though. I got fired when my parents stopped giving me rides. I tried to walk it once, but I was so sweaty and exhausted by the time I got there they wouldn't let me inside. I was a fat dude. I got winded walking to the cupboard to get a Twinkie. Two miles was a little much.

Aside from the weight, not much has changed for me. I'm still poor. I still want to escape from my life. Life on the streets is like *Groundhog Day*. You have nowhere to go and nothing to look forward to, aside from your next meal. Time stands still. I'd do just about anything to be employed. I'd wear a suit, a costume, a hair net, a face mask. If it meant I'd have a job, I'd shovel anything, anywhere, and I'd do whatever it takes to keep it. Besides, what could possibly be more humiliating, and pay less, than what I do now?

CHAPTER 2

We wander aimlessly toward Boston Common, past a series of trees strung with tiny white lights, shivering in the dark. I kick a pile of snow. "Where to?" I finally ask.

"I need to get sozzled, that's all I know. The drink is my only comfort these days." Liam looks at me with cheerless eyes, hugging his jacket to his chest. His comment stings.

"How about Downtown Crossing?" Downtown Crossing is a shopping area near the theater district. I like it this time of night because there isn't heavy foot traffic and it gives us a place to hide.

"Sounds good to me."

We walk down the narrow cobblestone street that leads to our destination. We walk by a woman selling her services, and she starts to proposition us. She has crows feet and a fake orangey tan. She snaps her gum and walks circles around us. I can tell she's as high as a kite. When we tell her we have no money she storms away.

Liam and I sit on one of the concrete planters in front of the food court. The area is desolate and dark, except for the streetlights casting slabs of yellow light on the snow. Luckily the wind isn't as bad here. The buildings keep it out somehow.

Liam removes a bottle of cheap whisky from his bag and uncaps it, taking a long, desperate pull. He knows better than to offer me some. I don't touch the stuff because of my father. I don't mind it when Liam drinks though, because he's a happy drunk, and he needs someone to look after him when he gets out of hand. It gives me a purpose.

We sit there in comfortable silence for a while, our breath hanging in front of us like lace. I pick at the soles of my sneakers, flopping loose in one long, rubber strip. They glued them together for me last spring at the Boston marathon, but the wetness of winter ate away at the adhesive.

I ran the marathon last year for shits and giggles. I took the free shuttle to Hopkinton and ran as a bandit, without a number. There was free Gatorade, oranges, power bars, music, and every few miles they'd tell us the score of the Red Sox game. It was amazing. Everyone held up signs and cheered us on and for those three and a half hours, I actually felt good.

At the end of the race they gave out bags of food—drinkable yogurts and fruit and crackers and granola bars and cheese—and these silver foil blankets that are really warm. They had a free medical tent and they took care of the blister that ran the entire length of my foot. They bandaged up my bloody nipples. I got shin splints, side stitches, and I puked twice. But it was still one of the best days of my life.

Since I came to the city four years ago, I've grown four inches and dropped close to a hundred pounds. The constant hunger was part of it, but exercise was another. It didn't take long for me to realize you fight to stay alive on the streets. Kain wasn't the only one to beat me up. They all did. They pummeled me until I couldn't take it anymore. I was sick of being tormented, and angry, *so angry*, at everyone and everything. Working out was my escape.

"So, what's the craic, friend?" Liam's eyes are warmer now, and his cheeks have a rosy glow.

"Craic?" I eye him skeptically and give an easy chuckle. Sometimes I think the buzz is contagious. My head feels lighter now, and I didn't touch a drop.

"I've never used that one before? Ye know, craic. News, gossip, whatever you kids are calling it these days. What's new with you?" He takes another drink and flashes an impish grin. Liam is the definition of a light weight, probably because he weighs a buck forty soaking wet.

"Same old same." I slide the elastic further down my ponytail so I can tug my hat tighter around my ears. The chill is starting to set in.

"Yer a good fella, Charlie," he says, patting my back."

"Right back atcha buddy."

"I know I don't say it enough, but I'm lucky to have ye. If it weren't for ye, I'd be pulp by the river."

Liam's referring to the fight with Kain. When I saw it, I stepped in immediately. I had to. I knew the poor chap on the ground didn't have much time.

Liam lifts his bottle in a toast to me. "To friends."

"To friends," I echo casually, lifting my imaginary glass. Case in point: Liam's a happy drunk. The more sauced he gets, the sappier he becomes. At first it made me uncomfortable; but I'm used to it by now.

"Charlie?" He sits straighter, wiping the silly smirk off his face.

"Yeah?"

"Are ye scared to die?"

I let the words sit in my mouth a minute. Death has always scared me. I don't think your soul moves on. I don't believe in an afterlife, so the prospect of dying is terrifyingly final.

"I'm not." He answers. "It's a welcome alternative to this feckin' place." He leans back, crushing the spruce tree. "What's yer thought on cremation?"

"Cremation?"

"Yes, burning dead bodies and scattering ashes, all that gas." He props the bottle on his knee.

"Why are we talking about this?" I ask uncomfortably.

"Just answer the question, gobshite."

"I guess I never really thought about it."

"I want to be cremated." He says with resolution.

"Ok," I answer, because there's nothing else to say.

"If I die before ye, Charlie, will ye burn me? Scatter my ashes somewhere?"

I hesitate, blowing warm air into my tattered, fingerless

gloves. This is morbid. "Fine," I appease, to prevent the conversation from going any further.

I'm thankful for the group of college girls approaching. A new focus. They're all bundled up in pea coats and bright scarves, clicking along the cobbled street in their heels.

They pass by, laughing, obviously inebriated and walking arm in arm. One of them catches my eye. She's tall and leggy, really hot. I stare at her but she doesn't make eye contact. It's like we're invisible to them.

"Wow, did you see the blonde one?" I ask once they're out of earshot. Liam shakes his head, clearly not impressed, so I fight the urge to continue. They start singing as they turn the corner.

"I can play a Christmas song," he offers, breaking out his harmonica. He brings it to his lips and starts to play. I sit back and close my eyes.

Liam's very talented. He makes twice as much as I do on an average day because of that thing. He runs through a gamut of songs, some I know, some I don't. I recognize Jingle Bells and Hark the Herald Angels Sing, Frosty the Snowman, Rudolph the Red-Nosed Reindeer. He makes it seem effortless, even after heavy consumption of alcohol. When he's not looking I take the bottle of whisky off the ledge and tuck it in his bag.

While he's playing, a middle-aged couple walks by holding hands. They're talking in low whispers, with their heads close together, not paying attention to anything but each other. *Fuck I'm lonely*, I think to myself. Liam watches me with a serious expression. He looks from me to the couple and back, letting out a long sigh. I'm sure he's lonely too.

"What do you think they'll serve tomorrow?" Liam asks. He's referring to the Christmas Eve luncheon at South Parish Church. We go to their soup kitchen every Tuesday night, but since Christmas Eve falls on a Tuesday this year, they're serving lunch instead of dinner. This allows workers to spend the holiday with their families.

"I don't know. Probably same as last year. Roast beef,

potatoes, boiled vegetables, pie." It's a mouth-watering image, and I pause to wipe the drool off my lips.

"What was Christmas like as a boy?" Liam asks inquisitively.

"Not the happy occasion it is now, that's for sure."

"Same shite?"

I wiggle my feet, trying to get sensation back in my toes. "No, it was worse. My parents told me Santa didn't come to our house because I was such a bad kid." My eyes settle on an illustration of Santa Claus, done with window paint on the face of a store across the street. "I was actually relieved when I found out he wasn't real."

Liam nods, his eyelids starting to droop.

"No wonder I have more issues than a Playboy magazine." I joke. "What about you? What were the holidays in Ireland like?"

"There is one I remember." His eyes get distant before the smile reaches his lips. "I was a young fella, living with a couple in Dublin. They couldn't get pregnant," he explains, holding the harmonica tight in his lap.

"In Ireland, on Christmas, you decorate everything with holly. We put holly all over the house, in every room, even outside, and they told me the fairy folk came out at night to find shelter in the branches.

"I kept watch for those fairies every night, but they never came. Then one night my foster parents brought me outside to see the berries were gone. They said it was the fairy folk that ate them. I was awful sure of it at the time," he says. Telling the story makes him happy. There's a glimmer of something I've never seen before in his eyes.

"They let me light the candle, too. Another Irish tradition is that you leave a candle in the window on Christmas Eve, welcoming Mary and Joseph and other travelers into the home. We ate roasted goose and sausages and pudding, and then after the meal we put out milk and raisin bread and unlocked the door.

"They taught me that a traditional Irish Christmas lasts

twelve days. Every day they gave me a small gift. One day they took me to the pictures. On the twelfth day they gave me this harmonica." He shivers and retrieves his bottle of whisky. The joy leaves his face.

"The oul wan was pregnant two months later and they sent me back." He holds the bottle high. "Nollaig Sona Duit, Merry Christmas," he cheers and drains the rest.

~~~

Liam passes out shortly after that. I bend down and lift him onto my shoulders, thankful for the fact he's so thin. I carry him to the side of the building and set him down, giving him the protection of an awning. As I put him on the ground he embraces me back fiercely. I want to cry.

My body's numb, and aside from the deep throbbing in my fingers and toes, I can't feel a thing. It's now freezing rain, and the drops are so cold they shatter like glass when they hit the ground.

The worst part about living on the streets is that there's no familiar place to go back to. You can never really relax or get a restful night's sleep. There's nowhere to call home. At least in my trailer I had that.

I take out the wool blankets they gave us at one of the shelters. I lay one over Liam and the other over myself. I'm on the line between asleep and awake when I hear yelling from a group of men walking by. They're carrying briefcases and wearing suits, swaying from side to side as they walk through the square. I duck under my blanket to block out the noise but they see me. The tall one nudges his friend and starts laughing, pointing me out.

"Look, it's a hobo!" He calls, looking to his friends for support. "Should I give him some money?" He digs into his pocket and pulls out a fistful of change. "On second thought, why should we work sixty hours a week, while they sit there expecting handouts?"

I stare back at them blankly, my fists clenched beneath the

blanket. I remind myself there's only one of me and four of them.

"Oh look, they're gay," the other one exclaims, laughing at his own pathetic joke. The other two eye each other reluctantly, and then urge the first two along.

"Merry Christmas, bottom feeder," the first one shouts as he throws his change. The coins sting like fish bites on my ankles. He spits when he walks by.

"Fuck you!" I yell when they're too far away to hear. Liam stirs and rolls over, tugging the blanket over his head. I frantically collect the sixty-five cents. Then I lie back down beside him and try to fall asleep.

CHAPTER 3

I wake up on Christmas Eve morning to sub-zero temperatures and concrete so cold, it penetrates my bones. I squeeze my eyes shut, willing it away. When I finally sit up, I find Liam pissing on the building a few yards down.

"Morning," I shout, clutching the blanket to my chest.

"Mornin,'" he calls back, zipping his fly. "It's feckin cold out here!"

I nod in agreement and rub my face, sitting upright against the wall.

"The clock down the way said seven o'clock, so we better move out, lest there's a line."

I remember our upcoming lunch and start to salivate, licking my lips. They're so dry and cracked they itch. I scoop up a handful of dirty snow and shovel it in my mouth, trying to sate my thirst.

"Alright, let's go," I say as I zip my blanket inside my pack, alongside the limited contents of my life.

We immerse ourselves in the morning buzz of the city—burping buses and taxi cabs, overusing their horns. I watch the ebbs and flows of people going to work on Christmas Eve. The girls wear leather coats and brightly colored scarves. The guys have on expensive jackets and carry briefcases. They all listen to headphones. It's a sea of businessmen and women, all carbon copies of each other. I count twelve people typing away with gloved thumbs on their phones.

We cross the freshly salted streets and make our way toward Beacon Hill. Soon the high-rises turn to old-fashioned post lights and dark cinnamon brownstones with American flags out front, snapping in the wind. Living the American dream, I muse with sarcasm.

South Parish is on the flat of the hill, where it stands like a castle, with intricate windows and sharp edges of red and tan brick. For some reason, churches make me uncomfortable. It's something about the jagged steeples, high ceilings, and eerie, almost cult-like chants that creep me out. I eye the building from afar and get a chill.

Already, there's a ribbon of people twisting down the street. We jump in the back of the line and wait, while my stomach roars with hunger

"Hey Charlie," someone shouts from the front of the pack. He smiles at us and waves eagerly. It's Shaggy, an ex-marine who wears long matted dreadlocks and walks around in army fatigues. He's a real nice guy, but a few nuggets short of a Happy Meal. We see him at soup kitchens and the occasional shelter, and he'll tell us stories about his dog, Scooby. They all happen to be Scooby Doo episodes I remember from childhood.

I wave back and then look around at the rest of the crowd. There are a few new faces, but most of them I've seen before. There's Cory, the girl with the shaved head that gives me dagger looks all the time. She's standing in line with a group of people I don't recognize. Luiz is standing in line a few people behind her. He's a middle-aged man with crooked teeth and bad breath. Story has it that he moved here from Mexico with his wife a few years ago, and then she kicked him out for another man. He only speaks Spanish and he's drunk most of the time so he smiles a lot. He seems like a decent enough guy.

"Weeee, toot toot!" A voice calls behind us. Liam and I turn around to find Ethel, or Beth, or Harriet (her name changes depending on the day) wheeling her shopping cart toward us. I reach out and grab it before she rams it into my heels. The cart is full of plastic shopping bags and soda cans and other miscellaneous junk she's collected over the years. I think she has some form of dementia. I back away because she reeks of urine.

"Howya Ethel." Liam dips his head in greeting.

"It's Harriet!" She croons, and then starts to dance around her cart, lifting her skirt a little too high. Her face reminds me of a dried fruit.

"I've been workin' on the railroad, all the live long day..." Ethel habitually breaks into song. I think Liam has a soft spot for her, because he saddles up beside her and joins in on his harmonica.

"Oh look, carrot top has a girlfriend." Kain says as he comes up beside us. Harriet screams and hits herself. "Shut up, old bird," he says as he pushes her and swipes Liam's harmonica.

"Hump off," Liam says as he reaches for it back.

"What's the matter migrant? You don't like me making fun of your gal?" Kain laughs and dangles the harmonica over Liam's head.

I can't stand it when he bullies him like that. I walk up to Kain and grab him by the neck, slamming him into the tree beside us. "Give my friend his harmonica back or I'll make you wish you were dead." I knock his head into the tree for emphasis.

Kain takes a swing at me and I back away. He's not much bigger than Liam. He's just a skinny, trashy white guy with a big mouth and an even bigger ego. People are only afraid of him because he packs heat. I know he wouldn't be stupid enough to pull out a gun here.

Kain shoves me. "You don't know who you're messing with," he barks as he backs away. He gives me a sinister look and tosses the harmonica over his left shoulder. Liam fetches it like a golden retriever.

"We're done here." I retort.

"You're a dead man." Kain says as he pats the coat pocket where he keeps his weapon. I nod with a come-and-get-me grin. He growls and pulls a pack of cigarettes from his jeans.

14

He lights up in front of me, takes a drag, then crushes out the butt on Liam's bag.

It kills me that he comes to the city and steals money from us when he has enough at home to buy cigs. That's definitely the point he's trying to make. Kain lives in one of the subsidized housing projects in Jamaica Plain. He has a home. Yet he's determined to come to our neighborhood and take our hotspots, lie to our people. I once heard him telling a group of tourists that he needed the money to pay his son's medical bills. Kain doesn't even have a kid.

I glare at him, ready to deck him if he gives me another reason. Lucky for him he doesn't. He just flips me off and takes his sweet time walking to the back of the line.

~~~

As it approaches noon, I watch the front door, waiting anxiously for it to open so we can go inside to fill our bellies and get warm. It's like watching paint dry. My eyes dart from back to front, front to back, scanning the crowd for familiar faces.

Someone in the front of the line catches my eye. It's a man, maybe my height, with a face so mangled it's hard to stomach. It looks like someone took a torch to it, and all of his features melted together in a mass of dimpled flesh.

I cringe but I can't take my eyes away. He's holding hands with two young kids, a boy and a girl, one on each side of his body. They're both happy as clams. They don't seem to notice their father's deformity.

I wonder what his story is. Did his wife die? Was he born like that? It could have been a car accident or a bullet to the face. Whatever it was, it will take some serious reconstructive surgery to fix. An operation I'm sure he doesn't have the money for. For the first time in a long time, I feel lucky.

The boy leans into him and hugs his leg. Then he reaches around and takes his sister's hand, pulling her away from Dad and onto the lawn. They have to be related, they look too much alike. I'm sure they look like their father, too, but you can't tell.

The two of them chase each other until they're breathless, falling into the snow in a fit of giggles. I see a flash of black wool in my peripheral vision. The girl in front of them turns around. She has curly blonde hair and the bluest eyes I've ever seen. She's stunning.

She kneels beside the kids and pulls an egg of silly putty out of her bag. The kids open it, and fight over it like it's the coolest toy in the world. She takes it from them and warms it in her hands. When they reach for it impatiently, she flashes a breathtaking smile of exultation, one that will be engrained in my mind until the day I die. She's beautiful.

"Liam, look." I elbow him in the ribs until I get his attention. We've never seen this girl before. I wonder if she's homeless, like us, or from a low income family. I don't see anyone else with her.

"Ow, what the feck." Liam looks at my face. "What's the matter with ye? Yer all shook looking."

"Over there, look at her." I point, not thinking that she'll catch me. She looks up and smiles because she does.

I duck my head and look away. Liam chuckles with an odd, almost resentful expression on his face. "I'm scarlet for ye, fella. You took a reddener when you saw that one."

The girl stands up and looks the mangled man in the eye. She doesn't flinch. Instead, she makes friendly conversation while they wait for the doors to open. I can't tell what he's saying, but it must be funny. The girl tilts her head back in easy laughter and I feel an unfamiliar pang of jealousy. The wrinkly indentation where the man's lips should be curls under in a smile, and for an instant he reminds me of an elephant. Spit dribbles down his chin but she doesn't seem to notice. It hits me that I'm jealous of a man in this condition.

"I've never seen her before," I think aloud as I watch her. Her cheeks are red from the cold. She tickles the little girl, making her curl up like an armadillo. Her giggles pierce the air. The younger brother fights for her attention, standing behind her and pulling at her coat. She pulls him into her lap.

"You're acting the man as usual." He says with a casual air of indifference.

"No, this is different. *Look* at her."

"She's a fine thing, but nothing special."

Nothing special? I do a double take. She's heartbreakingly beautiful, and young, maybe sixteen or seventeen. That's the age I was when I left home and hitchhiked to the city.

"Oh look, they're opening the doors." Liam's voice sounds far away.

The women adore her as much as the men. As everyone files into the church, the ladies chat her up. The men are too intimidated to speak, but like me, they can't take their eyes off of her. Liam must be blind.

"My name's Sarah," I overhear her say as she crosses the threshold, disappearing from my sight. She sounds kind.

Liam and I enter the church shortly after that. The place is so warm and comfortable it brings moisture to my eyes. The hallway opens up into a big room full of tables dressed with white tablecloths and upside down paper cups. Off to the side is the assembly line where you get your food. The smells are intoxicating—gravy and butter and cranberries and freshly baked pies. I inhale deeply and imagine this is what it feels like to be high.

I scan the room but I don't see her anywhere. My stomach sinks. Then I see a flash of blonde rounding the corner on the opposite side of the room, coming from the bathrooms. The woman she was originally standing behind waves her over but she declines appreciatively and walks toward the back of the line. She approaches us because we're near the exit, blocking the door. She pokes her head around us but the area is so concentrated she can't get through.

"I was trying to be nice and go to the back, but I didn't realize the line was so long," she says to me with a giggle. "Look, it snakes all the way down the street!"

My breath catches in my throat. She's even prettier up close. Her skin is pale like Liam's, but she doesn't have the magnitude of freckles, just a small dusting on her nose. I stop staring and pull my hat off out of respect. "Please," I say softly, signaling for her to cut me in line. She looks from the door to me, accepting her lack of options, and then smiles sweetly. She smells nice, sort of a mixture of sweat and flowers.

"Thank you very much," she replies, and shimmies into the open space in front of me. Her head barely reaches my chest. I look at her and I feel self-conscious. My hair's greasy and matted, I surely have hat-head, and there's probably food in my beard. I haven't showered in weeks so I know I'm rank as hell.

I curse myself for being so unremarkable, with my dark hair and gray eyes. This girl's completely out of my league. She's the majors and I'm little league. She's the Marriot and I'm Super 8. I don't stand a chance.

My only comfort is the fact we've made our way to the serving table. Everything looks so good. Sarah scoops a big mound of mashed potatoes onto her plate. Before she can move on to the next thing, the Asian girl in front of her turns around. "'Scuse me. No Engrish." She points at her baby. "Food. Eat." She brings an imaginary fork to her mouth. "Baby."

"Oh. You need baby food," Sarah translates. She waves over a volunteer and explains the situation. The woman nods and smiles, and pulls the young mother out of line. She says "mgòi" to Sarah as she walks away. The line starts to move again.

Liam smacks me and gives me a hard time for not paying attention. "Were you even listening to me?" He asks. I turn around to see what he's babbling about and I catch the toothless man behind us staring at Sarah's ass. For whatever reason, it makes my insides burn with fury. I glare at him until his eyes hit the floor.

"Easy down, hardshaw. Jealousy's not a flattering color on ye." Liam jokes. That strange, almost envious, expression returns to his face. "What's with ye today?"

"He was staring at her and I didn't like it." I say between

clenched teeth.

My eyes follow Sarah as she carries her plate to one of the tables. Despite my unease, I feel this odd compulsion to talk to her, like a magnetic force willing me in her direction. It's a feeling I've never experienced in my twenty some-odd years of life. I've never been with a girl before so I don't know the first thing to do. I'm absolutely terrified.

I get my food and linger around her table, waiting for Liam and weighing my options. I wish I'd cleaned myself up. Liam shoots me a look that I return with a shrug. Repulsive or not, I have to talk to her. I shake away my insecurities and sit down across from her. Hopefully she has a whale's sense of smell. Liam sits beside me and sighs.

"Hi again," she says sweetly as she looks from me to Liam. "Thank you so much for letting me get in front of you in line, I really appreciate it."

"Not a problem," I answer quickly, sounding as nervous as I feel.

Liam rolls his eyes.

"My name's Sarah, what's yours?" She asks, taking a bite of her roast beef.

"Charlie," I respond, no longer feeling hungry.

"It's nice to meet you Charlie." She looks at Liam. "And your name?"

"Liam." He says frigidly, as he continues to shovel food into his mouth.

"That's a nice, Irish name. I like your accent," she says politely as she returns to her lunch. My eyes linger on her until she looks up from her plate. I look down. A smiling woman with white hair comes to our table and fills our cups.

"Thank you," Sarah and I say in unison. I look at her and blush.

"The people are very nice here." Sarah concludes. She tips her head back to drink, and her hair falls like a scented waterfall down her back. "The church services are nice, too."

"Really? I bet the—"

"Shut your gob, Charlie, and eat," Liam interrupts. "You

don't even believe in God."

I hang my head quietly in submission. I feel Sarah's eyes burning into the top of my head. I start to eat my meal. Once I have a taste, it takes hold of me and I can't stop. I finish off the entire plate in less than three minutes.

When Liam and the rest of the table go back for seconds, I decline their offer to join. Like Sarah, I'm "going to let things settle." Obviously Liam sees right through me and gives me a discouraged look, but I don't care. I'm sitting here with the nicest girl I've ever met.

I lean back in my chair, a muddle of nerves, and try to think of something intelligent to say. Luckily Sarah beats me to the punch. "So are you from the area, Charlie?" She questions, like it's the most regular thing to ask a homeless person.

"No, I'm from New Haven, Connecticut." I answer while I fumble with my napkin, my eyes fixed on the table.

"Oh wow, Connecticut! I heard it's beautiful there. What's it like?"

Where I'm from it's filthy, dark, and depressing, that's what it's like. "Um, it's nice," I lie, cursing myself out for being so painfully awkward. Unfortunately, it isn't something I can control.

"I'm from Maine. The way life should be," she says with a giggle. "Have you ever been?"

I shake my head and say, "No, but I hear it's nice." I look up and make eye contact, getting that anxious jolt to the heart.

"We call it God's country. But Boston's beautiful, too." Unlike me, she seems so relaxed, so laid back. She rests her elbows on the table and looks me in the eyes, smiling. She prods me further.

"So what brought you to Boston?" She asks, leaning in closer.

The brittle, cranky, white-haired man with the bamboo cane pops into my head. I crack a smile. "My grandpa brought me here for a Red Sox game when I was little. One of the best days of my life."

I can see myself sitting there beside him in Fenway Park,

dangling my legs off the seat and watching him with adoration as he teaches me about the game. He told me what 'can o' corn' was, and how to throw a curveball, and he explained to me why Babe Ruth was one drunk, brilliant sonovabitch. We ate hotdogs and peanuts and swore at the umpires until it was time to go home. It was a really great day.

"What was he like, your grandpa?"

"He was a hard old man, actually. He was a General in the military back in his day and I guess it made him that way. For whatever reason, he seemed to like me quite a bit. He said he'd always wanted a son and all he got was my mother." I pause to gauge her reaction. It stays the same so I continue.

"He took me fishing, and to football games and he'd tell me funny jokes about Grandma. She died when I was in second grade. That's when Grandpa came to live with us. He refused to cook or clean for himself, and no one else would take him in so my mom had to.

"I was excited about it, but my parents weren't. They hated him, actually. One morning I woke up to find him slumped over the kitchen table, face-down in his scrambled eggs." I get that familiar sinking feeling in my chest. "I yelled for help and shook him and tried to wake him up but my mother told me he was dead. I asked if he'd eaten something bad and she dared me to try it, but it had a funny smell. I think they poisoned him." Sarah's eyes bug with surprise.

"Your parents? Your mom would kill her own father?"

"I wouldn't put it past her to do something like that. One time she told my father to shoot the dog because I wouldn't clean my room."

"He didn't really do it?" She asks nervously. I'm not sure why she's so interested in all of this. Her eyes never leave my face, not once. I keep my head down as I speak, pushing around crumbs on the tablecloth, but I see her looking out of the corner of my eye.

I nod sadly in response to her question, staring at my plate. She looks down too.

"So what did you do? About your grandpa, I mean."

There's something about her that puts me at ease. "What could I do? I was a kid. I cried and I yelled and then my parents beat the living sh—daylights out of me. 'Real men don't cry', my father said as he railed on me. He told me if he ever saw me doing it again he'd shoot me like he shot the dog."

Sarah reaches her hand across the table and rests it on mine. My pulse quickens. "I'm really sorry Charlie. I'm sure your grandpa's in a better place now, with your grandma; and your dog too." Even though I don't believe what she's saying, there's something about her words that makes me hopeful.

The others make it through the line and back to the table. When they sit down, I close up tight like an oyster and Sarah returns to her meal.

"The line's awful long up there. We had to wait behind all the first timers passing through." Liam says with his mouth full.

Sarah looks troubled. "Should we get up? Let them have our seats?"

"Nah. This is why ye get up early and wait in line. That 'ill teach 'em." Liam swallows his food.

The homeless population has grown significantly since the recession. I steal a glance at all the people huddled in the corner and sigh. One woman holds a plate under her chin to catch crumbs as she devours her meal standing up. I sit there and weigh my goodwill against the gnawing hunger that still plagues my stomach. I take one look at Liam and then go up for seconds.

~~~

I sit back and pat my pregnant-looking belly. I'm so comfortable it's hard to care about anything else. Liam says I could be carrying twins in there. What can I say? When you're starving all the time and then you gorge yourself, your stomach swells.

The volunteers let us loiter for a while and enjoy the heat. Lots of people stay, and most of them make their way over to

Sarah. She's one of the most tolerant people I've ever met. She hasn't made judgments about anyone, not even Shaggy, who's currently talking her ear off about his escapades. She just smiles and nods and humors him with stories of her own. If he's annoying her, she hides it well.

Kain saunters over and puts his hand on her shoulder, claiming his territory. I notice with satisfaction that she shies away from it. Shaggy jumps like he's sitting on hot embers and Kain steals his chair. *What did you do to him?* I mouth across the table, but he just laughs and sits down.

Kain puts on a good show, trying to convince Sarah he's not the scum of the earth. I stare him down, gripping the tablecloth because I know better. He winks at me when she's not looking.

Before I get a chance to cut in, they tell us lunch is over. We're herded to the door like cattle as they start to clean the room. I catch Sarah filling her napkin with leftovers. She slips the wad in her purse. *Clever girl.*

"It was really nice meeting you both," she says when we reach the doorway. She has a way of making people feel good without even trying. We walk out together and she turns to me and smiles, leaning in for a hug. "Bye Charlie," she says as she wraps her arms around me. "Merry Christmas."

"Merry Christmas." I echo back, stunned. When she pulls away I just stare, like a freak, because I don't have the balls to tell her what I really want to say. *I have to see you again...*

Before I can say it, she's waving goodbye and scurrying away, in a hurry to go wherever it is she's going. I watch her leave with an anxious feeling, wondering when I'll get to see her again. I look at Liam with wide eyes. He puts his hand on my shoulder in silent support, and then leads me away from the church. I walk away warm and full of something I can't put into words. I've never been in love before but I suspect it feels something like this.

CHAPTER 4

Since I met Sarah on Christmas Eve, I haven't been able to think about anything else. I've been having vivid dreams about her. Dreams that have me waking up gasping for breath. I have to find her.

I stand on the Esplanade, knee-deep in snow and panting like a dog. I just finished a five mile run along the river that didn't go so well. Liam and I fasted for two days so we could save enough money for razors and alcohol, and it did a number on my energy. I'm so weak I can barely stand. I reason that if a foot of snow won't stop me, nothing can.

I jump up and grab a tree limb, angling my face to the pearl gray sky and falling into a pull-up. It looks like it's going to snow again. I pull myself up with a groan and wonder where she is and if she's safe. I can't get her out of my head. I've never had feelings like this before. When I was five, I asked my mom after a beating if she loved me as much as she loved my father. She took a drag off her cigarette and told me no. Maybe this is how she felt about him.

I land ungracefully on my hands and knees. I never liked running in the winter. My body parts are frozen, my throat's scraped raw, and there's snow in my sneakers. I brush off a bench with my sleeve and sit down. Running is one of the few things that makes me feel this way: giddy, charged, alive, and yet completely miserable at the same time. I take a deep breath and watch my breath curl into vapor around me.

There's something oddly beautiful about the snow, the way it sparkles like diamonds in the sun. I fashion a snow cone out of the pile beside me and suck it dry. After the thaw, the water fountains will work again, but until then I have to work with what I have. The outhouses are out of service right now, too. I meander over to the side of the boathouse and pull down my jeans. In the meantime, I'll continue to squat in the snow like a dog.

~~~

"Hey buddy," I shout to Liam, who's bent over his journal in the food court of the Prudential Mall.

"Howyiz," he says as he slams it shut and smiles up at me. "Did you leg it in the snow?" We both turn to the window. It looks like we're in a snow globe with quarter-sized flakes.

"Yeah, it just started. If it keeps coming down at this pace, they're gonna close down the trains." I pull out a chair next to Liam. "How's the crowd?"

He just shakes his head. Post-holiday crowds are usually a good way to make money, with all the returns and cashed checks and good cheer; but the fact Liam's sitting in the food court with his nose in his journal should tell me something.

"You think it's the storm?" I ask.

"Yeah. It's supposed to be a bad one." His eyes follow a man in a gray suit, walking to a table with a plate of Indian food.

I dig a book out of my bag, trying to ignore the ferocious growling in my stomach.

"*The Jungle* again?" He asks mockingly. "I don't know how ye read that. Yer a lot smarter than me, I suppose. I was lost on the first page."

"It's a good book, man." I defend. "And I read a lot." My eyes wander to the diner and his heaping plate. I can smell the curry from here. I breathe it in and lick my lips. "Besides, I can relate to the main character. He has a shit life like ours— living in poverty on the streets of Chicago, struggling to find work and support a family."

"He's not real, Charlie. It doesn't count." I shrug. "I'm so feckin' hungry!" Liam exclaims, reading my mind.

"Me too." I open and close my fist. "I was thinking, maybe we could go to a day-shelter and clean up today. You know, get some chow, wash our clothes," I suggest.

"Good idea. I'm awful manky." He pinches his nose for emphasis.

"Yeah, me too. I can't even remember the last time we showered." I shake my head in disgust. I don't even want to know Sarah's first impression of me.

The man in the gray suit keeps checking his watch. He pulls out his phone and does something to the screen with a stylus. He grumbles and checks his watch again. Guys like him have more important things to do than eat.

I watch him like a hawk, as the fork goes from his mouth to the table and back, a mere exercise, a waste of time. He's not enjoying it. He looks stressed out. I can't pull my eyes away. I'm the opposite of discreet. He looks over at me and I pretend to read, shoving my nose in the book.

My theory proves true. His plate is half-full when he dumps it in the trash and takes off at a near sprint for the doors. My only set back is that these trash bins have swinging doors, so it's harder to pull stuff out. If I'm lucky, the receptacle is full enough that I can reach in and pick it off the top.

I stand up and make my way over to the garbage can. Liam nods, appreciative that it's me and not him this time. I'm fully aware of the middle-aged woman in the back right corner, staring me down with disgust as I bend down and feel around, up to my elbows in garbage. The employees working the counters whisper and laugh. It makes me anxious but I'm much too hungry to stop.

My fingertips find the edge of the plate. I curse when I realize it's tipped, because the bag's only half full. That makes things much more difficult. I drop my head back and dip in my other arm, pressing my chin against the swinging door. I try to scoop as much rice back onto the plate as I can, ignoring the other things my hands are touching.

The smells seeping out are fresh, and mostly spicy-sweet, but I catch a whiff of something off that makes my stomach curdle. I gag reflexively. I've dug through dumpsters a hundred times worse that this, so I have a pretty strong stomach; but sometimes you just can't control it.

I maneuver the plate out of the awkward opening. There's a chicken bone on the plate that I pluck off, along with a balled up napkin covered in sauce. For the most part, it looks like the meal he was eating five minutes ago. Unfortunately, I've only recovered about half of it. Liam and I will only get a couple bites each, but hopefully that will be enough to calm our appetites until we get to the shelter.

I drop the paper plate in front of Liam. "You owe me," I tell him as I hold out my arms, now covered in spicy orange sauce. He jumps up to grab napkins and forks.

It's hard to care that everyone's staring when all I can focus on is the food in front of me, and how badly I want it. My stomach grumbles in anticipation. I sit down and shovel in a fistful of rice, moaning in ecstasy, sauce dripping down my chin, thinking to myself, hey, this is how the Indians eat it.

CHAPTER 5

It's still snowing when we get in line at the St. Peter Center. I'm more content than before, but not satisfied by any means. I shake with anticipation. I can't wait for a hot shower and a warm meal.

I nudge Liam. "Maybe we can start going to night shelters, too. I mean, if it's supposed to continue to snow." He's eyes me suspiciously. "What?"

"Ye hate shelters. Ye said there are too many people and rules and not enough privacy." He lets it process for a minute. "Yer still looking for her, aren't you?"

I shrug and flash a guilty smile. He shakes his head in disbelief. "Ye have a bad dose, my friend. Yer one sick fella."

I grin wildly. "I bought the razors this morning at the grocery store," I announce, changing the subject. "I had just enough, too. Talk about a test of willpower. It took everything I had not to steal a rotisserie chicken."

"Yer in a bad place." Liam says bluntly.

"What?"

"Shaving yer head for a doll?" He underscores.

He's right. I'm going to shave my beard, and my head, because I'm sick of looking homeless. If I ever see her again I want to look less like a Neanderthal and more like a man. I need all the help I can get.

"I can see your woman parts from here," he scoffs.

"Easy! So I like her, big deal. Last time I checked, it's ok

28

to like girls. You should try it sometime."

He winces.

"Stop being thick, Charlie. Ye met her once. She's not yer girl so move on. Yer acting the maggot as usual."

"Agree to disagree, *friend*. At least I have feelings. Do you even know what those are?" I get right in his face. It was meant to be a joke but he doesn't take it that way.

"Hump off!" He says, pushing me back as hard as he can. I stumble and catch myself with one hand.

"What the hell was that for?" I shout. Liam drops his backpack and I do the same. Before he knows what hit him, I have him pinned down in the snow. He tries to push me off but I'm much stronger. I take a fistful of snow and whitewash him.

"Effin' bowsie!" He calls. "I was only slagging ye, get off!" I loosen my hold and he rolls out from under me. Maybe I overreacted, crossed the line. Liam's all I got. It's not his fault he's scared of girls, or jealous that I met one and he didn't. Maybe he's afraid he's going to lose me if we find her again.

"Sorry man," I apologize, getting to my feet. Liam's smile is different, stilted somehow. I cock an eyebrow, questioning it, just before I notice the hand behind his back. He whips a snowball at my face and tackles me to the ground. We start all over again.

I spit and roll him onto his back. The snow swirls around us as we wrestle on the lawn. When we're both too winded to continue, we fall onto our backs and laugh. I can't stop. I'm soaked through and having more fun than I've had in a long time.

We brush ourselves off and get back in line. We're so close now I can smell the food. My guess is spaghetti, or chicken parmesan, because there's a hint of basil, definitely tomato, and mozzarella cheese. This is another game Liam and I play, and one that I never lose. It's to my advantage that I used to be three-hundred pounds.

They make us wash up before lunch because we're both dripping wet when we get inside. The community showers remind me of the locker rooms at the YMCA. Our middle school took us there once in the sixth grade. Men on one side, women on the other.

I take a towel from the stack and stuff my wet clothes in a locker. I cinch the belt on my robe and take out my razors. Some of the shelters provide robes to wear while you do your laundry, since a lot of us only own the one outfit. Luckily, this is one of them. Liam hangs his robe on a hook and drops his towel. "Ye coming?" He asks over his shoulder.

"I'll be over in a minute," I respond to his naked backside. It's bony and you can connect the dots with his freckles. *Don't be mean to him anymore*, I tell myself.

I carry my bag of razors to the sink. I'm not really sure how to use them because I didn't start growing facial hair until after I left, but it looks pretty straight forward. I lean over the sink and bring one to my face, dragging it over the wiry black hair on my chin. The blade doesn't move easily and it burns like hell, ripping the hair from the root, one strand at a time. I curse when the blade catches on something, sending a stream of blood down the drain. A chunk of hair falls with it, and I notice tiny bugs crawling around inside. Disgusting.

I flip over the package to read the instructions. Apparently generic brands don't have those. I splash soapy water on the gash and watch my beard shrink like a wet rag. Hmm, ok, maybe you're supposed to clean the area before you shave it. In the mirror, I watch my cheeks redden at the stupidity. I shake my head and put my face under the faucet. I use the hand soap to grease up and I strain out all the bugs. The next time I run the razor across my skin, it moves like a knife through butter. Mats of hair fall into the white porcelain bowl.

It takes the entire package of razors to finish the job. Plus, I think I clogged the drain. I stand back and examine myself in the mirror. I'm looking back at someone else, someone I don't recognize at all. I can see the sharp line of my jaw bone, and my eyes seem bigger, brighter. I'm not fat anymore. I squint at the semblance of my former self. It's not me.

I run my hand along the smooth surface of my head, wincing as it touches down on nicks and cuts. The bald skin is lighter than the rest of my face, which is tan from exposure to the sun. I feel out in the open. There's nothing left to hide behind and this makes me uneasy.

I clean up the mess and get in the shower. There are two emaciated men inside, watching me as I tilt up the shower head to accommodate my height. Their bodies look like raisins. All the elasticity is gone and the skin just hangs there, sloppy and loose, flopping over their shriveled junk. I try not to look. That's the thing with being homeless. No one here has any dignity left so we strip right down and bare our dirty, imperfect bodies for everyone to see. At least at the Y you have a choice. You can wash up with your swim trunks on and wait until you get home to shower. Here you don't really have that.

To make matters worse, there are a lot of creepy guys that come to these things and they stare, and I mean really stare (head tilts even) at you when you're naked. It took me a while to get used to it, to accept they have mental problems and just ignore it. The first time someone really *looked* at me, I put my clothes back on and showered in them. Everyone laughed at me and I assumed it was because of my weight. The second time it happened, I sent Shaggy to the emergency room with a broken jaw. We've obviously gotten past it but it was rough. I guess he liked his hospital stay so much, he tracked me down and thanked me for sending him there. When I saw those empty eyes I felt terrible. That's why I've been nothing but nice to him since.

Liam looks over, and I see the surprise on his face when he notices me. He goes from six o'clock to noon and covers up in embarrassment. I don't fault him for it. Those things have a mind of their own.

I close my eyes and let the water run until it's scalding hot. The sensation is overwhelming, like a full-body massage. The water sluices over my head, down my chest, between my legs. I roll my neck from side to side and pump a generous amount of soap out of the dispenser, lathering up my arms and legs. It smells like pine trees and spearmint gum, so I try a taste. Not great but I've had worse. I swish it around in my mouth and spit it out while I watch the grime pool at my feet.

"Nice tan lines," Liam jokes from across the shower.

"Shut up. At least I'm not translucent," I call back, catching a glimpse of old balls.

"Kiss my arse." He gives me the finger. "Now hurry up so we can eat." He gets out and wraps his skinny ass in a bathrobe. "Come on."

I ignore him. I plan on showering until I'm pruney. I scrub my bald head and think about Sarah. I turn my back to the entrance and take care of business while Liam sits in the locker room and waits.

CHAPTER 6

If there's one thing I've learned from my stint on the streets, it's that being homeless somehow alters your perception of time. Instead of days rolling into weeks, then months, then years, you find yourself living from day to day, meal to meal. Seconds turn into minutes, minutes turn into hours, and hours eventually turn into days. Somehow the hands on the clock move with more resistance.

It's been a month since I saw Sarah and it feels like an eternity. I'm starting to think I made her up. I ponder this as I feed two dollars into the ticket machine and update the balance on my CharlieCard, Boston's reusable subway pass. She's in my head and I can't get her out.

At the gates, I scan my card and take a seat on the platform. I take a quick inventory of the other passengers. Girls don't usually give me a second glance, but lately, when I ask for train fare, they hand it over willingly. There's a girl looking at me right now. Maybe there's something to be said for the military haircut. The red-head smiles at me and I look away. Whatever it is, girls are still terrifying.

I roll the plastic train ticket over in my hands, dissecting the picture on the front. It's this goofy guy with a sideways grin hanging out the window of a train. Grandpa told me way back when it's supposed to be Charlie, the man from the song (hence the name CharlieCard). He told me it's about a man who can't get off the train because he doesn't have enough money for exit fare. Charlie didn't have it that bad, though. I still remember one of the verses Grandpa sang to me:

Charlie's wife goes down
To the Scollay Square station
Every day at quarter past two
And through the open window
She hands Charlie a sandwich
As the train comes rumblin' through.

The train comes to a screeching halt and I make my way to the front car. The subway is an escape for me. If I ride the T inbound and outbound, and I never leave the station, one dollar and seventy cents buys me several hours of heat. It's a place where I can read my library books and relax and get out of the cold. Sometimes I get on the train and pretend I'm important, like on my way to work or something, and I'm reading to fill the commute just like the people in scrubs and starchy shirts beside me. For those few hours, in my mind, I'm no different than anyone else.

As I walk up to the half-empty train, I recognize with a smile that Keisha's on shift. Keisha's a friend of mine, or at least I think she is. She waves enthusiastically as the doors unfold in front of me.

"Hey Charlie! How you doin' handsome?" She asks, and then her jaw drops. "Oh. My. Lord. Look at you!"

I take the seat to her right, where I usually sit, behind her but still in her peripheral vision. My hand instinctively moves to the top of my head. The hair has grown out since I shaved it, but only slightly. It's bristly but still close cropped, and I have a thin layer of stubble on my face. It just goes to show that I'm not an innately hairy guy. I don't have any hair on my back or chest, and it took me years to get my beard to where it was weeks ago.

"I decided to bic it," I state, pulling my backpack onto my lap. "I figured it was time for a change."

"Well, Mama like!" I feel my cheeks change color. "Look

at those pretty blue eyes you were hidin' under there. Like liquid sapphire. Honey, if I was younger, I'd be all over you," she says with a chuckle, her neck wrenched around so she can see me.

I don't believe her. Keisha always talks to me like that, like I'm something to look at. That's not to say I don't enjoy it when she humors me...

"So was your grandson born yet?" I ask quietly, changing the subject.

"He don't want to come out. She's a week past her due date and still no baby. I'm ready to start a fire under there and smoke it out!" She makes me laugh.

We make our next stop and Keisha talks over the commotion while people file in. She talks about the weather, her dead-beat ex-husband, her landlord raising rent, and this new recipe she tried the other day. I toy with the straps on my pack until she's done. At the first lull in our one-sided conversation, I ask the question that I always know the answer to.

"Any new job openings today, Keisha?"

"Sorry Charlie, not today. But I'll let you know if I hear anything. They have your resume, and it looks great, so I'm sure they'll call once we get out of this damn recession."

The whole sentence is one big lie. First of all, my resume is not great. It's shit. It's hand-written on the back of a bank loan application. Second, if I couldn't get hired as a Boston lobster mascot, where I'd be completely concealed from the public, it's stupid to think I stand a chance anywhere else. And third, they won't call me because I don't have a phone. Or a phone number. Or an address, for that matter. I don't know why I ask.

I thank her politely and pull out my book, trying to hide my disappointment. She continues to talk my ear off while I read. I don't mind. There's something comforting about it anyway.

I glance out the window. We emerge from the dark tunnel and into the light. A cluster of passengers wait at the next stop, clutching their scarves and watching intently as we approach. I keep a watchful eye out for her, always, but once again I'm beyond expectation. She isn't there.

"Look at these angels," Keisha comments, scattering my thoughts. "They just tug right at your heartstrings."

I watch a pair of grubby white kids climb the stairs and sit across from me. The boy helps his younger sister into the seat because she's too small to reach. He looks like he's maybe five or six years old and he holds her hand protectively. His eyes never leave her face.

The girl's adorable. She has chocolate corkscrew curls and brown eyes. She looks over at me with a bashful grin and hides her face in her brother's arm. He says something to her in hushed tones, presumably about me. I watch them from the corner of my eye for a few more minutes, observing their behaviors. I like to people watch.

My attention's broken by a salty, greasy smell wafting from the back car. I crank my neck to find a crumpled red and white bag with yellow arches sitting on an empty seat, ironically beneath a sign that asks passengers to pick up after themselves. I mentally thank the person, whoever it is, for their disregard for others.

I bring the discarded bag back to my seat and dig around inside, finding a handful of fries but nothing else. It's not uncommon for riders to leave behind coffees and half-eaten sandwiches. As the saying goes, one person's trash is another person's treasure.

The boy watches me as I eat. I offer him a fry and he motions for me to give it to his sister. He trusts me. Few people do.

The little girl leans out and takes the fry, licking her lips with anticipation. She makes a loud sucking noise while she eats. Her joy is tangible. You can feel it in the air.

I hand over the bag and her eyes widen with shock. "Go ahead, take it." I say, trying to make my voice sound small and childlike. She takes the bag.

"Say thank you," her brother urges.

"Thank you." She says obediently.

Her brother smiles, watching her eat like she hasn't eaten in weeks. This may be why he lets her have them all. In a simple paternal gesture, he collects the trash from her when she's done.

CHAPTER 7

I've switched trains six times. As it approaches rush hour I spot the Villanuevas, in their authentic Mexican garb, stepping up to the platform. Occasionally, they pick my train and entertain me for a while. The father has this big accordion, and an even bigger smile. One of his sons walks around shaking maracas, while the other one does a jig with his feet and the wife collects change. I can barely stand while the T is moving, let alone do all of that. The accordion squeezes out a Spanish song and I listen with my eyes closed, pretending I'm somewhere else. It's nice.

You see a lot of families from the projects come into the city to earn a living, and you have to respect it. If I was good at something I'd do that, too. I'd much rather showcase a talent than hold out a cup. Liam makes a lot more than me because of his harmonica. When we're together, people look at him different than they look at me.

I take in the darkening sky. It's still early, but I have to meet Liam at Government Center so we can get in line for dinner. We're going to a shelter tonight because it's supposed to be one of the coldest nights of the year. The heater beneath the seat blasts my legs and makes me have to pee. I listen to the music and my eyelids get heavy. I lean my head against the cold window for a second. I'm only resting my eyes…

When I wake up I don't know where I am. I stand up in a panic and shove my way out of the train. I bend over and put my head between my legs, trying to scrub away the images, but thinking of nothing else. The dream was about my father. It was terrifying.

I float in autopilot through the gates, up the stairs, past the man sitting on a bucket, jingling his change, out of the station, and onto the street. I regain my composure when I see the nameless man curled up, absent his dog, on the stairs out front.

I realize with a sinking feeling that I got off at the wrong stop. I'm staring at a Copley sign. I need Government Center. Now I have to walk the rest of the way in the cold. *Dammit.*

I meander away from the station with a chip on my shoulder, trying to remember that I had a good day. It's mind-numbingly cold outside. It hurts to breathe. I hug my coat tight to my sides and step into the crosswalk.

I'm halfway across Dartmouth Street when the girl standing on the other side of the cross street catches my eye. She's back-to, holding the door at CVS. My eyesight isn't great but something about her looks familiar. The blonde hair, the pink plaid scarf, the black...coat. I freeze like a deer in headlights.

It takes the honks of oncoming cars to snap me awake. I run and duck behind the bronze statue of John Copley so she won't see me. Now that I've found her, I have no idea what to do next. I poke my head around the side of the statue, and stare at her like a blind man seeing light for the first time. She's achingly beautiful, even more so than I remembered. Her cheeks and nose are candy apple red, and bright next to the pale yellow curls that spill out of her hat. She laughs easily with a woman at the door. She doesn't fit in here.

The lady smiles at her with a mixture of adoration and pity, sliding a few bills into her cup. Sarah lifts her head, her eyes level with mine. I think she might have seen me. Although, her body language doesn't suggest that she has. She chews on her bottom lip for a minute, takes a deep breath, and then slips inside the store.

I cross the street, keeping a safe distance behind her. I'm nervous. When I enter the store, I spot her in the first aisle, filling her basket with granola bars and bottled water and fruit cups. She looks thoughtfully over her selections and then counts her change to make sure she has enough. My heart's beating really fast.

"Hola Charlie, còmo está usted mi amigo?" I jump when I hear Luiz. I can tell it's him by the raunchy breath. Sarah's head starts to turn and I duck into the next aisle, safely out of sight. Luiz watches me with a puzzled look on his face.

"Hi Luiz!" Sarah says, averting his attention from me. My heart's pounding a thousand beats per minute.

"Holaaa bastante senora. Còmo está usted?" He asks with a toothy grin, leaving my sight. I listen from my shelter of tissues and paper products.

"Bueno, y tu?"

"Muy bueno ahora que I' m aqui con usted, mi senora bonita. Aunque, it' frio de s esta noche." He wrinkles his nose and then scratches his mustache. "Qué usted está haciendo aqui?"

There's a short pause. More Spanish. A polite laugh. She has no idea what he's talking about, nor do I.

"Well I have to go meet someone, but it was nice seeing you, Luiz. You take care of yourself, ok?" *She has to meet someone?* My heart sinks.

"Espero ver su belleza otra vez pronto, amor. Buenos noches hermoso. Estancia caliente!"

Sarah gives him a hug and makes her way to the cash register, while I follow, row by row, at the other end of the store. I stop at the health care products and leer like a creep. It's just so nice to see her. And surreal. She dumps a wad of ones and about another buck fifty in change on the counter, which impresses me. Granted this is a prime location, but that's more money than I usually make in a day. I wonder how long she stood out there.

She collects her bag and her change and she leaves the store. I'm reluctant to follow, but I can't help myself. I give her five seconds and then wave goodbye to Luiz as I barrel out the door.

The cold air hits me like a punch in the face. I crank my

neck from left to right, searching for blonde hair, until I finally spot her crossing Boylston, moving toward the outbound train station that I'd come out minutes earlier. If she goes in there I'm screwed. I don't have enough money for train fare.

To my relief, she doesn't enter the station. She stops a few feet short and sits down next to the mute in front of the library. He doesn't have his dog today. I keep walking so I don't look like a stalker, moving slow and watching them. She opens the CVS bag and gives him the fruit cups and bottled water. She hands him the granola bars. Then she pulls an overstuffed napkin out of her pack and gives him that, too. She laughs like he's saying something funny to her. I'm several shades of confused. Then I see his lips moving and there's actual sound coming out. *He talks?*

In all my time here, she's the first person I've ever seen him talk to. She re-adjusts his blanket and pulls his hat down. I only catch bits and pieces of the conversation from where I stand in the opening to the Old South Church. I pretend to read the mass schedule with both ears open.

She asks about his day and he mumbles a response while shoveling food into his mouth. He looks awful. He's gray and drawn and really depressed, worse than I've ever seen him. Sarah keeps asking him questions. Trying to get answers out of him is like pulling teeth. He keeps asking about Sasha.

I can see they're both shivering. I want to tell her to get out of the cold and go find a shelter, preferably the one Liam and I are staying at. But at that same moment she stands up and says goodbye. She says she's going to pick up Sasha on Wednesday. He looks up at her the way a baby looks at its mother, with a mix of wonder, helplessness, and fear.

Talk to her, I coach as I cross the street and follow her in the opposite direction. The wind is strong, whipping her from side to side as she tries to jog away from it. I finally build up the courage to call out her name but she doesn't hear me. She keeps her arms wrapped tightly around her body and her head down.

I don't like the thought of her out here alone at night. I feel protective of her, like I imagine you'd be with a little sister. I rationalize that I need to know she's safe so I continue to follow her. She takes a turn toward the river. When she walks past the sign that says the Esplanade is closed after dusk, I start to question her judgment. She's too trusting, too naïve. She looks for the best in people and few of the vagrants around here have any good in them to find.

I stop on the stone footbridge over the lagoon and watch from afar. Luckily there was a thaw earlier in the week so a lot of the snow has melted. The river's still choked with ice because of the freeze. It has to be at least ten below zero, or worse with the wind chill factor. It's *cold*. Weather fluctuations in Boston are typical, and very very dangerous.

Sarah's sitting on top of her backpack on the dock, looking up at the stars with her hands clasped together. It looks like she's praying. She's talking in a faint whisper and I try to give her privacy. I only want to keep her safe.

I follow her line of sight to the sky. The air's clouded by my breath, but the sky's clear. You can actually see stars tonight. You're hard pressed to see them anywhere else in the city. It's beautiful.

Sarah snaps her head around, surveying the area. I dive to the ground. With the cold stones against my chest it hits me that I've crossed a line. I have to get out of here. As I get to my feet I hear a rustling behind me. I duck down in a defensive position, following the noise. There's a man walking towards Sarah. I move closer to see who it is. Five-eleven, dark hair, dark eyes. I stop dead in my tracks. I read an article the other day about a BU student who was raped down here on the bike trail. The picture of the man was fuzzy, but in the shadows I see the resemblance. *Of course it's him.*

"Kain, you scared me. What are you doing here?" Sarah asks politely, her teeth chattering from the cold. My hands ball into fists.

"Prolly same as you. Mind if I join you?" He moves closer and I take a deep breath, trying to restrain myself until she needs my help. She can take care of herself, I repeat frantically. *If she realizes I'm here, I'm just as bad as he is.*

"Um..."

He moves in quickly, standing over her, as she cowers back. "Hey, hey, hey," he soothes. "I really like you. You ain't gotta be scared of me."

Rage fills me like an injection.

"Oh, I'm not. I was just leaving. It's awfully cold out here. You should go somewhere warm, too," she says as she gets to her feet.

"I can keep you warm right here," he says, putting his hand on her arm. She tries to move around him but he stops her. When she tries to run he grabs her and pins her against the snow.

"Please, get off me, I have to go," she begs, but he only tightens his grip. She cries and tries to wriggle out from under him. He moves his face close to hers and she thrashes from side to side, avoiding contact. He shushes her over and over again. When he presses his lips against hers I almost lose it. All of this happens in the five seconds it takes me to get there.

I lunge at him like an animal. I grab the neck of his shirt and lift him off Sarah, turning him toward me. Then I cock my fist and break his nose. He drops to the ground like a brick. He takes a swing on the way down and catches my jaw.

"Sonovabitch!" He screams. He holds his nose while the blood drains through his fingers. "You're gonna regret that," he mumbles viciously, clutching the ground. I rub the side of my face. He actually got me pretty good.

"If you ever go near her again I'll kill you." I threaten calmly.

"Fucker, I'd *love* to see you try," he growls, scrambling to his feet. I trip him and kick him in the stomach. Twice. He curls into fetal position, gasping for breath.

I turn around and look at Sarah. She's clutching her bag and shaking. Her eyes are wet. They meet mine with a flicker of recognition that quickly fades. *She thinks I'm a monster.*

"I'm sorry Sarah. I didn't mean to…"

"Can I go now?" She asks softly.

I nod. She's gone before I can even finish the sentence.

CHAPTER 8

On my way to Government Center, I see the cheerless realities of life on the streets in New England. For some reason, it seems worse when you're an outsider looking in, when you see someone else curled up in a doorframe, or on a park bench with an umbrella to stop the wind, or on a statue, hugging the marble to feel safe. It's not uncommon to see people hunched over on stairwells, attempting to get a restful night's sleep, or nestled into garbage piles in the dumpsters, leaving a small enough crack to let out the smell.

Tonight I don't see as much of it as usual. The life-threatening temperatures drive the homeless into shelters like ants. But it's still there, and always will be, and I take an odd comfort in that.

The shelters will be overflowing tonight. I'm talking bodies upon bodies, sleeping on tile, pressed against the body parts of strangers, wearing wet boots and jackets and trying to block out the sickening smells of sweat, BO, and poor hygiene. Liam and I will be on top of the pile, thanks to me. I was supposed to meet him hours ago. There's no way there will be any cots left by the time we get there.

Despite the nasty sleeping arrangements, my body screams for it as the icy wind renders me useless. It's getting harder to move my limbs. I find Liam sitting on a curb on the outskirts of Faneuil Hall. He looks over at me with watery eyes and an eye-crinkling grin. My eyes follow his smile to the brown paper bag in his hand. Self-sabotage.

"You're drunk, Liam? What were you thinking?" I berate, letting the hard reality of the situation set in. I rub my hands together. I can't feel any of my appendages.

"I'm sozzled. And *you're* late," he says with a sloppy smile.

"I'm sorry about that, but it doesn't give you the right to go get drunk, you moron. Now we can't get into the shelter! What are we supposed to do now?" Liam shrugs with an innocent expression on his face.

We can't get into the shelter because it has a sobriety requirement (most of them do), and Liam's unmistakably drunk. Pine Street doesn't have one, but they have limited space and they raffle it off mid-day, so we're shit out of luck there.

I run through the limited options in my head. Churches lock their doors by now, stores won't let us in, bars have cover, the library's closed this time of night. I consider and then instantly disregard another alternative. T stations provide minimal heat, but only until one AM when they lock up. I've heard stories about bums sneaking into the tunnels at night and starting fires, but if you fall onto those tracks you'll be fried to a crisp, and there are stories of that too. I've never tried it before and I don't want to take that chance, especially not with drunko tonight.

"You do realize we're going to be sleeping outside tonight? I can't feel my body Liam. It hurts to breathe."

"The whisky is warmmmm," he says with a chuckle. "Ye want some?" He sloshes the bottle in front of my face. He's gone.

I sit down on the curb beside him with a sigh. "I saw Sarah tonight."

"I know ye did," he responds flatly, his smile wiped clean. He lowers his head. "I was there, lookin' for ye, and I saw ye followin' that wan toward the river."

"You did?"

He nods and takes another swig, avoiding eye contact.

"I had to follow her. She was going to the river at night, it was a rape sentence. You would have done the same thing." I rationalize.

"Maybe, maybe not," he says, getting to his feet. He looks down and scrutinizes me for a minute, blinking away the buzz. "You get a punch to the gob?"

I touch my cheek. It's swollen. I wipe away the smear of dried blood under my left eye and say, matter-of-factly, "Kain showed up." Liam's eyes widen and he stumbles to the side. "He tried to, you know, with her and he…he was gonna hurt her." My body tightens at the thought.

"I, I, I bet'ye banjaxed him beyond'll help," he muses, slurring with pride.

"Something like that." I respond. The smile touches my lips briefly and then disappears. "It doesn't matter anyway," I explain, "I let her walk away, just like that. I didn't even talk to her."

"She's juss a girl, Charlie," he whispers.

"Nope." I say harshly.

"Then yerr a rrright eejit for letting 'er go," he mumbles.

"I know," I agree. I don't want to talk about it anymore.

Liam takes another haul off his bottle and nearly topples over backwards.

"Why don't we settle in somewhere, go to sleep so we can forget about how damn cold it is." My breath swirls in front of me in white puffs.

Liam finishes his drink and throws it on the frozen ground, smashing the bottle into a million pieces.

"Let's go." I repeat with more force. I take his arm and drag him like a rag doll to the steps of Quincy Market. Ordinarily, Faneuil Hall would be the last place I'd want to crash, but it's a freezing cold Monday night and the place is a ghost town. That, and Liam's too drunk to move much further.

I pull out Liam's blanket and drape it over him. He's already curled up like a fortune cookie at my feet, shivering uncontrollably. He's built like a ten year old girl, which doesn't provide much in the way of insulation. I wedge my cardboard square beneath his body. Maybe that will help.

I lay beside him on the platform outside the entrance. The second my back hits the concrete I gasp. I pull the blanket tight around my neck and fight through it. Since I don't have a pillow, the cold seeps right through my hat. I'm so uncomfortable. What I'd give to have my hair back.

Sounds get louder as my other senses shut down. Liam's shallow breathing is overshadowed by the pulsing music of one of the bars down the way. I hum along with the song to take my mind off the pain.

My teeth are chattering now, too, and I can't stop shivering. I look over at the helpless version of my best friend. His eyes are still open.

"Chhharrlie…?"

"Yyeah?"

"I dddon't knnow wwhat I'd ddo wwithout ye, Chharlie." He tries to disguise his emotion with the casual tone of his voice.

"You ggonna make it over there?" I ask. It's hard to think of anything but the cold.

He nods and tries to communicate something, but I can't decipher his quivering speech. I scoot closer to him so we can share body heat. He leans into me.

"Dddd'ye know wwwhat wwould hhhelp?"

"Wwhat?" I ask.

"Ifff wwe ttook off'r ddrrawers and shhared bbbodyheat." He stares at me with a look I don't entirely recognize. It's intense. And dead serious.

"Tttake off our cclothes?" I repeat with a chuckle, dissolving the moment. "Ggood one, man." I curl my body into a tighter ball, averting my eyes.

Liam responds with a breathless laugh, but the laughter doesn't touch his eyes. "I wwas only sslagging ye," he says, making a face for comic relief. But there's something alarming about the emptiness of his words.

"I knnow," I lie. I turn my back to him and squeeze my eyes shut. My fingers and toes ache too much to dwell on what just happened. The only thing I want to do is fall asleep and dream of a warmer place.

"Nnight bbuddy," I say, stifling a yawn. I can feel my body shutting down, slowing down, pulling me under.

"Nnnight Chharlie," he whispers, patting my side. "I love ye."

I do love Liam, like a brother, but I don't say it back. It's arctic and it takes too much effort. That's what I tell myself. Instead, I lay there like a dead fish, pretending to be asleep.

CHAPTER 9

I don't sleep well. I drift in and out of consciousness until the sun comes up, piercing through the clouds and trying to break the cold. The temperatures are comparable to the night before, but without the wind chill so it feels warmer.

My body's numb, desensitized from the neck down. I sidle up next to Liam and rub my limbs to get the blood flowing again. They start to tingle, which quickly gives way to aching as they thaw. I curse and look over at Liam.

He lays there motionless, a pool of something yellow by his mouth. I furrow my brow. Liam never sleeps later than I do, no matter how drunk he was the night before. And I didn't think he was drunk enough to get sick. Although, he did say some crazy things. I nudge him but he doesn't move.

I roll him onto his back and something grips me. It squeezes my chest until I can't breathe. He doesn't feel right. His body is stiff, and cold, and there's a grayish tint to his skin. There's a patch of frostbite snaking down his cheek.

"Liam?" It's more of a question than a calling. "Liam, wake up." My voice is hollow, distant. "Liam," I say a little louder, "wake up, dammit. Wake up."

He doesn't even flinch. I lower my ear to his cracked blue lips. Nothing. I jam my fingers into his neck, feeling around for a pulse. Nothing. *No, no, no, no...*

I rest my head on his. It's really cold and his hat smells like scalp. I'm not detached enough to think. My eyes jump around. I touch his cheek, his hair, the scratchy fabric of his scarf, searching for something I know I'll never find. My hands ball into fists on his chest and I grab a fistful of his jacket, pulling myself down to his level. I lay there, desperate, waiting for the easy rise and fall of his chest.

The sound of a siren interrupts my waking nightmare. I sit up. People walk by, on their way to work, pretending not to see us. I know what it looks like but I don't care. How could I? The stores are going to open soon and more people will file through. I have to get him somewhere. Anywhere but here. Why? *Because he's dead.* All of a sudden everything else seems unimportant—the people, the noises, the weather. All of it falls away. It rolls off of me like water over an umbrella.

My whole world comes crashing down, crushing me with the weight of it. I start hyperventilating, fighting for breath, telling myself to get it together. *Don't make a scene. People are looking at you and right now you need to be discreet. Focus, dammit, focus.*

I slump over and pinch the bridge of my nose. I close my eyes. *This can't be happening.* But it is. I take a deep breath and peel off his blanket. It still holds his smells, both the good and the bad. I clutch it to my nose and take them in. Then I shove it into his backpack and roll that one inside of mine.

I get underneath him and throw his body over my shoulder. His arms fall limply down my back. I eye the soiled cardboard square and decide to leave that behind. The frost slows the decomposition process, but Liam's body still has a smell. The more I think about it, the more suffocating it becomes.

I lug my best friend all the way to the river. It's early enough and cold enough that no one stops me. I guess we're too convincingly homeless to question, because I've carried the passed-out-drunk Liam across the city like this before.

It's bitterly cold down by the water, and mist curls off the ice like smoke, creating an eerie, ghost-like shadow. For all intents and purposes, it's perfect weather for what I'm about to do. I step cautiously onto the ice, trying to keep my balance. We slice through the fog with small steps until we reach the

Longfellow Bridge. I walk far enough beneath the massive structure that we're secluded, cut off from the world and shielded by mist.

I lay Liam down gently on the bumpy, pockmarked surface of the frozen river. I curl over him in fetal position, rocking back and forth. I whisper apologies and curses and use the ice like a punching bag until my fists are raw. His body wheezes in weak protest. I fall back on my heels with exhaustion.

Some time later I open my eyes. I stare down at his lifeless body and something changes inside me. I don't recognize it. This isn't him. This isn't my goofy, outspoken, Irish best friend. He's gone. I focus on my breathing, in and out. My heart twists in pain because I know what I have to do.

I leave Liam and return to the bike trail, where I snap off some kindling for the fire. My arms are full of branches when I get back. I dig around for my lighter and all the free copies of the daily Metro I have floating around. Newspapers are good for wiping your ass when you don't have anything else.

I crumple up the newspapers and arrange the kindling on Liam's body. When I stop to think, I mean *really* think, about what I'm doing, I freeze. I want to cry but nothing comes out. Instead, I yank my fist back without thinking and I strike the ice, two, three, four times. It's a hard hit and it hurts like hell. I take off my glove and stare at the wounds, reopened from last night. The throbbing pain refocuses my agony on something rational, something real; because the nightmare I'm living in can't be.

I look at Liam and I throw up. I don't have anything in my stomach so I dry heave, over and over again until I've purged myself of all guilt, all emotion. I feel empty, like someone's pumped my stomach full of air. I have to get away from here. I throw down the lighter and run.

I emerge from the mist like a bat out of hell. My muscles are cold but I move quickly. I gain traction when I hit the trail, my run turning into a full-on sprint, a pace I can't maintain for long.

I run until I collapse. My head hits the frozen ground with

a thud and everything starts to spin. I'm hungry and exhausted and I feel like I'm going to die. It happened to my best friend, my brother, so why won't it happen to me?

I need help. I can't deal with this alone. I'm only twenty years old. Liam was my rock and now I don't have anyone. I lean my head back and close my eyes, willing death to take me away.

"Charlie, are you ok?"

I hear the voice of an angel. *I'm losing it.* But when my eyes snap open, there she is, looking down at me.

"Sarah?" I rub my eyes. I blink. She's still there.

"Are you ok?" She asks again.

"I don't know." I answer truthfully. My voice is flat and frightening. I'm gasping for breath. "How did you...I thought..."

"I saw you with Liam and I followed you." She says openly. "It looked like you needed help."

I nod, getting to my feet. I know if I open my mouth I'll lose it. So I walk to the bridge in silence, and Sarah follows me.

The sight of my best friend, covered in sticks and newspaper and starting to decompose, never seemed more real than it does right now. Sarah gasps in horror. "Is he?" She swallows.

My face must be answer enough.

"So he's not just..."

I bite my lip and shake my head violently, pleading with her to stop.

"Why are you..." She points at the lighter laying a few feet from the body.

I clear my throat. "I promised."

She doesn't understand.

"I don't want them to find him and throw him away like a piece of garbage. He wanted to be cremated." My voice breaks on the last word.

She nods and stares at him, wide-eyed, letting it all sink in. After a few minutes she moves in closer and kneels beside him.

She clasps her hands together and closes her eyes.

"God of mystery, whose ways are beyond our understanding, lead us, who grieve at this untimely death, to a new and deeper faith in your love, which brought your Son Jesus through death into resurrection of life. Amen." She looks at me and I shake my head. I have nothing left to say.

I watch the scene unfold like a movie. It's in slow motion and I have no control over the events. Sarah takes the lighter in her dainty hands and lights the paper, one corner at a time. The flames lick the branches and spread slowly across the pile, dancing over his body and putting off a moderate amount of heat. The air smells like campfire and cold winter air. I hold my breath.

As the fire gets larger, it shivers and touches down on my friend. It melts his skin the way it melted my favorite G.I. Joe in second grade. It smells like burnt toast, melting crayons, blood, bile, and week old trash all bottled into one. It's revolting. The feeling it evokes in me is indescribable. I can't watch anymore. I'm going to be sick. Sarah touches my arm and I turn away.

When I turn back, her eyes are soft and apologetic. She knew I couldn't do it myself so she did it for me. She's my rock today.

"I'm so sorry, Charlie." She takes my hand and rubs my knuckles with her thumb. My hand looks so big next to hers. She looks up, and I control my expression. *Don't, I can't...*

"I know how close you were with Liam and how much you're going to miss him. But everything happens for a reason, I really believe that. We just don't always know what it is until later on." She looks at me and my bottom lip quivers.

Sarah draws me in for a hug. I know what's coming but I don't have the strength to resist. She's like oxygen. I need her more than I've ever needed anything before in my life.

She's so small and warm. She fits perfectly in my arms. My eyes well up and spill over. I can't stop the tears. I crumple in her arms, gripping her coat and holding onto her like a life raft. I allow the weakness I've fought to crush me.

Sarah holds me for a long time, comforting me with platitudes and telling me everything's going to be okay. When she finally lets go, I pull away, our faces only inches apart, and I wonder what's next. I get my answer quickly. Out of the corner of my eye, I see the first crack in the ice. The ice around the fire is melting. *Liam's going to break through.*

Sarah notices this at the same time I do and we look at each other in panic. I grab my bag, then her hand, and we run across the ice, slipping and sliding, escaping only minutes before it pulls in the remnants of Liam's body.

We reach the shore, tired and out of breath. I look apologetically at Sarah. "What?" She asks.

"I put your life in danger."

"You saved me. You're always saving me," she says with a knowing smile. "You did the best you could." She says, and squeezes my arm. "He knows that."

I look from her to the ground. "I don't know."

We stand in awkward stillness for what feels like an eternity. I try to think of something to say, anything to keep her from leaving, but my mind is a sieve. I can't seem to hold onto a complete thought. Sarah teeters in place like she's looking for an out and I panic.

"You don't have to go anywhere, do you?" I ask desperately. It's nice having her here. I've waited so long for this, and yet I'm too distraught to think about the implications. I'm completely guarded. All I know is that my best friend just died and Sarah's the only person in the world I can lean on.

"No, I don't have to go anywhere," she reassures. I nod appreciatively, wiping the moisture from my eyes. "Let's go somewhere." She says, taking my hand like I'm a child. There's nothing romantic about it but beggars can't be choosers.

We walk along the bike trail, to the old BU boathouse and back, talking, about what I don't remember. I'm just grateful that the snow is gone. I don't have the strength to lift my feet.

Sarah drags me to a shelter and makes me eat. The food feels heavy as it goes down. It has no taste. But I leave feeling slightly better, not as empty as I did before.

We linger in the lobby when we're done with our meals, trying to savor the heat. I plop down on a bench and she joins me. I stare at the overstuffed pack in my lap, willing it to open. I finally yank the zipper, with a mixture of sadness and anger, extracting Liam's bag from inside.

I hold the small backpack like it's human. I touch the cigarette burn from Kain, and then I put my fingers through a hole over the left shoulder strap. I didn't mean to do it. I was a kid, we'd just met, and I was waving my pocket knife around like a sword. I was laughing too hard to have any sort of depth perception. Liam used his bag like a shield and I caught the edge of it. He pretended not to care. But I saw the look on his face and I knew better. The memory tugs at my heart.

I get a whiff of him. Sweat, whisky, and skin. I swallow down the lump in my throat. Inside there are very few things: his journal, harmonica, a newspaper, his blanket. I find a few pennies at the bottom and tuck them in my pocket. I take out the harmonica. I hold it like a sandwich, the way he taught me, and bring it to my lips. I blow into it and it makes a dreadful sound. I get a few looks as people file out the front door.

"Do you play?" Sarah asks. To my surprise, I actually forgot she was there. A smile tugs at the corners of my lips. It's the feeling I get when I look at her.

"No. He tried to teach me a couple times, but..." I shake my head. We're quiet for a moment and then I say, "There was this one song he really liked. It was an Irish song called Danny Boy. Have you heard of it?" She nods.

"He used to play that and I'd sing along, kind of as a joke, but it made him happy."

"I'd love to hear it sometime."

"Oh, I don't know." My stomach seizes with fear.

"Maybe another time then," she says sweetly.

I pull out the journal and run my hand along its destroyed, black leather binding. Another one of Liam's most prized possessions. I wish he could take these with him.

"Hey, Charlie?"

"Yeah?"

"Can I take you to church tonight?" She asks as she fumbles with something in her lap. "I think it might make you feel better." She looks at me with those big, beautiful eyes and I'm defenseless.

"You're going, regardless?" I ask. The thought of her leaving is too much to handle.

"Yes. I have to go." She replies.

"Then I'll go, too."

CHAPTER 10

Sarah takes me to an old church in Back Bay. She says it's one of the few places in Boston that holds a six o'clock mass. I look up at the daunting structure, with its columns and heavy arches and massive, tomato red tower. *I'm really dreading this.*

"Did you know this area used to be a tidal marsh?" Sarah asks animatedly. I think she can tell I'm nervous.

"No, I didn't know that."

"Yeah, all of Back Bay was. They filled it in." She looks up in awe. "There are four thousand wooden supports under this thing, all under water."

"Really?"

"Yeah, isn't that cool? I learned that on a duck tour of Boston a few years back."

I want to hear more. I want to know everything about her. Where she came from, how she got here. Church bells break my train of thought. I panic when I see people start filing into the church.

Sarah gives me a consoling look. "Ready?"

No. I bob my head in assent. Then I hold my breath and follow her inside. I've never been to a church service before so I don't know what to expect. I've never even been inside the chapel. Just the area where they serve the food.

We walk into a high-ceilinged room full of long benches. The space is quiet and warm, and oddly romantic. A child robed in white follows a red carpet to the front of the room, where he lights the candles, framing the podium with soft light. There are colors everywhere. Light from the street pours through the stained glass, creating a kaleidoscope effect in the room. I pause like a child seeing something for the first time.

Sarah reaches up to pat my shoulder. "Charlie, we can sit down now," she whispers, as a line takes shape behind us.

"Oh, sorry," I mumble as I take the piece of paper she's handing me and follow her down the aisle. I pull off my hat. This is nothing like my preconceptions. I thought I'd come in here and feel strangled, claustrophobic. Instead I feel oddly safe.

Sarah claims a bench near the middle and I slide in next to her. She unwinds her scarf and leaves it in a pile with her hat and mittens. Her hair's mashed to one side, but somehow it still looks cute.

"What's that for?" I ask, pointing to a folding table in the front of the room. There are two silver trays on it. One has three loaves of bread, and the other has shot glasses of dark purple liquid. I start to salivate.

"Oh, that's for Communion. The bread represents the body of Jesus, and the grape juice symbolizes his blood." She goes into more detail about the history, and I nod along politely.

More people file in and greet each other. Sarah waves to a couple of them, while I try to remain as inconspicuous as possible. The place is getting pretty crowded.

We're silenced when a man in a robe takes the podium. He says his name is Reverend Frye. He's a plain vanilla kind of guy, balding with a paunch and jowls like a Saint Bernard. He smiles widely at the congregation and bellows, "Good evening!" Loud enough for all of Boston to hear.

"Good evening," Sarah answers back politely, her hands folded neatly in her lap.

The minister welcomes new faces and then two old ladies go up front to talk about bake-offs and garage sales. When they finish Sarah reaches for the scarlet books in front of us.

She hands me one. "Hymnals," she mouths, and tells me to turn to page two-hundred-nineteen. Before I know it, we're singing a high-pitched song about God. I stop singing and turn to Sarah. I'm too stunned to continue. Her voice. It's like velvet, and full of so much range and emotion. It makes the hairs on my arms stand up.

The Reverend returns to the stand and does a brief segue into Communion. After that he gives his main speech. I try to follow his message but my eyelids droop as sleep deprivation breaks my defenses. It's so warm in here...

My head falls against my chest and jolts me awake. I straighten in my seat and look at Sarah. Her head's down like everyone else's. Frye speaks, with his eyes glued to the podium, until he gets to the resounding Amen and the organist starts up again. Everyone lifts their faces to Frye and reaches for their hymnals. The church comes alive with music. I don't know why, but the song induces a mixture of sorrow and joy, a most intense combination. *I've heard this one before.* Where, or what it's called, I couldn't tell you; but I've definitely heard it.

I sing along with Sarah. When we get to the chorus, something inside me lifts. I know it sounds crazy but I feel Liam all around me. In the air, in the music, in my chest. The sensation's so powerful I can taste it. I close my eyes. When I open them I'm smiling. I pull up my sleeves to examine the goose bumps that cover my arms.

"Are you ok?" Sarah asks, touching my leg. The service is over.

I nod and dab my eyes discreetly. I look around. There's nothing out of the ordinary. No white light, no translucent figure floating around the room. No proof. Just a feeling.

"So what did you think?" She asks when we get outside.

"It was—" I search for the right word. Different, non-confrontational, warm. None of these seem like good answers. "I'm glad I went," I substitute.

Her face lights up like a Christmas tree. "Well I'm glad you went, too."

We wander away from the church in silence, neither one of

us knowing what to do next. I want to beg her to stay with me, but I'm too frazzled from what went on inside. *Did I make that up?* If so, I have bigger problems to deal with.

"Charlie, look!" Sarah's standing by the Copley fountain, pointing at a barren flowerbed. I gasp. It's a cluster of shamrocks, poking up through the frozen ground.

Sarah giggles. "Charlie, you look like you just saw a ghost."

"Do you believe in that sort of thing?" I question cautiously.

"Spirits? Absolutely," she answers like it's a perfectly legitimate question. She bends down and picks the cluster. "Here."

I handle the clovers like they're delicate glass. After several seconds have gone by I ask, "What now?" It's more of a general question, but Sarah offers to buy me dinner.

"No way." I respond too quickly. "I mean, I'm not really that hungry. But we can get something for you?" I suggest, hoping I can tag along. I just don't feel right letting her pay.

"I'm ok," she lies. I can hear her stomach rumbling.

"Ok." I teeter on my heels until she says the inevitable.

"I guess I should probably go now."

I clamp down on the clovers. The voice inside me screams at ear-splitting decibels to make her stay. "Please don't go," I ask pathetically.

Sarah looks at me with what can only be described as pity. "Ok, I'll stay," she replies.

We stand there in silence until Sarah starts walking. I follow blindly. "Sarah?"

"Yeah?"

"I can't go to a shelter tonight." Just the thought of it, being crammed in a confined space, on top of each other like M&Ms. It makes me claustrophobic. I can't deal with people tonight.

"I know," she replies casually, like she's known this all along.

"But you should go to one." I suggest, going back on my original plea. It's not fair of me to keep her in the cold all night. "There's Rosie's place, or Pine Street for women." I make sure to mention only women's shelters.

"On second thought, Pine Street has the lottery and you have to be eighteen—"

"I am eighteen," she interrupts.

"You are?" I ask, clearly shocked.

"Yeah, I turned eighteen in November." She explains. "It's ok. I get that all the time."

"So, are you going?" I ask hesitantly, not wanting to hear the answer.

"To a women's shelter?"

"Yeah."

"What about you?"

"I'll be ok here. Somewhere. I'll find a place."

She thinks it over as we continue to walk. "No." She shakes her head. "I'm not leaving you. You shouldn't be alone tonight."

CHAPTER 11

We end up at the edge of the Common, on the brighter side near Lowe's Theater. Sarah points to a gazebo a hundred yards away. It's still lit with twinkly white lights from Christmas.

"We could sleep here tonight." She suggests. "That way we don't have to sleep on the ground."

I look at her and I'm struck with simultaneous elation and fear. Elation because she's thought this through, and fear at the very thought of it, spending the night here with this beautiful girl. I know she'd never like me in that way; but there's still a hopeful feeling inside that spawns my fear.

She catches me with the deer in headlights look on. "If you don't like it…"

"No, it's great. Perfect, actually." My eyes linger on hers. She's breathtaking. She smiles nervously and looks down, her rosy cheeks getting redder.

"Perfect," she says quietly. She walks over to the gazebo and I follow, my feet crunching on the frozen grass.

"Charlie, look!" Sarah bounces up and down.

"What?" I ask with a chuckle.

She holds up a Styrofoam to-go container that must have been sitting on the ledge. I don't have the heart to tell her people leave those all the time so they don't have to carry them around. They're usually empty when I find them.

"God works in mysterious ways, Charlie," she says when she sees my dubious expression. I don't mind her persuasion, but I'm confident that my religious beliefs, or lack thereof, are not something she's going to change.

"Don't get your hopes up," I warn, but she has already popped the lid. She extends a full meal of marinated chicken, rice pilaf, and some sort of green vegetable I probably won't like. It's untouched. To top it off, there's a clean set of silverware and a wet nap taped under the lid. Her look says, *see, I told you so.*

Sarah can't contain herself. She puts down the food and jumps into my arms, catching me off guard. I hug her back, trying not to squeeze too tight. I really, really like this. Sarah drops the embrace and backs away. Her breath is surprisingly unsteady.

We stare at our feet for an unendurable minute. My mind's a jumble of thoughts. At the forefront is the one that wants to read into what happened. Behind that is the one that wants to do it again.

Sarah scatters my thoughts with the slice of her hand. "Yoo hoo, earth to Charlie. Are you ready to eat or what?"

"Yeah, sure," I say distantly. In autopilot, I sweep frost off the gazebo floor with my sleeve. I lay a blanket down and we sit beside each other, Indian-style, with our arms touching. Sarah says grace and opens the to-go container like it's a first edition of the Holy Bible. A blast of spices and butter and chicken fat hit my nostrils. I suck it in like heroin. I'm hesitant to take the first bite because I know I won't be able to stop.

Sarah takes a forkful of rice and closes her eyes, savoring the flavors. I want to kiss her. I watch her with concentrated interest. I keep thinking about our hug. She sighs and hands me the fork. I rip off a piece of chicken, and with shaky hands I bring it to my mouth. A whimper escapes me when it hits my tongue. Sarah smiles at me. I smile back. The sexual tension is gone.

We go back and forth like this until everything is gone. The Styrofoam is clean by the time we're done with it. We devour every grain of rice, every last fleck of rosemary. I lean back on my elbows and sigh, feeling both satisfied and sleepy.

"Charlie?"

"Hmm?"

"Nothing, nevermind." She shoos the thought away with her hand.

"No, what?"

Sarah looks down, averting my gaze. Her eyelashes are so long they cast shadows on her cheeks. "I'm really sorry about what happened today. That's all." She mumbles something into her scarf about him being in a better place.

My stomach muscles clench. She has good intentions, I know this much. But she just took the knife of truth and sank it in my chest, turned it around, pulled it out. It leaves me feeling exposed. I haven't thought about Liam in almost an hour.

Sarah recognizes her mistake right away. Panic flashes across her face in a deep shade of red. She keeps saying she's sorry but I barely hear it.

I feel my mind slipping, back to my best friend, and I remember it all—his accent, his pointy ears, the way he covered his mouth self-consciously when he laughed. He was there, holding his bottle of whisky, telling me how sozzled he was and saying he loved me. The image shutters and switches, like a changing slide in an old projector, and I see the hollow-eyed, crusty-lipped, purple-skinned Liam from this morning. I open my eyes and everything fades. He will never be that living, breathing version of himself again.

I watch with mortification as a string of silent tears hit my jacket, one by one. I bury my head in my hands. *Dammit.* My shoulders shake as I fight for breath. I'm not crying. I'm hyperventilating.

Sarah kneels in front of me. She hooks her thumbs around my ears and takes my face lightly between her hands. "It's going to be ok," she says softly. She wipes my cheeks with mittened hands and I allow myself to look up. She's leaning over me and her pupils are dilated, revealing small slivers of blue. I can see the white lights reflecting off her corneas.

She's looking at me funny, watching me, her eyes suddenly intent.

It might be my heart wrenching vulnerability, or out of mere pity, but she kisses my cheek. I can't breathe. Our physical proximity makes it hard for me to concentrate. Our faces are only inches apart now. She angles her face toward mine, slowly, cautiously. I lick my lips. I've never kissed a girl before, and I don't know the first thing to do. Is that what's happening? I'm not even sure. Sarah seems hesitant. Maybe she doesn't want to. Maybe I'm imagining the whole thing.

She whispers my name and my heart rate quickens. I hold perfectly still, listening to her breathing, waiting to see what she's going to do next. I close my eyes. I can feel her head lowering, so I adjust mine accordingly, meeting her somewhere in the middle. I wait for her to kiss me. I try to be patient but this is much worse than hunger for food.

Despite my inexperience, I take her chin and guide her mouth toward mine. Our noses bump and I tilt my head more to one side. When my lips finally find hers, they part, just as hers do, adjusting and readjusting to the feel of each other. Everything around me disappears.

We touch each other's faces and kiss slowly; until my feelings for her take over. I pull her into my chest and kiss harder. I don't think I can stop. I want to swallow her whole, keep her inside me and carry her around forever.

Sarah pulls back, startled and slightly out of breath. "I'm sorry," I gasp, reaching instinctively for my lips. They're buzzing. She shakes her head, wide-eyed, content. If I didn't know any better, I'd think she has feelings for me. My heart pounds in my chest.

After a bloated minute of silence, Sarah yawns. "Tired?" I ask, hoping that's not the case. She nods. I take out the second blanket and extend it to her. She takes it reluctantly with a look that says, *what are you going to sleep with?* I take out the crumpled foil blanket from my marathon. "It's warmer than it looks," I tell her.

She leans forward and I think she's going to kiss me again.

Instead, she wraps her arm around my neck. She hugs me, and I get this rush of feelings. They're so intense I can't hold them in. Uninvited, the words, "I love you" tumble off my lips.

"What did you say?" She asks, pulling away. I hide my face. This time *I'm* the one blushing.

I back up until we're an arm's length apart. "Uh, nothing. I didn't say anything." *Real smooth, Charlie.*

"Ok," she appeases, knowing damn well it's a lie. The right side of her mouth twitches with a smile. "Goodnight, Charlie."

~~~

Sarah's sound asleep beside me and I'm jealous. It's not only the absence of Liam, but also the presence of Sarah that keeps me awake. I want to keep an eye on her. I have to. I have this irrational fear that if I close my eyes she'll disappear.

It's the best and worst day of my life. My body churns with grief and guilt, but watered-down versions of what I felt before Sarah showed up. I unzip Liam's backpack and pull out the journal again. I imagine him lying where Sarah is, smiling and rambling on about anything at all in that silly Irish accent of his. I miss him intolerably.

Maybe reading this will make it feel like he's here, I think foolishly, as I peel back the first page.

The first few passages are about turning eighteen; flipping off his last set of foster parents; the flight to America. You can tell it was a very angry time in his life. The pages are riddled with threats and Irish curse words. I get caught up on some of the slang, but I understand most of it.

There are Irish poems, quotes, songs. I skip over these. He delves modestly into his job at The Playwright pub, and the aftermath of getting fired. He never told me it was because he stole from the cash register. Nor did he tell me his roommates in Southie used to call him a fag and beat him senseless. I always assumed his scars were from his father.

After forty or so pages he mentions me for the first time. I smile when I see my name. He's referring to the fight. He calls Kain a gammy eejit and talks about how I saved his life. I keep reading, and I'm puzzled by some of the description. *Very trim and strong, copper skin, fierce eyes.* I'm none of those things. I frown at this passage but keep flipping. It's an entry much later that stops me like a slap to the face.

My name's written all over the margin, in different sizes, different fonts. Some of the i's have hearts instead of dots. I frown at his doodles before reading what's written beneath them. *Today I'm awful jaded. Yer the only one I can speak the truth to and I'm tired of it. I can tell myself to feck off all day long, but it's lying next to him at night that kills me.*

I scratch my chin, pretending it doesn't make sense. A few paragraphs later: *Charlie makes a holy show around the floozies. He gawks at them and never shuts his gob about it. He looks at wans the way I look at him.*

My heart rate accelerates.

I would die for Charlie. He's the only fella to ever love me. Just not in the same way I love him.

I drop the book like it's suddenly ablaze. It's too personal. It compartmentalizes all of his private thoughts and feelings and I shouldn't be reading it. I should have left it alone.

I don't understand. Liam loves me like a brother, the same way I love him. I take off my hat and scrub what little hair I have left. I put it back on. *What?* I stand up and leave the gazebo. I walk around the park with my hands on my head and I take deep breaths. I try to deny it all but somewhere deep down I recognize the truth. I guess on some level I always knew. My head just never caught up with it.

I feel sorry for him. I should have seen the signs. It must have been terrible carrying that around. I talked about Sarah constantly because I thought I'd explode if I didn't. He must have felt that way all the time. No wonder he never liked her.

I curse myself out for reading that damn diary. It only rubbed salt in wounds that were rubbed raw hours ago. I kick the ground and grit my teeth. *How could I have been so stupid?* I desperately want to run somewhere, let it all out. But I can't leave Sarah here alone. Instead, I drop to my knees and do push-ups. I summon the strength from his memory and I pump until I can't pump anymore. When I'm done I stand up, sore and exhausted, and I return to Sarah. I curl up beside her on the cold, hard platform and I cry. The crack in my heart splits open, leaving a gaping hole that I know will never fully heal. I'm not gay. But tonight my heart is broken.

CHAPTER 12

My head's groggy and my eyes feel weird, sticky almost. I rub them and realize my eyelashes are crusted together with ice. *Where am I?* I snap my head to the left, looking for something. What, I'm not sure, but my hand lands beside me on the empty pile of blankets. Liam. Instinctively I grab my belly, trying to contain the nausea.

I roll onto my side and groan. It's a clear, cold morning and everyone's going on with their lives as usual. I don't want to move. My head's congested, I have a migraine and my whole body aches. This must be what a hangover feels like.

I lean on the handrail for balance. I wonder if any of it happened, or if my recollection of yesterday was all a dream. I lick my lips, searching for evidence, and I taste her cherry chapstick. I swivel around, clutching my shiny blanket and scanning the park. She's not here. My heart sinks to my toes and I start to panic. It could be one of two things: she decided last night was a mistake, or someone took her.

I bound off the steps. There's no time to reason through this. If there was, I'd ponder how Kain could have taken her without me waking up, or how he would have known where we were in the first place. I would consider that number one is the more probable choice. But there isn't time and I'm not rational at the moment, which is why I run around the park, searching frantically. My legs are stiff from the cold but I keep going. I think the worst. I see him, unzipping her jacket, kissing her, having his way with her, and my pace quickens.

I complete the loop near Tremont street but still no Sarah. I fold over on a bench with my head between my legs, panting heavily and feeling defeated. I'm trying to think of where he'd take her, why he'd come here, why she didn't scream...

"Charlie?"

I lift my head slowly. It's her! "Hi." I say casually, trying to catch my breath. I don't want her to see how positively ecstatic I am to see her. "Morning run," I explain, thinking that seems less pathetic than going berserk looking for her.

Her eyes are soft with sleep and her hair's a little crumpled around her neck. She runs her fingers through it when she sees me staring. I look away.

"I got breakfast," she announces, holding up a Dunkin Donuts bag.

"What?"

She repeats herself.

Wow.

"How are you feeling?" She asks as we walk side by side back to camp.

"Good," I answer shyly, still taken back by her gesture. I can't remember the last time I had breakfast.

I sit on the steps and she joins me. She takes an orange juice and a breakfast sandwich from the bag and starts to unwrap it. It smells like ham, egg and cheese on a toasted bagel. I'm right. *Liam would be proud*, I think sadly.

Sarah cuts the sandwich with her plastic knife and hands me half. I accept it reluctantly. "Are you sure?"

"Of course I'm sure," she replies cheerfully. "I had a little money leftover and we have to eat," she reasons before taking her first bite. I follow suit. That's a good enough reason for me.

I sink back against the stairs. "Did you sleep well last night?" I ask with my mouth full.

"I slept fine. Did you sleep ok?"

I shrug, wondering if I'll ever have a good night's sleep again.

I lick melted cheese off my fingers and toss our trash in a nearby receptacle. When I get back, Sarah's folding blankets in the gazebo. She lifts my bag and Liam's journal falls out. I stare, like it's a ticking time bomb ready to explode. Sarah catches my expression.

"What? Charlie, are you ok?"

I'm at a crossroads. Do I preserve Liam's secret and lock this one up, or do I tell someone, get this enormous weight off my chest? I know what I should do. It's private information, I should keep it that way. Then again, he's dead.

"Liam's gay." I announce before I have time to think it through.

"He is?" Sarah straightens up with the journal in hand. She processes this. "Well, that's ok. It doesn't really change anything, does it?"

"No, it doesn't. But I didn't realize he was gay. I read about it in his journal," I confess. "He said he was in love with me.".

"Oh." Her expression changes.

"Yup." I tuck my chin inside the collar of my jacket.

"And you didn't know?" She asks.

"Nope."

"Did you, were you, I mean—"

"No, no, nothing like that. He was like a brother to me but nothing more. I like girls," I clarify, blushing.

Sarah's face is unreadable. She nods and zips my backpack, with the journal tucked safely inside.

"Am I terrible person?" I ask when she hands me the bag. "I mean, I violated his privacy and read something personal. That was wrong, wasn't it?"

"You're not a terrible person. You wanted to know more about your friend. Did you ever read the Diary of Anne Frank?"

"Yeah, we read it in school."

"That was extremely personal but it told her story. On some level she knew people would read it. I bet Liam felt the same way. He probably wanted you to know."

Maybe.

"Charlie, I have to go now. I have to be somewhere in half an hour. Are you going to be ok?" She asks.

"You're leaving?" I get that fluttery snap of panic in my belly. I know I should accept that being happy isn't in the cards for me, but I don't want to. "When will I see you again?" I ask in a fit of desperation. I practically throw myself at her feet.

Sarah smiles and says, "You can come if you'd like."

"Ok." I answer much too quickly. "I mean, sure, I guess." I cover my mouth in embarrassment.

"Let's go then," she says sweetly, reaching for my hand. "We don't want to be late."

CHAPTER 13

We bum money for train fare and take the red line to South Boston. It dumps us off at West Broadway, which eventually connects us to this narrow, unmarked street with a small brick building on the corner. Sarah grins as we approach it. She won't tell me where we're going because it's supposed to be a surprise.

"Can you tell me now?" I inquire when we get to the door. It's unmarked and it smells like a pet shop—a mix of animal dander and dog food. I hear barking inside. "Is this an animal shelter?"

"Oh no, are you allergic?" She starts to panic. "I wasn't even thinking, I—"

"No, I love animals. I used to have a dog, remember?" I touch her shoulder and she relaxes.

"Oh good. Yeah, that's right." The broad smile returns to her face. "I do too, love animals I mean. I volunteer here once a week. The people are really nice." She puts her hand on the door knob and hesitates. "Do you still want to come with me?"

"I do."

She pulls open the heavy green door and we go inside. The animal smell is much stronger in here, but I'd bathe in it to stay in this warmth. The old heating vents in the corner groan as they crank out heat. We stomp our boots and shrug out of our coats. I help Sarah with hers.

"Sarah!" A gray-haired woman walks over and gives her a hug. Her arms are doughy and covered in cat scratches. She looks like mother goose. "And this is?" She asks, sizing me up with kind eyes.

"This is Charlie," Sarah answers as she removes her gloves. "I'm Sarah's...friend." I'm not sure this is accurate. Can you be friends with someone after one day? What if you kissed? I feel myself blush.

"It's nice to meet yah, Chahlie. Are you here to help us out for the day?" I nod.

"Unfortunately, like I tell Sarah, we can't pay yah, but you're welcome to the muffins. Home-made. Maggie brought 'em in this mornin'."

"Oh no, I don't need any money." I say, looking for the muffins. "I just appreciate you letting me stay."

"It's nasty out theyah, isn't it?"

"Yeah."

"Well my name's Ruth, and I appreciate the help. If yah need anything, anything at all, yah let me know."

"Thank you."

"Hey Pam, Maggie, get ova heyah! Sarah brought a friend." Two middle-aged women greet us at the door. "Chahlie, Pam, Pam, Chahlie," Ruth introduces.

"It's nice to meet you," she says. Pam must be a smoker. Her face looks like a boiled vegetable, and she has yellow fingers. My mother looked like that, too.

"It's nice to meet you, too." I repeat politely.

"I'm Maggie," the other woman says. I don't know Maggie but I instantly like her. She has one of those faces. It's compassionate and motherly, and she looks like someone you'd want to read you bedtime stories. She extends her hand to me and I shake it. It's very warm. "Are you from around here, Charlie?"

"Uh, no, I'm from Connecticut originally."

"Don't tell me you're a Yankees fan," Ruth interjects. It's more of a demand than a question.

"No way. I've been a Red Sox fan since I was four years

old."

"Thatta boy," Ruth says with an exaggerated sigh of relief. "My granddaughter's datin' a Yanks fan. I told her I wouldn't go to the wedding." I laugh.

"Oh, Sarah, we found a new cat yesterday." Pam says, changing the subject.

"Really?"

"Yeah, another tattered tom. He was all dirty and emaciated and his ribs were stickin' out, the poor thing."

"Aww, can I see him?" Sarah's expression softens.

Pam gets the cat from the back room. The creature she's holding is one sad excuse for a cat. He has bald patches all over his body and one of his ears is sliced clean off. He cries this heart-wrenching cry when Pam hands him over to Sarah. She cradles him very gently in her arms.

"Baby, what happened to you?" Sarah whispers as she kisses his head. The cat nuzzles into her chin and starts to purr. "Charlie, do you want to hold him?" She asks.

"Uh, no thank you," I respond awkwardly. I'm afraid I'd break the poor guy.

Maggie lifts the cat out of Sarah's arms. "We should probably take him back anyway. It was very nice meeting you, Charlie," she says warmly as she disappears into the back room.

Sarah leans into me and whispers, "Maggie's great, isn't she?"

I turn the question around on her. "Where did you come from?"

"Maine. Why?"

"No, I mean, I didn't know people like you existed. You seem too good to be true."

"What?" She asks, clearly embarrassed. She falls back on nervous laughter.

I look down, like I always do when I'm uncomfortable. "I'm not trying to embarrass you or anything, it's just, I mean, you help me, and then you bring me here, and you're good with animals. You're perfect." I lift my head, slowly, until our

eyes meet. Sarah makes sure no one's looking and she kisses me. It's quick but sweet.

"Do you want a muffin?" She asks.

"What?" I feel dizzy. Sarah grabs my hand and pulls me into the kitchen. She stops and we stand there, staring at each other. I can hear her heart beating. Or maybe that's mine. I want her more than I've ever wanted anything. She takes a step forward and I reach out, trying to grab her but she's already pinned me against the refrigerator. She gets up on her tiptoes and kisses me again, harder this time, with her hands locked behind my neck. My hands tangle in her hair. I'm shaking. I feel my face contort into something resembling pain, but it's not pain, it's elation.

When she finally releases me I take a deep, uneasy breath. The room's spinning. Sarah's breathing heavy, too. She smiles at me and touches my cheek.

Before I know what's going on, she hands me a muffin and walks out of the room. *What just happened?* It takes me a minute to regroup. I run my hands over the peach fuzz on my head and take a deep breath. Sarah comes back.

"Do you want to help me with something?" She asks.

"Ok," I answer, feeling confused. I'm still holding the muffin.

"We have to give Sasha her shots and I'm not good at sticking the animals." She leans against the doorframe with her hand on the door.

"You want me to jab a needle into a cat?"

"It's a dog, actually," she says with a guilty expression.

"Oh boy." She has to be joking.

I follow her into the main room, and she starts giving me the tour. "So this is the reception area. That's the supply closet. That room over there is where we keep the animals we're trying to find homes for. This one," she says as we enter a white room with an operating table, "is for the sick animals." I eye the cages at the back of the room. A gaunt Siamese cat stares back at me with empty eyes.

"We have a voluntary vet that comes in once in a week. He

teaches Maggie, which is great for us. We get a lot of homeless people bringing in their pets." She says it so casually you'd never in a million years think she falls into that category.

"Wow, I didn't know they had that kind of service."

"Here she is," Maggie interrupts as she walks a medium-sized dog into the room. He's black with brown patches and he looks very familiar. I can tell he's in a lot of pain.

"Sasha!" Sarah exclaims and claps her hands. "There you are, girl." She kneels down beside the dog and tells her it's going to be ok. She looks up at me. "You remember Sasha, don't you Charlie?" I rack my brain. The name sounds familiar. Dogs, dogs, why would I know, who do I know that has a—it hits me. The public library guy.

"Oh yeah, I remember you." I say as I kneel down next to Sarah and scratch Sasha's neck. "I always thought you were a boy." She tips her head back and rakes her nails across the floor.

"Nope, she's a little lady. This is Sam's dog," she tells me. *Sam.* So he has a name. "It's actually Sam that led me here in the first place."

"Sam can walk?"

"No, he can't walk. His muscles are all atrophied." She affirms sadly. "But he asked me to bring Sasha here. She was coughing and having a hard time breathing and she wouldn't eat anything. I guess all she did was sleep. So he told me about this free clinic and asked me to bring her here. That's how we met."

"What's wrong with her?" I ask. Sasha tilts her head toward mine and licks me. Her tongue is dry like sand paper, more akin to a cat's tongue than a dog's. She stares up at me with sad, milky eyes. I gasp when I make the connection. "She's blind?"

"Yeah, but she's always been blind. She doesn't know any better," Maggie says over my shoulder, getting the shots ready. I hear cabinets opening and closing, and glass bottles being shuffled around.

"Then what's wrong with her?"

"She has heartworm." Maggie answers. Silence falls over the room. Sasha shrinks back when she senses the change. "It's a parasite that lives in the heart and lungs." Maggie explains.

"Is she going to be ok?"

"Most likely, but she's in a lot of pain. We have her on immiticide injections, which are kind of like chemo treatments for dogs. We have to give her one more today."

"Can't you do anything for the pain?" Sasha rolls onto her side and whimpers. I stoke her belly to put her at ease.

"Some animal hospitals administer xylazine, a sedative, but we can't afford that here." Maggie says this with a guilty expression. She swishes around the immiticide, and then pushes a needle into the center of the jar, drawing its contents out like a straw. Sasha drifts off to sleep, with her mouth drawn into a smile. I'm scared for her.

Maggie walks over to the silver operating table with her massive needle. "I don't really have to give her that, do I?" I ask Sarah. She shakes her head.

"No, we need you for your muscles." Maggie says, keeping the mood light. "Can you give us a hand lifting her onto the table?" Her voice is soothing and I try to focus on it as I get underneath the dog. "That's right, easy on the back. That's where the injection sight is." I lift her effortlessly onto the table.

"Wow, look at you. That would have taken all three of us," Sarah praises. I turn to her and crack a smile.

Sasha regains consciousness when she hits the cold surface. I hold her there, cradled in my arms, as Sarah strokes her and Maggie injects the shot. I look away when the needle goes in and I feel Sasha tighten against me. She lets out a long, painful howl. "There, there, girl. It's gonna be ok, you're getting better. I know it doesn't feel like it but you are." I soothe. I touch her with my thumbs. "You'll feel better soon, I promise." My voice catches on the last syllable. Then Sasha arches her back and throws up.

~~~

"Thanks for helping us clean the cages." Pam says appreciatively.

"No problem," I answer, pulling off one of my rubber gloves so I can scratch my nose. We're shoveling out dog shit together. I can't believe how much of it there is. The smell is terrible.

A cat on the other side of the room stares at me with weepy eyes. Her nose scrunches into a meow, but no sound comes out. *I'm not so different from you,* I think to myself. We have no home, nobody wants us, we sleep in our own filth. I flash a look that says *I know how you feel.* She yawns and licks herself.

There's a chorus of barks in the lobby. I guess they're done walking the K-9s. I laugh when I hear Ruth, the sweet silver-haired woman, swearing up a storm. I slop another scoop of crap into the bucket.

Sarah breezes into the room carrying an oversized bag of cat food. It's amusing to watch her maneuver something that's more than twenty percent of her body weight. She glances at me from across the room and smiles shyly. My heart starts to race.

"You need help?" I call from my cage.

"No, I'm good. Thanks though," she says with another smirk. I hear the sound of dry food on plastic as she fills the bowls. I watch her when she's not looking. She catches me and hides her face in embarrassment, grinning wildly. She tucks her hair behind her ears and turns away.

Pam's oblivious to the whole thing. I feel like we're passing notes in class, trying not to get caught. I see Sarah staring out of the corner of my eye. I tilt my head in her direction and raise my eyebrows. *I caught you.* She snaps her head back, and then looks again. This time she holds it. I try, but her eyes are too intense. I have to look away. She winks as if to say, *I win.*

Maggie pokes her head in the door, effectively ending our game. "It's almost five o'clock guys. How's it looking in here?" Pam tells her she's on the last cage. "Great, I'll tell

Ruth to round up the dogs."

Most people are happy for their work days to come to a close. I, on the other hand, could stay here all night. I remember how arctic it is outside and I slow my pace.

We lock up the dogs, and then I'm sent to the kitchen to wash up. As I'm scrubbing my fingerprints off, Maggie comes in.

"Hi Charlie."

"Hey Maggie."

"I want to give you this," she says as she extends a folded twenty dollar bill between her thumb and pointer finger. I stare back at her, dumbfounded.

"Why?"

"To reimburse you guys for train fare. To pay for your help. Whatever you want to call it. I know Sarah won't take it so here you go." She sees my dubious expression and puts her hands on her hips. "Honey, if I needed the money I certainly wouldn't be working here," she says with a chuckle. I hesitantly accept the cash.

"I don't, I mean, I probably shouldn't but..." I'm so grateful I can't articulate it. "Thank you. Thank you so much."

"You're very welcome, sweetie." She nods and pats my arm. We walk together to the front door, where everyone's bundling up to face the cold. I'm not going to tell Sarah.

"I had an idea," Ruth suggests, while she winds a wool scarf around her neck. "Why don't you two stay heyah tonight?" She motions toward Sarah and me. "It's supposed to be below zero, and the sheltahs are probably full by now. It makes more sense than stayin' outside and freezin' to death." My stomach tightens. I see the panic on Sarah's face.

"I think that's a great idea," Maggie chimes in. Pam concurs. "What do you two think?"

I look at Sarah desperately, pleading with my eyes. *Please agree with me on this one.* There's nothing I want to do more.

Ruth opens the door and the cold rushes in. "Ok." Sarah says reluctantly. "But you're stuck with me tomorrow then."

"Ok, fine, we'll let yah work tomorrow, too," Ruth says mockingly, as she drops the key in Sarah's hand. "Just remember, I'm not condoning any funny business tonight, yah heyah me?"

"Of course not!" Sarah turns a fiery shade of red.

"Oh, leave 'em alone, Ruth. They're good kids," Maggie says as she buttons her coat. She heads towards the door.

"Wait!" Sarah stops her. "I just remembered something. I promised Sam I'd bring Sasha back tonight."

"Oh, sweetie, she's in no condition to spend the night in the cold. She not supposed to exert herself, remember? Not for a month. That walk's way too long."

"But I promised, Maggie, and Sam shouldn't be alone tonight. Maybe if we could somehow keep her warm. She loves him, too, Maggie, and he's been counting down the days."

"It's not much warmer in the cages," Pam reasons. "At least he'll have a warm body to lie with."

Maggie sighs. Her heart's as big as Sarah's. You can tell she hates letting people down. "Take all the blankets in the closet, all four of them. I want that dog swaddled all night long, you hear me?" Sarah agrees enthusiastically. "And I'm sending you back there tomorrow morning to check on her."

"Of course, Maggie, thank you!"

"You're welcome." She huffs for dramatic effect. "Charlie, you're gonna to have to carry her to Sam, can you do that?"

"Yes, ma'am."

"Good. Then I'm going home." She gives us both hugs. "We're putting our faith in you tonight, so make sure you lock up if you go out for dinner, and don't let anyone in. Don't burn the place down!"

"Check, check, and check," Sarah says, rolling the key around in her hand.

"So little faith, Mags," Ruth teases.

Maggie ignores her. "You have my number?" She asks. Sarah shakes her head.

"You know where the phone is?" Maggie asks as she fishes

for a piece of paper in her purse.

"For heaven sakes, Maggie," Ruth cuts in, "it's right theyah."

"Oh all right." She mutters as she shoos Ruth away. She writes down her number and hands it over.

"Great, let's go," Ruth says as she ushers Maggie out the door. Pam follows. We thank them as they float out into the cold.

"Be safe!" Maggie cries.

"Don't do anything I wouldn't do." Ruth says with a wink.

"See you tomorrow!" Sarah calls out. I wave goodbye. I wonder if she's as nervous as I am. We look at each other briefly, then watch the three of them walk away.

CHAPTER 14

My arms are tired by the time we get to Sam. We didn't think the cramped riding quarters of rush hour on the T would be ideal for Sasha, so we ended up walking the entire way back to Boylston Street.

Sam's hunched over, hugging a tattered blanket to his chest, shaking from the cold. The look on his face when he sees us fixes a knot in my chest. It's one of pure joy. His bottom lip quivers and he extends his arms to the pile of blankets in mine. Sasha's head pokes out of the side and she whines in anticipation. I get choked up. Sarah's already misty-eyed but she's smiling. She greets Sam with a hug.

"Hi Sam. We brought her back!"

"Sasha," he says, dragging out the last syllable until I place her in his outstretched arms. His voice is grainy but soft, not what I expected.

"You have to be very careful with her though," Sarah explains, "she's in a lot of pain. She had her last injection today so go easy on her lower back. We'll be back tomorrow to check on her." He doesn't seem to be paying attention. He's stroking her head. Sasha plants a wet one on his face.

"Sam?"

"Yeah, I'll be good to her." He assures when he finally looks up. He sounds like a child, making promises so his parents will let him keep the stray animal.

Sarah pulls a Ziploc bag of dry dog food out of her coat

pocket. "She already ate today, but take this. It should last you for a while." She finds muffins in her bag and hands them over. "These are for you."

"God bless you child," he says as he takes the food. He digs right in and takes a bite. "So *this* is Charlie," Sam mumbles as he spits crumbs in my direction. He smiles with recognition. Sarah's cheeks turn red.

"I'm sorry, how rude of me. Sam, Charlie, Charlie, Sam."

"Sam Ophir IV, it's a pleasure." He extends his hand.

"Likewise," I respond as I bend down to shake it. "It's nice to have a name behind the face." I sit beside Sarah on the cold concrete.

"Fifty years," Sam blurts out. "We've been together fifty years." In the silence that follows, I try to decipher this. Dogs don't live that long.

"You and your wife?" Sarah presses.

"Yup, me and Sasha. Fifty years."

"But Sasha's a dog," I point out, wondering what I'm missing. Sarah flashes a look that says *just go with it*. I ask him what his wife's name is.

"Sasha." He answers, slightly annoyed. He gets this distant, starry-eyed look on his face. "I met her when I was ten years old. Married her when I was eighteen." He gets quiet for a minute.

"She died of leukemia," he says softly. "M'not sure how I lived through it, really. Almost didn't. I stopped working, eating, paying my bills. After I foreclosed on the house I found myself here. I sat here, day after day, and let the depression eat me alive." Eventually, the smile in his eyes reaches his lips. "The cops don't like me much. There's somethin' about a grown man cryin' that keeps 'em away." He chuckles and we wait for him to continue.

"May 14th, our anniversary." He stops. "I know it was May 14th because someone dropped an issue of the Boston Globe and I saw the date. I was ready to end it. Roll myself into the street and let the cars get me. But before I could, she showed up lookin' for me." He pats the dog. "She

85

was hangin' around the road there, listenin' to the traffic with her ears perked up. She was makin' me nervous, that close to the road an' all, so I whistled her over.

"When I saw her eyes my heart stopped. I called out her name and she came right over and started lickin' me, like she'd known me my entire life. That's when I knew."

"Knew what?" I ask.

"You're leaving out a very important fact," Sarah reminds him. She wraps her arms around her knees and waits anxiously for the next part.

"Oh, right," he says as he strokes the dog. He pauses for effect. "My wife was blind her entire life." The hairs on my arms stand up. Sarah stares at me expectantly but I say nothing. Instead, I look at Sasha. She's snoring, coiled up in Sam's lap like a cocktail shrimp. Her mouth curls into a smile.

~~~

We sit with Sam for another hour while he regales us with stories from his past. Come to find out, he has a pretty colorful history. His great grandfather was born into slavery in Tennessee, where he worked on a tobacco plantation during the Civil War. When he was freed in the 1860's, he moved north to Lancaster, Pennsylvania and started working on another plantation there. He passed down his expertise to his only son Eugene, Sam's father, who eventually got into the tobacco business himself. Sam took over the family business when he was twelve years old, the year his father killed himself. He doesn't get into who runs the business now. I figure it's better not to ask.

"So I married Sasha and we loved each other for fifty years," he continues, bringing the story full circle.

He waves a hand absentmindedly in our direction and says, "You two should go." He doesn't sound angry but he looks tired. "You've heard enough of me. Go get warm somewhere.

I pull the wool blanket out of my bag. "Take this. We

have cover for tonight. You're going to need it more than we will."

Sam accepts it graciously. It's meatier than the towel he's holding now. Sarah wraps him in it and we say our goodbyes.

We catch the tail end of dinner at St. Peter's, then we head back to the animal shelter. I'm riddled with nerves the whole way. I want to hold Sarah's hand but I'm too chicken shit to do it.

The back of my glove brushes her arm and I move closer. I reach for her but she keeps talking, oblivious to what I'm trying to do. I take a deep breath. I press my palm against hers and our fingers touch. Sarah looks down. She takes my hand and our fingers interlace expectantly.

Before I know it, we're standing in front of the green door. Sarah finagles the key in the lock with her free hand. She pulls me toward her, kissing me lightly on the lips before we enter. It sends a ripple through my chest.

"It's just me!" She warns the animals, but barking ensues. She flicks on the lights. They hum as they come on, lighting the tiny space.

"Is the heat on?" I ask, watching my breath crystallize in front of me. Sarah shrugs and tells me it doesn't feel like it. We leave our coats on and go to investigate. Ten minutes and two rounds of the floor plan later, still no thermostat.

"Should we call Maggie?"

Sarah bites her bottom lip and checks the clock on the wall. "It's almost nine, she might already be in bed."

"True." I rub my arms vigorously. "Maybe we could find a few more blankets around here."

"We gave them all to Sasha." She says solemnly. Her body's trembling from the cold. "Maybe we should call," she reconsiders.

While Sarah goes to call Maggie, I swallow another muffin and use the restroom. I wash my hands for a long time, letting the water run to scalding temperatures. Steam floats up to the mirror and I clear a spot. My eyes reluctantly meet their likeness on the other side. They're different. I'm different. I turn off the faucets and towel off. I've never seen myself smile before.

Sarah and I converge in the lobby. She looks worried, guilty almost, like she's letting me down. "Charlie..."

"What's wrong?"

"She didn't answer. Should I try again? I know she's a heavy sleeper."

"That's ok, we'll be all right. Unless you want to?"

"No, I was more worried about you." She replies.

"Don't worry about me. This isn't the first time I've gone through the night without heat." I touch her shoulder for reassurance. "We can sleep on the carpet. You can have my blanket. It's certainly better than sleeping outside."

"True." She drops to the floor and props herself up on one elbow, looking at me. I sit beside her and drape the blanket over her legs.

"Tell me something," she says, pulling her knees to her chest.

"Like what?"

"I don't know, something interesting, something no one else knows."

"Hmm." I'm not good at this game. I quickly come to the realization that I'm not very interesting.

"Like...what do you want to be when you grow up?" She asks.

Ha. Homelessness certainly wasn't an aspiration of mine. "I used to want to be a pilot."

"Used to?"

"Yeah. My best friend Peter and I used to sit in my mother's car and pretend it was an airplane. We'd play with the knobs and stuff. She'd get so mad at us." I chuckle at the memory. "Especially when she got in to the radio cranked and the heat going full blast. It was a guaranteed beating every time, but it was worth it."

"Did your parents beat you a lot?" Her expression softens.

"Oh yeah. Well, my father mostly, but yeah, all the time."

"Did you ever tell Peter?"

"He knew. He told me to close my eyes and pretend I was flying when it happened. That's what he did. It helped a little, but it still hurt like hell. Heck. Sorry." I never had to watch my mouth around Liam. Sarah shrugs it off.

"Do you and Peter still keep in touch? I mean, do you know where he is?"

I remain quiet for a long time. I pick at the lint on the blanket and then slowly roll my neck in her direction. "It's embarrassing."

"I won't laugh," she promises.

"Well, let's just say it was a sad day when I found out my only friend wasn't real. Peter was imaginary." I reiterate.

"Oh Charlie." She touches my arm. I decide not to dwell on the subject.

"What about you? What do you want to do?"

She doesn't have to think about it. She already knows. "I want to help people. Kids, mostly." She pauses. "Kids like you growing up. I want to get them out of abusive situations and into good homes."

My defense mechanism kicks in. I don't want to be her pity case. "What about Liam? He bounced around foster homes his entire life, and some of them were worse than my parents." I argue.

"That's what I want to fix," she explains. She sits up and folds her hands neatly in her lap. "You told me you wanted your parents to get divorced so they'd send you away. Don't you think other children wish for the same thing?"

"I guess."

"Why did you leave Connecticut?"

"I stayed until I couldn't take it anymore."

"Don't you think kids should have the same option?" She reaches for my hand. "I'm sorry you had such a terrible childhood. I hope you know it's not your fault. None of it is."

"I guess," I respond in a feeble attempt to agree. Social work is actually a very selfless aspiration. She'd be dedicating her life to helping others, which is fitting.

"Anyway, enough about that," Sarah says with a flourish of

her hand. She takes off her hat and tousles her hair. It falls in loose waves down her back.

My eyes go to her mouth. *Just do it, Charlie. Kiss her.* My heart thumps in my ears.

"So I have to be honest about something," Sarah cuts in.

"What?" I ask, breathless, and also a little relieved.

"This is all new for me. These feelings. I mean, I've had crushes on guys before but never like this. I don't know what it is about you—"

I lean in to kiss her, stopping her mid-sentence. She puts a gloved hand on my cheek and kisses me back. I wrap my arms around her and ease her onto her back. We kiss for a while, until I feel her stir beneath me. I stop and pull away, gasping for breath.

I ask her if she's ok. I'm distressingly hot, but my worry trumps all. I can't bear the thought of screwing this up. "I'm sorry, Sarah," I say before she can answer. I resume my upright position and wait.

Her expression softens. "You don't have to look so terrified, Charlie. I've been coming onto you all day." She sits up and clamps her knees to her chest. "It's just, I don't feel right doing this here. We promised Ruth, that's all."

That's all? I let out a sigh of relief. "Ok, we don't have to." I consent much too quickly, eager to please. I liken myself to a dog. My face is readable, and my heart's on my sleeve. If I had a tail, it would be wagging right now.

In the awkward silence that follows I struggle for words. Food, house, weather, blank. I've got nothin'. Then the old trailer where I grew up pops into my head and it gets me thinking. I pick at the carpet fibers and ask, "Sarah, why are you here?"

"What do you mean?"

"I mean, why are you living in the city, alone? What brought you here?" I can't imagine her parents being anything like mine.

"Oh." She looks down. "My mom died in a car accident and I didn't know where else to go. I hopped a bus from

Portland to Boston with babysitting money, and here I am."
She smiles weakly. I can tell there's more to the story than that.

"Didn't you have other family you could live with?"

"I didn't want to be a burden."

"I'm sure you wouldn't be—"

"I only have my aunt Nancy. She lives in Bangor, northern Maine, where my mom grew up. Her husband's on disability and they have an autistic son. She has enough to worry about, without adding a teenager to the mix."

"No grandparents?" I ask sadly, thinking of mine.

"They live in Italy," she clarifies. "They moved back after I was born because they didn't agree with my mother's decisions. I only met them once, when I was three. I don't even remember it."

"What about your dad?" I press.

Her chin drops and she says, "I don't have one." She moves a piece of hair out of her face. "I mean, I do, but I don't know anything about him." She answers my unspoken question. "Neither did my mom."

I don't get it. One night stand? Sarah shakes her head knowingly. *Ohhh.* I get a pit in my stomach.

"All I know is that I was conceived behind a grocery store in Lewiston. She was a junior at Bates and on her way back to the car when he grabbed her. I guess he caught her from behind because she never saw his face." She wipes away tears with the back of her hand. I feel incredibly uncomfortable.

Sarah pulls a folded photograph out of the front pocket of her bag. It's a picture of a woman holding a baby. It must be her mother.

"You look a lot like her," I say, trying to make her feel better.

She sniffles. "You think so?"

"Absolutely. You both have blonde hair and blue eyes."

"That's the northern Italian in me. But that's pretty much where it ends." I ignore the cage of butterflies and reach for her hand. I caress her knuckles with my thumb.

"If it helps, I think you're stunning. And your mom raised you well."

"Really?"

"You're the nicest person I know. I bet you broke a lot of hearts back in Maine."

She laughs and wipes her nose on her jacket. "No. I never had a boyfriend."

I'm dumbfounded. I tell her that's very hard to believe. She shrugs.

"What about your friends? Don't you think they're worried about you?"

"They don't know I'm gone." I wait for her to explain. "I grew up in Bangor so that's where all my friends are. Then last year my mom met Tom, this doctor from Portland. "He was ok, I guess. I always felt like the elephant in the room, but he was nice enough to me. And my mom adored him."

"So you moved to Portland and had to make new friends?"

"Yup. And shortly after the move my mom died, so I had no ties there. It was just as easy to leave."

"Well if it makes you feel any better, I lived in my hometown until I was seventeen and I still had no ties. Not a single friend or family member that cared."

She squeezes my hand. "They were stupid not to."

I shrug.

Sarah stifles a yawn. "Heart to hearts are exhausting. You ready for bed?" She asks, rubbing her eyes.

"Sure," I reply halfheartedly. I don't want it to end. When I'm with her, I forget how cheerless life is.

"Good, because I'm spent," she says, using her arm for a pillow. She spreads the blanket over me. "Let's share."

We curl up together with our one blanket and try to forget the cold. Now that we're still, that's harder to do. I think of Liam. He would have liked this place.

"Charlie?"

"Hmm?"

"I had fun with you today."

"I did too." I reply, smiling. I reach into my pocket and

touch the twenty dollar bill. "Sarah?"

"Yeah?"

"Maggie gave me money today and I took it." I admit, feeling ashamed. "But if you want me to, I'll give it back tomorrow. I was only thinking we could save it for an emergency. In case there's no food or something. But if—"

"You're cute."

"I am?" I ask incredulously.

"You are. Thanks for telling me," she says and then rolls over. *Is she mad?* She didn't sound it.

She swivels her head around and says, "We can save it," putting special emphasis on the 'we'. "But don't take any more from her, ok? She doesn't have as much money as she leads you to believe."

"No, I won't." I answer quickly, feeling relieved.

"Ok, good." She smiles and touches my hand. Then she leans her head on me and closes her eyes.

CHAPTER 15

Someone's touching me. *Leave me alone,* I imagine myself saying, but nothing comes out. There's that annoying poke again. More urgency. My eyes snap open and the cold air smacks me in the face. It seeps through the blanket. My breath circles in front of me as I try to make sense of what's going on. I hear my name. Someone's calling my name.

"Charlie," she breathes, "I ccan't feel anything." Sarah touches my stomach over the blanket.

"Wass wrong?" I mumble as I slowly regain consciousness. I stare in her direction until my eyes adjust to the dark.

"It hhurts. Everywhere hhurts," she says through chattering teeth. I squint into the moonlight and examine her skin. I can't tell the color, but I see that it's covered in gooseflesh. She's shaking. Her whole body's trembling. I snap out of my haze and start to panic.

"We have to get you somewhere, now, out of the cold, to the hospital or something. I can take you." I get to my feet and start lacing my shoes.

"Nnnoo, I ddon't wwant to go outside. It's even ccolder and it's too ffar to walk," She says desperately. "It hhurts to move. I wwant to sstay here."

I bend down and wrap her in the blanket like a burrito, conceding my share of it. "Does that help?"

"It hhurts to mmove," she repeats. She looks up at me with watery eyes and tells me she's scared. My heart sinks.

"It's ok, I'm going to help you." I scan the room frantically. *Think, think,* I urge. I can't go through this again.

"What about body heat?" I ask, stone-faced. I'm thinking of Liam. *If we took off'r drawers and shared body heat, he said.* I laughed, but he didn't. Maybe I killed him. I file away the thought and return to the nightmarish present. I have no idea how I'm going to suggest this to Sarah.

"Wwhat do you mmean?" She presses.

"Umm," I delay as my cheeks redden in the dark, "I have an idea. Well, it's not really mine but I think it might help, if you want to try it, I mean." I don't sound convincing at all.

"Wwhat is it?"

"I guess if you share body heat, like skin to skin, the heat spreads faster."

"Wwhat do you mmean?" She presses.

"Like, we would have to take off our clothes, and, kind of hold each other, I guess. So our skin's touching." She goes silent. I wait for her to slap me.

"I swear I won't look at you or touch you or anything like that. No funny business, I promise. I just want to help." Believe it or not, I actually mean it.

"Ppromise?"

"I promise."

"I ddon't know. I, I—"

"Do you trust me?"

"Yyes. I ttrust you," says in the midst of a full-body tremor. "Just make it stop."

"O-k," I stutter. *She's actually agreeing to this?* I'm going to be with a naked girl. She's going to see me naked. I'm in utter disbelief. And scared shitless.

"Can you help me?" Sarah asks as she fumbles with her buttons. My breathing accelerates and I nod in response to her question.

"Wwe can leave our underwear on, rright?"

I nod again. That's less embarrassing. "Maybe I should go first," I suggest, "so you don't have to sit there in the cold." She smiles and I take that as my cue to undress. She looks away and I remove my jacket and then my shoes. "Damn, damn, damn," I blurt when the cold hits my skin. I can see my breath. It's freezing. The poor animals, I think as I remove my pants.

I'm balled up in my yellowing tightie-whities, shaking just as hard as she is and feeling several degrees of awkward. Sarah tells me to take the blanket but I don't. Instead I lean in and kiss her blue lips, not knowing what else to do. She reminds me that she needs help with her clothes.

"Rrright." I slowly unpeel the blanket and unbutton her pea coat. She cries out in discomfort and I try to hurry. I'm scared. I don't want her to die.

I look to my left as she lifts her arms and I pull the shirt over her head. I see her bra in my peripheral. *Oh God.* I'm too nervous to be aroused. And too cold. I know that sounds absolutely insane, but it's true. This is not how I imagined this happening.

I have her lie back and I unbutton her jeans. I yank them off and throw them onto the heap of clothes beside us. I roll onto my back and close my eyes. I give her the signal, but Sarah whimpers in response.

"I cccan't mmmove," she says again. I sit upright and pick her up. As I draw her into my arms I see her, naked except for her bra and underwear, and it's the most beautiful thing I've ever seen. I feel guilty. I try to erase the perfect image from my mind, but I can't.

I pull her on top of me and she lays flat with her arms tucked in. She's so cold. It's like hugging an ice cube. She brings her hands to my chest and I gasp when they touch me. I don't think it's working.

I'm quickly proven wrong. The pain gives way to a tingly sensation, like a flame beneath the skin, spreading across every inch of our bodies. It's intense. To top it all off, my face and neck are on fire. I'm blushing profusely.

Sarah vocalizes her pleasure at the temperature change. With a jolt of alarm, a certain mistimed body part awakens.

"Sorry, sorry, sorry. Ignore that please," I beg, more than a little embarrassed. Graciously, Sarah pretends nothing happened.

I reach for my jacket and drape it over Sarah's back. The inside is still warm. She thanks me and says that it's working. I wrap my arms around the outside of the jacket, hugging her to my chest. She's so small I can practically touch the floor with my fingertips. She lays her ear on my chest and I kiss the top of her head.

"I can hear your heart." She murmurs. "It's beating really fast."

We lay in silence for a few minutes. "Sarah?"

"Yeah?"

"Why did you go to the river alone the other night?"

"I go there to talk to my mom. It's the only place in the city where you can see stars," she says sleepily. I tilt my head to look at her. Her eyes are closed.

"Well it's really not safe there. I'd feel more comfortable if you didn't go there anymore at night…unless I'm around." I realize I probably sound controlling. "I mean, you can do what you want, but I think your mom would agree, too. It just makes me nervous, that's all."

She presses her lips to my skin. "Ok," she agrees.

"Really?"

"Mmm hmm. On one condition," she adds

"Anything."

"You have to sing to me."

"What do you mean?" I ask nervously.

"That song you like. Danny boy. You said I could hear it another time, so what better time than now?"

"Oh I don't know—"

"Please?" She asks in the sweetest voice imaginable. "It will help me get to sleep."

I think about it for a moment, then I come to the conclusion that I'm unable to deny her anything she asks for. "Fine, but you can't laugh at me. My voice is terrible. Trust me, it'll hurt your ears."

"I'm sure I'll live," she says with a yawn. She nestles her

face into my neck and hugs my sides. It's quite possibly the best feeling in the world, being here with her like this.

"Ok, but I'm not good with the whole Irish accent part so—"

"Just sing for me," she commands, teasing.

"Fine. You asked for it." I clear my throat and start to sing. My voice cracks on the first line. *"Oh Danny boy, the pipes, the pipes are calling. From glen to glen, and down the mountain side."* Sarah touches my hand and I get distracted. She prompts me to continue.

"Tis you, 'tis you must go and I must bide. But come ye back when summer's in the meadow, or when the valley's hushed and white with snow." When I close my eyes I picture Liam here. I can hear his harmonica playing in the background. *"'Tis I'll be here in sunshine or in shadow. Oh Danny boy, oh Danny boy, I love you so."*

CHAPTER 16

With time, things start to thaw around me. The ice melts, the snow disappears, and winter slides into spring. Things get worse before they get better. Liam's death hits me in increments, as I see things that trigger flashbacks. Sarah helps me through it and I fall deeper in love with her every day.

In those next three months, we develop our own routine. Day shelters on Monday and Thursday, Tuesday dinners at South Parish, and at the St. Peter's Center on Wednesday, volunteer at the animal shelter on Friday, visit Sam on Saturday, and church on Sunday. In actuality, we visit Sam almost daily, and we're at the animal shelter more like two or three days a week, but it helps to have some structure in our lives. It makes us feel more normal.

It's a beautiful spring evening and the sunset's taking over the sky. The clouds look like cotton candy, with swirls of lilac, magenta, and rose. *I hope Sarah gets here in time to see it.* She's supposed to be meeting me in government center.

While I wait, I tap my foot in time with the saxophonist playing below. We met him for the first time a few weeks ago. He said he plays on the weekends, to earn extra cash for his family. He's really good.

Sarah emerges from the mouth of the T station, looking for me. My face lights up when I see her. She quickens her pace and jumps into my arms.

"Hey you," I whisper in her ear before returning her to the

ground. We kiss and she takes my hand in hers.

"Did you have a good day?" She asks.

"Better now," I say with a cheesy grin.

"Me too." She crinkles her nose and kisses me on the cheek. "I made quite a bit." She adds cheerfully.

"Of course you did."

"Oh stop it. You do better when I'm not around, too."

That's doubtful.

Sarah squeezes my arm. "Ready to go?"

"As ready as I'll ever be."

"Come on," she says as she tugs me down the stairs. We pass a crowd of tourists watching a guy on a unicycle do tricks. She swings our interlocked hands.

"Remind me why we're working here again?" I ask as we enter the ring of shops and restaurants and bars. It's no secret to her that I hate crowds. Accordingly, I *hate* Faneuil Hall, particularly on Friday nights.

"Nice try. I already told you it's personal. I just need the extra money, that's all."

I don't like secrets. They make me uncomfortable, which is why my stomach hurts. I'd push harder, but we've already fought about it once, and I don't like fighting with Sarah.

As we look for a place to sit I eye the clientele: a sea of drunk college guys and middle-age bankers wearing suits and ties. *Oh goodie.* I spot Cory, sitting with an older man I don't recognize, working the other side. She shoots me a fiery warning and I wave back just to piss her off.

"This looks good," Sarah says as she points to an empty patch of sidewalk next to an ATM machine. We sit down and I keep my eyes peeled for trouble. Out of the corner of my eye I catch a grungy guy with a bandana staring at Sarah.

"Charlie, what's wrong?"

"Nothing. Sorry, I'm fine" I lie. I don't like all the looks she's getting. I pull out Liam's harmonica to distract myself. I've been practicing, so I can actually play a few songs now. I start with 'Amazing Grace', and Sarah gives me that starry-eyed look that I can't get enough of.

We sit there for a while, accumulating a small mountain of bills and coins. Sarah was right. This place is a goldmine. She leans her head on my shoulder and I think, *this isn't so bad.*

No sooner had I said that, we're interrupted by a string of catcalls from the left. I look up, expecting to see Kain, but instead it's a spiky-haired metro-sexual with diamond stud earrings and seersucker shorts. *Ugh.* Sarah squeezes my hand.

"Sweetheart, don't you want a real man?" He asks with a chuckle.

"What do you want?" I bark, wound up tight like a spring.

"Woah, easy down man, I'm just talking to her." He laughs and extends his hand to Sarah. Luckily she doesn't take it. I don't know what I would have done if she had.

I sit there, tight-lipped, with my fists clenched. I know I can take this guy. I tell him to back off, and when he doesn't, I get to my feet. Sarah grabs my arm and tries to yank me back down. "Charlie, no," she pleads.

"Wanna fight tough guy?" He asks, egging me on. I don't think he means it. He's too pretty to fight. I'd mess up his hair.

I'm angry but I can't deny the person holding me back. She's too important. If I went to jail she'd be alone again. So would I. These are things I never had to think about before.

I roll my neck and clear my throat. Then I back down from the fight. Metro man laughs and acts all tough, until Sarah tells him to leave. Her expression's much scarier than mine.

After he's gone, she turns to me and whispers, "thank you," but it doesn't help. She kisses my cheek. That doesn't help either. The thing that really irks me is that you touch one of these guys, you go to jail. But a homeless person dies, and no one gives a shit.

"Let's go." Sarah says, shoveling the money into her bag. I have enough to get what I need."

"What do you need?"

"Charlie, please." She says firmly. I apologize and take her hand, letting her lead me to wherever it is we're going. Two minutes later we're standing in front of The Store 24. "I'll be right out," she says. "Wait here."

"Ok," I reluctantly agree. *What could she possibly be buying that's so off limits?* I try my hardest to honor her wishes, I really do. I wait outside for what feels like an hour before I start to worry. I consider all kinds of ridiculous worst-case scenarios and then decide I'm going in.

A bell jingles overhead as I push through the door. I duck instinctively into an aisle so I don't draw any attention to myself. Of course the aisle I duck into happens to be the one she's standing in, looking at feminine stuff. *Yikes.* She stares at me, red-faced and horrified. I hang my head in shame.

"Charlie, what are you doing here?" I stand like a dog with a tail between his legs.

"Umm—"

"I asked you to stay outside," she snaps, the disappointment painted across her face.

"I know, but I was worried about you," I explain. This doesn't help. She puts the box of tampons back on the shelf and her hands on her hips.

"I trust you, now you have to learn to trust me." Her expression softens. "There are things a girl likes to keep private from her boyfriend, you know?"

Suddenly I'm grinning from ear to ear.

"What?" She asks.

"You've never said that before."

"Said what?"

"Called me your boyfriend."

She cracks a half-smile. "Is that ok?"

"Yes, very."

"Good." She kisses me on the cheek. "I'll be right back," she says as she floats away. Mid-stride she tosses a look over her shoulder and says, "I love you, Charlie." I reciprocate with similar ease. Even after a month of hearing it, it still floors me that someone like her could love someone like me.

I remember the first time she said it like it was yesterday...

We were sharing a cot at one of the night shelters during a bad storm. There was thunder and lightning every few seconds. Sarah got up to peek out the window, and told me how much she loves thunderstorms. I remember laughing, because as a homeless person that takes cover under trees and in metal dumpsters, they're not exactly a joyride for me.

She tiptoed back to bed with this mischievous grin. "What?" I asked self-consciously. Cots were lined up like crooked teeth all around us. Luckily, there was a lot of snoring going on.

"Nothing," she said, shaking her head and smiling even wider. "I'm just happy, that's all." She climbed back on top of me (the only way to sleep two people on those things) and tucked herself under my arm.

"I'm glad you're happy," I replied as she trailed her fingers up and down my chest.

"Mmm." Sarah lingered on one of my scars and I stopped her hand. "Those aren't pretty," I said, pulling her hand away.

"Why? I like your scars." She kissed the scar on my neck. Then she slid down the cot and kissed the one of my chest.

"You do?" I managed to ask through scattered concentration.

"Yep," she replied, moving up to my face again. She kissed the side of my forehead, where I was hit by a Colt 45 bottle freshman year. She kissed my cheeks, my eyelids, my nose, and then my lips. "Do you love me Charlie?" She asked, looking into my eyes.

"So much." I responded automatically, as if someone else was inside me answering the question.

"I love you too," she whispered into my skin.

~~~

Sarah comes back from the bathroom with her plastic bag and bumps me on the leg. "Earth to Charlie..."

"Huh?" Her touch jerks me back to the present.

"You were out of it. You didn't even hear me." She takes my hand and we start walking toward Boston Harbor.

"Sorry." I raise our joined hands and kiss her knuckles.

"What were you thinking about?" She asks.

"Nothing really. Just, uh, that really bad thunderstorm last month," I admit as we pass a guy playing the guitar on Atlantic Avenue.

"That was a good night," she says, looking out over the harbor. She sighs. The view is breathtaking. The water hosts a quivering reflection of the city.

I lob my arm over her shoulder and we meander across the park. We settle in on a bench facing the water and an offshore breeze. Sarah curls her body into mine and I pull her into my lap.

Muffled music floats over from Tina's, competing with the crickets. I close my eyes and listen to the sound of water lapping the docks. I think of Liam, and the time we came down here and slept in someone's boat. It was big enough to live in. And it had stocked shelves. I remember we talked with these pretentious English accents, eating like kings and pretending we were rich. That was a good night too.

I hold Sarah around the waist and kiss her cheek. Like she's read my mind, she twists around so she's straddling me. She smiles nervously.

"What's wrong?" I ask, breathless from her positioning.

She shakes her head. Then she hooks her hand around the back of my neck and pulls my mouth to hers. I kiss her with practiced patience. *Slow it down*, I remind myself when I start getting too aggressive, kissing too hard or touching too much. But she's different this time. She's not as hesitant. She puts her hand on my thigh, and I take that as a green light. My hands fumble eagerly with her zipper.

We're still kissing and it's hard to concentrate. I go underneath her shirt and touch her bra, dizzy with anticipation. Sarah tightens in my arms. "Please?" I breathe, wanting nothing more than I want this. She doesn't say anything so I keep going. I'm about to touch her when a high-pitched squeal pierces the air. Sarah shrinks back and all the color drains from my face.

"I'm sorry! Are you ok? Did I do something wrong?" She jumps up and turns away from me, crossing her arms. *What just happened? What did I do?* I don't want to ruin this. I need to make it right.

When she finally turns around, her expression softens. I

can only imagine what mine looks like. It's probably a pathetic mix of shame, desperation, and serious rejection. Neither one of us says anything. A worst-case scenario flashes through my mind. *Maybe I should leave.* I get up from the bench. I take a few steps and groan with discomfort.

"Charlie, wait!" I turn around. Sarah's coming toward me. When she gets there she stops and hangs her head. *Here it comes.*

"I shouldn't have done that without any explanation," she says. "It wasn't fair to you."

"What do you mean?" I ask, simultaneously relieved and confused with my guard intact. She sits on the ledge of a nearby fountain. I sit beside her. It's really hard not to kiss her when she's upset like this.

"My step-dad." She stops. I notice that she's shaking.

"Did he hurt you?" I ask, putting my arm around her. Her silence says everything. My body tenses as I realize I'm not going to like this.

"He was a mess after my mom died. Every time he saw me it hurt him, because I reminded him of her." She swallows hard. "Then, one night he got really drunk and told me I smelled like her. He said when he closed his eyes he couldn't tell the difference. He started...kissing me."

My insides are churning. I want to punch something, or start sprinting, one of the two. Sarah can tell I'm upset. She takes my hand in hers. "Did he—"

"No," she answers quickly, "but he got close. And if you hadn't stopped Kain..." She starts sobbing and it startles me.

"It's ok," I soothe as I rub her back.

"I'm sorry."

"Sorry for what?" I ask incredulously.

"I don't know." She wipes her nose with her sleeve. "What if I can never be intimate with you? What if I can't get over this? I mean, I just screamed when you touched me!" She hides her face and lets out a fresh wave of hysteria. I get down on my knees in front of her and pull her hands away.

"Hey. Shhh, listen. That will never happen with me. I'd

never do anything to hurt you, and I'd never let anything happen to you. If it makes you uncomfortable we won't do it. I'm not going anywhere, Sarah. I'll wait forever if it takes that long."

"Really?" She sniffles and flashes that beautiful smile I've been waiting for.

"Yes, really. When we met, I had a sign on my forehead that said damaged goods. But you still gave me a chance. I'd be a hypocrite not to do the same for you."

She climbs into my arms and I carry her back to the bench where we'll settle in for the night. As I remove her shoes, she rests her forehead on my shoulder and sighs. "I forgave him, you know."

"What? How could you?"

"I don't know. It was hard, but I knew he was hurting, too. I felt bad for him. It took forgiving him to make peace with it myself." She scratches her nose and stares at me sideways. "I left because I was making things harder. Because he couldn't take care of me anymore, not because of what he did."

It's hard to believe there's someone this selfless.

"Maybe you should do the same." She suggests.

"What do you mean?"

"Forgive the people from your past."

I chuckle and get to my feet. "Yeah, I don't know about that." I toss a rock at the water, watching it skip across the surface.

"Charlie, I'm serious."

I stop smiling. "I know you are." I sit down beside her and wait for a reaction. "You're not mad at me, are you?"

"Of course not. I just want you to be happy." She reaches for my hand.

"You make me happy," I say casually as I kiss her lips. She sidles up next to me and nestles her face into my neck. She tells me she loves me.

"I love you, too." I echo back. I pull her on top of me. I tell myself things are ok again. Everything's fine. But for some reason, I can't shake the feeling that something bad is going to happen. I just don't know when.

CHAPTER 17

Today's my birthday. I'm not going to make a big deal about it because I never do and it's pointless. But while I sit on the steps of Trinity Church, I realize I'm actually old enough to buy booze, and there's money in that. Underage drinkers come to me all the time asking me to buy them alcohol, thinking I'm older. All the homeless do it. It's an easy way to earn a quick buck. Or it would be if I had an ID.

I watch a blonde, curly-haired girl walk by and I think of Sarah. It doesn't matter anyway. She'd never condone it. Since we've been dating, it's like I have this blonde-haired conscience keeping me honest. She makes me want to be a better person.

"Thank you," I tell the woman as she drops change in my cup. Up close she looks eclectic, with braids and big jewelry and baggy clothes. Her clogs sound like horse hooves as she walks away. She takes them off on the grassy area in the middle of the square. She lunges into some sort of yoga position, encroaching on the two black labs fetching Frisbees to her right. Behind her is a sixty year old man wearing a dress. Nothing surprises me anymore.

My eyes wander to a family across the way. They're definitely tourists. Dad's holding open a map and pointing stuff out, while Mom smiles like she has Vaseline on her teeth. She puts her arm around her son. He shies away, embarrassed, while his sister looks around, absolutely mortified. They have no idea how lucky they are.

I stand up and peel off my shirt. It has to be ninety-five degrees out here, which is scorching for June. It's amazing that less than a year ago I was paralyzed at the thought of exposing my chest to the public. Sarah told me I'd make more money this way, which is questionable, but I'm too hot to leave it on. I look down at the semblance of a six pack. I still don't see myself that way. I feel like the fat kid that everyone's laughing at. Sarah says I'm crazy. Maybe I am.

I grab my stuff and cut through the square. There are fruit and vegetable stands, countless flower varieties, vendors selling Guatemalan sweet bread and tea cakes and freshly baked cookies the size of steering wheels. I take my change from the morning and buy a piece of fruit. I haven't gone to the bathroom in a while so I figure a mango might do the trick. *Happy Birthday to me*, I think sarcastically.

I sit down on the edge of the fountain, beside the plot of red and yellow tulips where the shamrocks had been. I eat my mango and people watch, letting the spray from the fountain cool me off. The kids splashing around in the fountain kick water at me. Not a bad way to spend my birthday, I suppose.

"Hey Charlie!"

I turn to find Shaggy bobbing his head to imaginary headphones behind me. His dreads are frizzier than ever. When he gets close enough to touch me he pats me on the shoulder. He's not wearing any shoes.

"Hey buddy. What happened to your shoes?"

"I wear socks in the summer." He says matter-of-factly. His eye twitches. That means he's not telling the truth. I cock an eyebrow and he caves. "They were taken," he admits, sighing loudly. I can venture a guess by who.

"Speaking of the devil," I say, noting the irony as I spot Kain walking down the other side of Boylston street toward the CVS.

"No. No no no no no!"

"What is it Shags?"

"It's *my* turn!"

"Your turn for what?"

"CVS! It's been two weeks since my last turn. He had his turn, his turn, his turn. Scooby! Not fair!" He calls across the street followed by a low growl. "Not...fair, not fair," he says quickly, sulking like a child.

"Hey, hey. It's ok," I reassure as I put a hand on his shoulder. "Come with me, we'll take care of it."

We cross three lanes of traffic to find Kain selling his sob story to a young couple looking for directions. They give him twenty bucks and a pitying smile, and tell him they'll pray for his wife. I wait for Kain to turn around, and then I greet him with a slow and exaggerated applause.

"Well look who it is," he says irritably as he shoves the money into his jeans.

"You're one sick fuck, you know that?"

He smiles and pulls out a Sears photo of two little girls. "Aren't they adorable?" He asks with a throaty laugh. "I stole it," he adds proudly.

"I mean it. You're going straight to hell."

"Noted," he says, rolling his eyes. "So you gotta point to this visit?" He asks, shoving the picture back in his pocket. "Let me guess. Good old Charlie's here to save the day," he says sarcastically, changing both his expression and his tone. "Except I wouldn't if I were you. 'Cause I ain't movin'," he snaps, glaring at me with disdain, warning me not to mess with him today. Something inside tells me to turn around.

Before I can process the feeling, Shaggy blurts out "my turn" and re-focuses my attention. Kain raises a fist in his direction and Shaggy moves behind me for cover. Kain laughs.

"What would this city do without you?" Kain asks. "First carrot top, then blondie, now this retard?" His expression is degrading as he looks over the shaking, whimpering thirty year old behind me. "Pathetic," he spits in our direction, wiping the residual off his chin.

"Look asshole, it's Shaggy's turn to work this corner and you know it, so get the hell out of here. Go back to your house," I snap, putting special emphasis on the last word. He comes at me like an animal cornering its prey, smiling a grinchy smile and laughing hard enough to piss me off. I put my hand out, stopping him from coming any closer. My open palm curls into a fist around his t-shirt. "Don't fuck with me, Kain, not today. I have no problem finishing you off right—"

I gasp. "You really want to finish that sentence?" He asks, grinding his teeth with anger. There's something cold and metal jammed into my belly. Kain cocks the trigger. "I dare you." He whispers.

I reach behind me and tap Shaggy with my finger. I tell him to run. He backs away hesitantly, keeping a hand grounded to my back. Kain yanks me into the brick wall beside an ATM bank. Shaggy moves with me but he gains enough distance to realize what's going on. He starts to hyperventilate. "Oh God, oh God, oh God," he repeats, over and over again, pacing in semi-circles beside us.

"You scream, you die," Kain threatens. He's smart enough to corner me in a way that shields the gun. A passerby would think we're having a heated discussion.

"Shaggy, go!" I urge. "He won't hurt you. This is between him and me, now get out of here!" I say more forcefully. He apologizes and lets go. As he darts out into traffic, almost getting himself killed, I notice the wet fabric on the crotch of his pants. My stomach sinks.

"What a sad excuse for a man," Kain says with a snake-like expression. He tightens his grip on the pistol he's pressing firmly into my skin. The indentation is starting to hurt. "Ain't much tougher than carrot top, though. It's a shame that didn't work out for you. What do they call them things? Bromance?" He laughs, thoroughly pleased with himself. My stomach muscles clench but I'm careful not to provoke him. He wants a reason to pull the trigger and I'm not going to give him one.

"Oh, did that upset you? But you have blondie now." My jaw tightens and he continues. "Thanks for that, by the way. You stole her from me and I didn't appreciate it much. What ever happened to bros before hoes?"

I laugh mockingly.

"What? We both had piece of shit fathers, fuckin' whore mothers. We ain't so different you know."

"Yeah we are." I snap.

Kain's expression changes. His eyes are angry again.

"What would you do if I killed you right now?" He jiggles the gun. "Who'd protect blondie then?" He flashes a wicked grin and says, "No one, that's who." He pauses for effect. "I think she'd come around."

The thought makes me sick. "Not in a million years would she like you," I spit, unable to contain myself.

"You're wrong!" He shouts. "If it weren't for you she'd be with me!" His voice drops off and I tilt my head in confusion. *Does Kain actually have feelings?*

When he sees my expression, he snaps. "Not like that!" The gun shakes a little. "I don't mean it like that. I mean, with you gone, I'd be able to finish what I started."

"You touch her, I'll kill you!" I threaten, unable to hold back.

"Not if I kill you first," he says with a shove. "You can't protect her if you ain't here." Just the thought of him getting close to her makes my blood boil. I tense up and he pegs me against the wall. He can say whatever he wants. *I'm not going anywhere.*

I eye the police officer sitting in front of Finagle-A-Bagel with a cup of coffee. He's facing the street in full-uniform, surveying the area. I have an idea.

"Looks like you'd better be careful." I smile. "Unless you want to spend the rest of your days getting raped in prison. That would be ironic, wouldn't it?"

"What the hell are you talking about?" He barks, keeping his eyes on my face.

"Look." Kain cranks his neck to follow my gaze. The cop picks up his steaming cup with both hands and takes a sip.

Kain swears as his dark eyes jump back and forth. He's searching for an escape. While he's distracted, I shuffle with small steps to the right. Kain follows me like a magnet, smart enough to keep me in his reach, but too dumb to notice what I'm doing. In a matter of seconds, the gun is visible to the street. A woman walking by gasps and backs away. The person behind her screams. There's a group congregating near us, too scared to come any closer, but unable to look away.

The cop gets up from his chair, reaches for his gun, and starts running toward us in alarm. Kain panics and takes a step back, muttering obscenities the entire time. I jerk away from him and yell "he has a gun!" as loud as I can. More screams. Kain looks at me with fire in his eyes.

"This ain't over," he hisses. He storms off, shoving through the screaming crowd. To my overwhelming disappointment, he get away before the officer has a chance to stop him.

CHAPTER 18

I'm back on the steps, thinking about how hungry I am, when I see Sarah approaching from the distance. She smiles when she sees me. She looks cute today, with her hair up in a loose ponytail.

"This is a nice surprise," I say as I greet her with a kiss.

"How are you?" She asks cheerfully.

"Better now," I answer, pushing the earlier incident out of my mind. "How are you?"

"I'm better, too." She's bouncing in place, holding a grocery bag.

"What's going on?" I ask with a chuckle.

"Happy Birthday!" She blurts, grinning from ear to ear. She extends the bag to me. "You thought I forgot, didn't you?"

I did. But no one's ever remembered before, so I figured the odds were good. I shrug my shoulders.

"Well I didn't! Here," she says, jiggling the bag. "Open it!"

"What is it?" I ask, feeling awkward as I take the bag. I'm secretly praying it's food. I look inside and there's a small plastic container and something bulky wrapped in newspaper. I can't believe she remembered.

I pull out the container first, charged with anticipation. I give Sarah a look that says, *what did you do*, but she urges me on. When I open it there's a piece of cake inside. It has raspberry frosting and chocolate sprinkles on top. I bite my bottom lip.

"There's a fork in there, too," she says quietly, "in case

you're hungr—"

"You're amazing." I interject. I lean down and kiss her, long and hard, drawing the attention of pedestrians and tourists. I don't care. I lift her off the ground and hug her until I realize it's so tight she can't breathe. She fakes a choking noise and I put her down.

She giggles. "Oh boy, there's more in the bag."

"Sorry."

"That's ok. Just open it!" She shrieks. Before I get the chance, she pulls out the second gift and hands it to me. I take a deep breath and proceed. It's at that moment, as I tear into the make-shift wrapping paper, that I realize just how much she owns me.

"What is…? No way. Are you serious?" I discard the last piece of paper and look at Sarah incredulously. She gets up on her tiptoes and kisses me on the cheek.

"Does it work?" I ask. She nods. "Where did you get this?"

"I found it," she says with a mischievous grin. "Someone threw it away."

I turn the radio over in my hands. It has a few nicks but overall it's in pretty good shape. I open the battery compartment in the back. I hope these last awhile. Batteries are mucho dinero. I turn the power button clockwise until it clicks into place. Sound cranks out of the tiny speakers as I test the volume. A poppy song I don't recognize is playing. It doesn't matter. I used to love music, and I miss it. My Discman was a permanent fixture to my body before my mother threw it through a window.

"I don't know how to thank you for this. No one's ever…" I have to stop. Sarah puts her hand on my arm.

"I love you," she says simply. I wrap my arm around her. "I kind of have another surprise, too," she admits.

"I don't know if I can take another one. You're making me soft," I warn, and then clear my throat.

"It's nothing special," she says as she stabs a forkful of cake.

"I don't know," I say hesitantly while I eye the food. She extends the fork to my mouth and then pulls it away. "You don't know?"

"Ahh," I moan as I reach for it, "so hard to concentrate." I lick my lips.

"So you're ok with the idea?"

"I don't even know what we're talking about," I reply idly.

Sarah giggles and backs away, taunting me with the most delicious dessert in the world. I free my hands and chase her briefly, more to amuse her than anything else. When I decide I want to catch her, I do, hugging her from behind and lifting her off the ground.

"Hey!" She squeals, kicking her legs and telling me to put her down. I do, but I keep my arm around her waist. With my free hand I move her hair aside and kiss her neck. The skin's dewy with sweat.

"Not fair," she breathes.

"Kiss me." I whisper.

I feel her turning around, leaning into my bare chest, searching for my face. I lean down to meet her lips, looking at her with all the intensity I can muster. When our mouths are only inches apart, I do the hardest thing I've ever had to do. I pull away. And then I grab her wrist and guide the fork to my mouth.

"Hey!" She chirps after I've clamped down on the fork. She lets go of the utensil and tucks the loose hair behind her ears, looking frazzled. I like it. "Cheap trick, Charlie," she adds, taking a deep breath. I just smile, holding the dessert in my mouth before swallowing, thinking *oh...my...God.*

CHAPTER 19

It's almost dusk and the setting sky is the color of lemons, casting an angelic glow on Sarah's face. "Where are you taking me?" I ask, surveying the area. We're close to Fenway Park, I know that much. I can smell the hotdogs from here.

"You'll see," she says with the radio tucked under her arm. The other one is linked with mine. "So impatient," she mutters as we cross Brookline Avenue and head toward the Fens. The bus dumps a boatload of people into the street. It's a sea of navy and red, fans sporting jerseys and face paint and ball caps with the stitched signature B.

"Are we going to the game?" I ask for the umpteenth time. There's no way we're going to the game. Tickets are next to impossible to find, and we could never afford one, not even if we worked Faneuil Hall for a month. But I still ask the question.

"You're a pain." She responds with a smirk as we cross the overpass to the Mass Pike. The area's more congested up here and it's making me anxious. An old man with a really long beard is handing out flyers about Jesus. He gives one to Sarah. She takes it politely and tucks it in her pocket.

A grown man on a tricycle whizzes by, honking his horn. He's covered in Red Sox paraphernalia. I lean into Sarah and explain that he's a legend around here. She smiles and says she's glad.

We're close to the green monster, the famous left field wall at Fenway Park. There are bars everywhere, and consequently, lots of drunks plugging up the street. All I smell is beer. I try to sneak a peek of the pre-game on the TVs inside. I tried that once, watching the game from out here. It didn't end so well. Apparently I was creeping out the customers and it took two, three-hundred pound bodyguards to tell me to leave.

We pass a child standing with his father, holding up signs for some sort of charity. They're not hurting for money. That's clear from the hundred-dollar jerseys they're wearing. The boy has a small cup in his hand. Sarah drops a few coins in it and I swallow...hard. We can't afford to part with any of that. The boy shies away from Sarah and says "thank you" behind the refuge of his father's leg.

"He's just shy around pretty girls," his father says coyly. I'm pretty sure he's hitting on my girlfriend. Sarah smiles. I take her hand, reminding him I'm here. Of course he looks like George Clooney and I look like pig-pen on Charlie Brown. It's a major buzz-kill either way.

The crowd disperses around us in all directions. The line opens up and we're finally there, staring up at it. The sign that I remember so clearly from my childhood. It says Fenway Park in white block letters against a backdrop of brick and green paint. It brings back a deluge of feelings. Nostalgia, longing, excitement, pain. Sarah reads my face and squeezes my hand. I'm so happy just standing here.

"Now I know it's not as exciting as the real thing," she starts sheepishly, "but I was thinking maybe we could sit out here and listen to the game on your radio. We'll still hear all the cheers and hits and stuff. I thought it might be fun." She eyes me nervously. "What do you think?"

"I think you're great." I tell her, overwhelmed by her kindness.

"Really? It's not stupid?"

"No, it's not stupid. It's very, very thoughtful." I put my arm around her and we fight our way through the crowds. We find ourselves in front of a souvenir shop and somehow get pushed inside. I look around in awe. I feel like a kid in a candy store, staring at hats and jackets and mini baseball bats and Wally figurines.

"Someday," Sarah comments, as she reaches out and touches one of the jerseys. "Someday I'll be able to bring you to one of these games for real."

"You really believe that?" I ask.

"Absolutely. Things will change for us eventually, I know they will. Don't you?"

"I don't know. I've given up on having expectations." I respond as I walk over to a pile of sweatshirts. The store manager watches me closely.

"That's sad, Charlie. You have to have faith that everything will work out. Otherwise, what's the point?"

"I'm happy now," I say, distracted, and squeeze her hand. The truth is, if things turn around for us, I lose Sarah. Right now I provide protection, companionship; I serve a purpose in her life. If she ever gets back on her feet she can do so much better.

"Well I'm glad you're happy. I'm happy too. Want to go get our seats?" She asks cheerfully, like we're actually going to the game. She's so cute I can't stand it.

"Sure." I've decided it's my birthday and I'm not going to sulk. If Liam was here, he would have called me a feckin' gobshite and told me to get over it. I chuckle to myself and follow Sarah out of the store. The air smells sweaty from all the people crammed together in the heat. I wonder if I blend in, or if I smell any worse than usual. I look over at Sarah apologetically. She doesn't seem to mind.

We walk down a small street parallel to the park. We pass a noisy bar full of fans, and I eye the clock. The game's about to start.

"How about right here?" Sarah points to a patch of grass behind the intersection of two sidewalks. People walk around us, picking up their step so they don't miss the game. It's not ideal but it's good enough. At least we're somewhat out of the way. And out of the way means we're less likely to get kicked out for loitering.

"Looks good," I answer, before I hunker in with the radio. I snap it on and find the station, which is difficult over the bellows of the announcer in the park. When I finally find it, Sarah claps and cheers and makes a big scene, and I get this intense urge to kiss her. There's a stray curl hanging in her eyes that I carefully brush away. She's so beautiful.

"It's starting!" Sarah exclaims. The Red Sox are about to throw the first pitch. She sits straight up, listening intently.

"I wonder who's pitching," I mutter, thinking aloud. I must have been talking when they announced it.

"Tim Wakefield." She answers. I stare back, impressed that she was paying attention. "What? I'm from Maine, not New York," she says with intentional sass. "My mom was a huge fan," she adds with a wink, then returns her focus to the radio. I don't know why I'm even surprised.

~~~

After the first three, scoreless innings, Big Papi comes to the plate and slams a triple to bring Pedroia home. Sarah and I go nuts. The radio announcer tells us it hit the wall in left field, then it was fumbled in error by someone on Seattle. What I'd give to see it live.

Sarah turns to me and says, "I love you," still breathless from all the screaming. She's grinning and her cheeks are flushed.

"I love you, too," I tell her, taking her hand. I play with her fingers as she launches into a story about her childhood crush on Nomar Garciaparra. I feel a tweak of irrational jealousy. She was ten. Am I really that insecure? Well, that's a definitive yes.

"Really? That guy?" I ask skeptically. "But he was so weird. Remember that thing he used to do at the plate? OCD much," I add as I tug at my imaginary gloves over and over and over again.

She laughs at me. "I thought it was cute."

"Cute? I don't see anything cute about it," I quietly

interject.

"I think someone's jealous." She teases with an enormous smile.

"Jealous?" I laugh like it's the most ridiculous notion in the world. "Me, a homeless bum with absolutely nothing to offer, jealous of a multi-million dollar professional athlete? No way!" I bark, trying to band aid the truth with sarcasm. I mean it as a joke, but Sarah doesn't take it that way.

"Charlie!" She scolds, "That's not true! Do you really believe that?" Kevin Youklis hits a homerun, but I pretend not to notice. Sarah's upset.

"I don't know, it's true isn't it?" I chuckle to dissolve the tension.

She puts her hands on her hips and shakes her head. "It certainly is not. You don't see what I see, Charlie, and I don't know why."

"Come here," I soothe as I pull her into my lap. "Thank you for my birthday, and for the game, and the cake, and everything." I kiss the side of her head. She turns around and leans her forehead against mine.

"You're welcome. You're a pain, you know that?"

"I know. But you still love me, right?"

"I guess." She kisses me on the lips. "We missed two homeruns you know."

"I know."

She asks, "Who got the sec—"

"What was that?" I interrupt when I hear glass shatter behind us. There's yelling coming from a bar down the street. I tell Sarah to stay where she is.

I go to investigate and I find two, very drunk guys yelling at each other outside. A third person stands there and watches as his friend instigates a fight with a much larger man.

Heated words go back and forth until the fists come out. I look around frantically for the bouncer. The smaller guy's getting the shit kicked out of him. His head keeps hitting the pavement. I run over to help, and I get clipped in the shoulder.

I stare at the wide-eyed, tight-lipped bystander and shout, "a little help here?" He ignores me and looks around. I shake my head, trying to pull the two guys apart. Luckily, they're not only tired, but drunk, which puts me at an advantage.

The bouncer comes jogging out of the bar five minutes too late. He's massive, probably six-foot-four, two-hundred and seventy-five pounds. "What's going on here?" He barks in a gravelly voice. He throws me off the pile and I smash my head on the sidewalk.

"No!" I hear Sarah shout from across the street. "He was helping!"

"Sarah, stay there!" I yell with my cheek to the pavement.

"What happened?" The bouncer asks the worthless third wheel. He points the finger at us.

"They were fighting," he says with a guilty tail-between-the-legs expression, placing the blame on the big guy and myself. "My buddy was just in the wrong place at the wrong time."

"What?" I snap, baffled at his outright lie. "Look at him!" I signal to the moaning kid on the ground. "You saw me come over to help. I was doing what you should have done in the first place!" I'm livid.

"The dirty kid started it," he says clearly, sticking to his story. I want to strangle him.

"I had nothing to do with it!" I stand up and walk over to him, fists clenched, ready for a fight. He looks alarmed by my reaction and he shrinks behind the bouncer like a little girl.

The gargantuan bouncer in the black shirt grabs my arm. "I think it's time for you to leave."

"But he's lying, I didn't start it. I just came over to break it up. This guy was watching his friend get pummeled and doing nothing about it. What about you? Way to be here—"

"Out!" He shouts with scary force. His breath smells like alcohol. The moron behind him snickers and I snap my head around. If looks could kill, he'd be charcoal.

I throw my hands up in defeat. "Fine. I'll go back over here and mind my own business."

He grabs my wrist and says, "No, you'll leave the premise

or I'll call the police."

"You've gotta be kidding me!"

"Charlie," Sarah squeaks from across the street.

The bouncer brings his thumb and forefinger an inch apart. "Look, I'm this close to escorting you out of here myself. And trust me, that's not something you want to be a part of."

Sarah crosses the street with the radio under her arm and a worried expression on her face. "Come on," she says softly as she grabs my elbow and pulls me away. The only reason I oblige is that I don't want her near them. I walk as fast as I can so I don't change my mind. Sarah has a hard time keeping up.

"People are cruel." She says with a scowl on her lips. She looks cute when she's angry, so much so that my fury subsides. It's hard to look at that crinkled forehead and tensed bottom lip without smiling.

"I'm sorry, Sarah."

"What do you have to be sorry for?" She snaps.

"I'm sorry I got involved. I promised you no more fighting and I ruined this nice game you had planned for us."

"Charlie, what you did was heroic. You were helping that boy. You have nothing to be sorry for. Don't even say that. Besides, I didn't see you throw any punches," she adds under her breath.

"That's true." I concur as I crunch through a pile of peanut shells. I reach for Sarah's hand. She takes it reluctantly. "If it makes you feel any better, this was still the best birthday I've ever had," I tell her as I squeeze her hand.

We walk away from the Green Monster, the cheering, the lights, and all the familiar smells. She smirks and replies, "It does."

CHAPTER 20

BEACH THIS WAY, reads a hand-written, arrow-shaped sign posted to the train station with duct tape. It's the first thing I see when I step off the air conditioned train into the sticky-hot summer air. We're on a covered platform, shaded from the sun, but it pours in at the edges, casting a buttery yellow glow on the tracks. It has to be ninety-five degrees out here.

Beads of sweat are already forming on my forehead. I wipe them away with the back of my hand and reach for Sarah through the other passengers. Flip-flops make clapping noises around us as people file into lines with their beach bags and folding chairs, and head toward the beach.

We climb the stairwell and exit the station. Up here the air feels thicker somehow. I breathe it in, sea salt and brine. This was Sarah's idea. I've never been to the beach before, so she thought it would be fun. I haven't decided how I feel about it yet.

I look forward through the muggy haze. Oily silhouettes hover over the pavement in front of high rises and fast food joints lining the boulevard. I watch hordes of people roaming the strip chomping on french fries and fried dough. There's so much going on. Radios blaring, babies crying, old men with paunches, wearing Speedos and sneakers, leering at pretty girls. All of a sudden my jeans and t-shirt feel suffocating. I roll up one and remove the other, stuffing it into my bag before the panic takes over.

"Show off," Sarah teases. "You just like all the girls staring at you."

"What?" I focus on taking deep breaths.

"You're lucky. If I took off my shirt I'd blind everybody."

"What are you talking about?"

She grabs my arm. "Blind everybody. Pale, pasty, blinding. If I took off my shirt I'd hurt people's eyes." She pats my bicep. "Are you ok?"

"I'd be ok with that," I answer, cracking a smile. "The whole blinding thing."

She pulls up her sleeves and says, "You might be ok with it, but I have to think of the well-being of the general public." I laugh, and then bend over to roll up her jeans. It's too hot. Although, she does look pretty cute all pink and dewy.

"Oh please, who are you kidding?" I ask. Sarah looks down at me and giggles. She knows she's gorgeous. She must.

The beach is only a short walk away. It's visible from here, glittering like diamonds in the sun. I squint to get a better look. A kid on a bicycle whizzes by as we zig-zag through the chaos. Vendors line the sidewalks, making it hard for us to get through. I take Sarah's hand and lead her to the rickety footpath everyone seems to be taking. We test its wooden planks, framed by sea grass and sand and buzzing insects, until we reach the entrance. I straighten up and sling my backpack over my shoulder.

"So this is it?" I ask, hanging onto my shoulder strap with both hands.

"This is it," she answers with a massive sigh. She looks distracted, but happy.

There in front of us lies one massive sandbox. It's not quite like I imagined it, with turquoise water and white sand. It's rougher, more commercial, and it's *really* crowded. It's a sea of umbrellas and leathery brown skin.

We find a patch of available beach along the shoreline and remove our shoes. My eyes skip back to the ocean. It's dark and immense, and loud, and it's unlike anything I've ever seen before. It's incredible. I burrow my feet into the hot sand. It burns so I pull them back. Sarah laughs at my reaction, and then charges toward the water.

"Wait!" I yell in panic, unsure of what she's doing. She splashes through the surf and then dives into a massive wave. It crashes around her and dissipates into a foamy white mist. The whole thing is graceful. I take a few steps closer, trying to find my footing. Seagulls wheel and dive overhead, laughing at me.

Sarah pops out of the water sopping wet. Her sweater's clinging to her chest and her hair's slicked back to her head. She looks incredibly sexy.

"Come in!" She calls from the water. "It's refreshing!" I walk toward her slowly. I'm not afraid of the water, per se, it's just that—I don't exactly know how to swim. I've bathed in the Charles plenty of times, but this is different. In the river I wade where it's four feet deep. And there are minnows, not sharks and stuff.

"Are you sure?" I ask. "Maybe we should lie on the sand for a while first.

"Charlie, you're sweating! You look miserable."

She's right. I'm boiling hot. *Ok, suck it up pussy, you can do this*, I tell myself as I start my sprint toward the water. I launch myself into the air like she did, but it doesn't end well. I flop awkwardly into the frigid water. It takes my breath away and causes me to suck all kinds of water up my nose. To add to the humiliation, when I go to stand up I lose my balance and get a wave in the face. It's far from pretty.

As I scramble to find footing, I feel Sarah's hand clamp down on my arm. She pulls my head to the surface and I proceed to cough and spit water all over her. "Sorry," I choke, trying to focus on breathing and getting the nasty salt-taste out of my mouth. Sarah does a good job holding back her laughter. There's no trace of it on her face.

"Are you ok?" She asks emphatically.

"Em-barr-assed," is all I get out. I cough and spit again.

"Oh, don't be! This is my fault. I didn't realize it was your first time in the water."

"It's not..." Deep breaths. "I've been...in the river before."
It's just my first time in deep, salty, shark-infested water, I think to
myself.

"Do you know how to swim?" She asks. I shake my head
sheepishly and she gasps. "I'm so sorry, Charlie!"

"Don't be. It's not like the water's even that deep," I reason
as I stand tall and it hits my belly button. "Wow, that's
embarrassing," I say with a laugh. Sarah's still frowning. "It's
not your fault. My jeans are heavy," I joke, trying to lighten the
mood.

Her lips curl into a half-smile. "I forgot you wore your fifty
pounders today," she mumbles as she tugs at my belt loops.
My jeans slip down.

I pull them up and lift her out of the water, seeking my
revenge. She wraps her legs around my waist and squeals as I
spin her around. The waves splash her denim-blue thighs as
she tightens her grip around my neck. I breathe in the scent of
her tangled hair. She says my name and we kiss.

"God, I love you," I whisper.

"I love you, too," she says back to me, blushing.

I walk her into shallow waters and put her down, kissing
the top of her head. Sarah moves away from me and starts
combing the ocean floor with her fingers. I ask her what she's
doing and she responds, "Looking for creatures," like that's a
normal thing to do.

She picks up a piece of sea sponge and shows it to me.
"Oh, look at this one!" She says, motioning toward something
else. I move closer, straining to see what she's looking at, but
hesitant because I'm not sure what it is. "It's just a crab,
Charlie," she teases, extending her hand. I lean way over to see
it and she whips a piece of seaweed at my head. I peel it off
my face and look up in disbelief. Sarah backs away with a
come-and-get-me grin. I lurch forward, and she turns and
runs, giggling uncontrollably.

My feet dig holes in the wet sand as I run after her. I look
clumsy as hell. I slip and throw out my left arm, catching
myself before I topple over, coating my clothes in sand. I

stand up and call a truce. Sarah inches over to me slowly, watching my hand. I drop the seaweed and wade back into the ocean to clean off. She joins me at my side. "I win," she mutters with a gloating smile.

"Mmm."

She puts her hand on my back and leans into me. "You know it's true."

Sucker! I lock my left arm around her waist and shovel water at her with my right. I splash her until she's drenched.

"What was that now?" I ask sarcastically.

She wipes her eyes and spits and says, "Oh, you're gonna get it now," as she slaps water at me. It's even harder to run in the ocean. I yank my legs in front of me, one at a time. It's like running through molasses. Sarah catches me and jumps on my back, trying to pull me down. I stand solid and laugh at her attempts, until she takes a lump of mud and slaps it against my forehead. "Fine, you win, you win," I admit humbly as I shield myself from another attack.

"That's right," she agrees with a chuckle as she hops down. Still panting, she adds, "At least now you know what you've been missing."

"Was it really like this as a kid?" I ask, crunching on granules of sand.

"Oh yes, it was so much fun! My mom used to bring lemonade and peanut butter and jelly sandwiches, and she'd wear this floppy hat with a pink bow that I loved. She made me put on sunscreen that smelled like coconut. I fought it every time, too, because what kid wouldn't rather be making sand castles and mud pies?" She rings the water out of her hair and says with a smile, "We'd always stop for ice cream on our way home. Peanut butter cup blizzards at Dairy Queen. Mmm, what I'd give for one of those right now."

There's a humid chill coming off the water, one that makes the hairs on my arms stand up. I notice Sarah shivering. I wrap myself around her and suggest we go lie in the sand to warm up.

"First, let's get some ice cream!" She croons, rubbing her

hands together with a glowing smile.

"We don't have any money," I reason, trying to feel her out. We usually don't like to beg on our days off, but at this point I'd do anything for a bite of...well, anything.

"That's ok. Desperate times call for desperate measures. And I'm starving!" She says through chattering teeth. I'm instantly on board. "I think ice cream's expensive here, but we can check."

We grab our things and make our way to the boulevard. The air smells like onions. We pass by the pavilions on the shore, stuffed with families, teenagers and obese people, eating fried lunches at picnic tables with red checkered table cloths. My heart goes out to them. At the same time, my stomach roars with envy.

We walk down the street in silence, taking it all in. A bikini-clad girl with long brown hair and huge sunglasses walks toward us, teetering on an expensive pair of high heels. She's in very good shape. Her hips swing confidently with each step, making her look like something out of a movie. I shake my head and look away, feeling guilty. I look over at Sarah in her wet jeans and clingy sweater and my heart goes soft. People are staring at us, but for different reasons.

"How about that one?" She suggests, pointing to an art deco building with pink and white striped awnings. I nod in approval. I don't care where we go, as long as it sells food and drink.

We walk inside, and we're transported back in time. It reminds me of a traditional 50's malt shop, or what I picture one looking like, anyway. My stomach sinks when I see that a kiddie cone costs $2.50. That's five dollars for the two of us to get the cheapest thing on the menu. I look over the clientele. A single mom with her two Latino children, a teenage boy with a few crumpled bills in his hand, an old man and his wife sharing a thick chocolate milkshake with two straws. What are the chances? I shrug and look at Sarah. She walks over to the old couple's sparkly table.

"I'm so sorry to bother you, but would you be able to spare

a couple dollars so we could get an ice cream, please?" The old man pretends not to hear her and continues sucking milkshake through his straw. His wife lifts her purse off the booth and pulls out a crisp one dollar bill.

"Here you go, sweetie. Enjoy," she says as she places it in Sarah's hand.

"Thank you so much. God bless you!" Sarah exclaims, clasping her hands together, as if the white-haired woman had actually given her enough money to buy an ice cream cone. I guess beggars can't be choosers.

"Let's try outside," she whispers as she tugs my arm toward the door. We exit the shop and bring our drippy clothes back outside. Sarah stands in front of the door with a puddle at her feet. A well-to-do family of four walks by and we ask them for help. The wife says "no thank you," with the flick of her wrist and they keep walking, grumbling as they go. We try the next several people that pass, and we get a couple quarters from one guy, some leftover pocket change totaling thirty-seven cents from another, and a lot of annoyed glances. One woman ignores us completely. Another one gives us attitude for getting paid to do absolutely nothing. I want to explain our situation. Tell her we'd give anything for a steady paycheck. That we work Wednesdays and Fridays for free. That we're both a product of unfortunate circumstances. But I don't. Instead, I watch as Sarah puts on a cheeky grin and thanks her anyway.

My stomach turns. You'd think I'd be hardened to rejection by now. You'd think I'd be used to it. But I can only take so much, especially today, on such a beautiful, wonderful day. I put my arm around Sarah and shake my head.

"I can't do this anymore. We've been out here for almost an hour and we only have four bucks. Let's just split a small, ok? I'm ok with a small."

"Oh. Ok," she says with a shrug, frowning slightly at the edge in my voice. I blame it on the hunger. It makes me grouchy sometimes.

We go back inside and order a small Peanut Butter Cup

sugar cone. The small is usually two scoops, but the girl behind the counter with the eyebrow ring gives us three. Three heaping scoops of hard white ice cream with peanut butter swirls. We thank her for her kindness and bring our cone to a table in the back. Sarah takes the first bite.

"Mmm." She closes her eyes and lets it sit in her mouth. I can't help myself. I lean in and kiss her, tasting the peanut butter on her lips. It's delectable. I brush the wet hair off her neck and linger there. She is too. Sarah shudders and says, "It's so good," in a barely audible voice. I put my hand over hers and bring the ice cream to my mouth. I take a big bite. Then I squeeze my temples as the cold goes right to my head.

CHAPTER 21

"Do you want to head back to the beach?" Sarah asks when we're done our cone.

"Sure." I raise our interlocked fingers and brush her cheek with the back of my hand. "You have some ice cream, right...there." I kiss the spot, triggering one of her easy blushes.

We stop at the public bathhouse on our way back, so we can get a cold drink of water and use the facilities. Now that we're dry, it's starting to get hot again. We head towards the water. After we've cooled off, we reclaim our spot on the beach. The sand sticks to our clothes like sugar on cookie dough.

"This is fun," Sarah remarks as she rolls onto her back and folds her arms behind her head. I sidle up beside her and lean on my side, looking down at her face. I bend down and kiss her forehead.

"It is," I agree lazily. I feel so warm and relaxed. I lie down beside her and look up at the crystal blue sky. A ribbon of white clouds stretches until it's too thin to see. I close my eyes and listen to the white noise in ebbs and flows as the waves crash against the shore. What a perfect day.

I wake up a few moments later with drool on my chin. Everything sounds loud and I'm covered in gooseflesh. My clothes are still damp so I know I haven't slept for long. I sit up and rub my eyes, trying to get my bearings. Sarah's snoring softly beside me.

I scan the parameter of the beach. This place is full of characters. There's a young, maybe thirteen-year-old, boy smoking a cigarette a few yards down. When he catches me staring, he stubs it out in the sand and flicks it in my direction. It falls short by about ten yards.

I stand up. I decide that rather than confronting the punk, I'm going for a walk. I walk the dark strip of wet sand in front of us, keeping Sarah in sight. It's much easier to walk on than the dry stuff. I pass a large Chinese woman, speaking rapid Mandarin on her cell phone, sipping sweet tea. She eyes me nervously when I walk by. I kick a piece of trash down the beach. There's a lot of it around here. I suck in the heavy ocean air. There's something rejuvenating about it, even if it is tinged with car exhaust.

I stuff my hands in my pockets and walk by two short-haired women sitting side by side in folding chairs with their faces tilted to the sun. They're chatting softly with their eyes closed. I look back at Sarah, who's now curled up on her side with her knees pulled tight to her chest. Behind her, there's a baby cruising around in his diaper. He's waving a shovel in one hand, and a Ritz cracker in the other. All of a sudden a bird swoops down and steals the cracker out of his hand. The baby starts to cry. I eye all the picnic baskets and coolers around me. *I'm tempted to try the seagull method*, I think to myself, as I watch his mother scoop him up.

On my way back to Sarah, something shiny catches my attention. I look down at my feet and I see the perfect shell. It's shiny, pink, and symmetrical. The hole at the top gives me an idea. I fetch a piece of sea grass and I thread it through the shell. I tie the ends, crafting a make-shift necklace. *It's the thought that counts*. I tuck it in my pocket, feeling good about myself, and I go back to her.

I kiss Sarah's forehead, trying to wake her up. I don't know exactly what time it is, but judging by the sun's position in the sky, it's after four. If we don't head out soon, we'll miss dinner tonight.

"Honey," a voice calls out behind me. A very concerned, white-haired woman peers over my right shoulder. She looks us up and down gently. "You two look like you're getting red. Would you like to borrow some sunscreen? I have some on my beach towel over there, if you'd like to follow?" She sounds sincere.

"Thanks for offering, but we're actually leaving," I respond, trying to sound as appreciative as possible.

"Oh, good. Get out of the sun, sweetie. Especially your friend there. You'll want to get some aloe on that."

I look at Sarah's pink skin with guilt. I should have done a better job monitoring it. I look down at my arms. Even I'm a little red.

"Sarah, wake up." I nudge her gently. She coughs and sits up, her hair all askew.

"Whazzapenit," she mumbles, all disoriented.

"It's time to go home."

CHAPTER 22

Steel gray clouds hover low overhead, with the promise of rain. We walk toward the park, feeling sunburned and stuffed. Dinner was unreal tonight. Corned beef, potatoes, boiled cabbage, carrots, bread and butter. A real Irish feast. I watch wistfully as Sarah places a hand on her protruding stomach, patting it like a pregnant woman. I can't help but smile. The wrinkled, frizzy-haired girl with the bright pink cheeks has my heart.

We settle into our usual spot on the common. It's wooded enough to give us some privacy, but adequately distanced from the halfway house outpatients howling and jacking off in the trees. I lay down our blanket and the two of us sit down to talk. We don't need a top cover tonight. The temperature is still in the upper eighties, with humidity like a wet towel against your skin. I'm sweating bullets. Sarah rolls up the heavy sleeves of her sweater, looking miserable.

"Tomorrow we'll set aside some money and buy you a t-shirt," I suggest as I grab a rope of her hair. I lift the ponytail so I can blow cool air on her neck. She sighs with pleasure.

"That would be nice," she says dreamily. "It's awfully hot in the city." Sarah collects her hair and twists it into some kind of make-shift knot on the top of her head. "My elastic broke," she explains. Gold veins of lightning streak the night sky, lighting the park like a floodlight. Thunder rumbles overhead.

Sarah gets that look in her eye, the one she had at the

shelter, the first time she said she loved me. I reach for my pack and take out the necklace I made earlier. I circle it around her neck and tie the grass ends together in the back. "I made this for you," I tell her shyly, cinching the knot.

She looks down to examine it. "Oh Charlie, it's beautiful! No one's ever given me jewelry before." She says as she puts her hand on top of the shell. "I love it!" She turns around to kiss me.

A warm breeze whips through the park and there's another clap of thunder, followed by a popping noise. I snap my head in the general direction of the sound, and through the darkness, I make out a shadow. It looks like Kain, with his arms outstretched, holding an imaginary gun. My heart skips a beat. *What does he think he's doing?*

"Charlie, what's wrong?" Sarah asks as she touches my arm. "You look like you just saw a ghost."

I look from Sarah back to the shadow and it's gone. I blink a couple times. Nothing's there. "Uh, nothing I guess."

I stretch out on my back, trying to get a hold of myself. Maybe I'm waterlogged. Sarah leans over me and stares, making me self-conscious.

"What?" I ask.

"Don't be self-conscious, Charlie. You're beautiful."

"Mmm hmm," I mumble, eyeing her like she's crazy.

Sarah rolls her eyes. "Oh come on. When I first saw you I had to catch my breath. You're gorgeous, Charlie. How is it that you have no idea?"

"When you saw me I'd cut my hair."

"No, before that. When I saw you on Christmas Eve, at the church."

"You thought I was handsome *that* day?" I ask incredulously.

"Yes. Try looking at yourself the mirror sometime," she says with a playful shove. "Those eyes, and that smile. Man! You could crack a woman's heart right down the middle, trust me."

I can't tell if she's joking or not. It doesn't sound like she is. "I don't smile much," I say.

"Who are you kidding? You smile all the time."

"I do?"

"Yes. Given our situation, you're one of the happiest people I know. Insecure, yes, and maybe a little pessimistic at times, but overall I'd say you're a happy guy." Sarah looks up at the darkening sky, then back at me. She wants something. "Ok. It's your turn."

I sit up on my elbows and ask, "My turn for what?"

"To tell me what you thought of me when we first met."

Oh boy, where to begin? I take a deep breath and smile. I remember it quite vividly. I was standing there with Liam when I saw her for the first time. She was beautiful. And she had the biggest heart, I could just tell. There was something about the way she smiled. It was glorious. She put her heart and soul into it.

My heart hammers in my chest. I play with the loose strings on my jeans as I admit to Sarah, "I was scared to talk to you."

"What?" She laughs.

"No, that's an understatement. I was paralyzed with fear. It was hard to focus on putting one foot in front of the other for crying out loud. Liam gave me a wicked hard time. I just, I'd never seen anyone like you before." I stop talking and take a breath. My hands are shaky with nerves, how stupid. "Look at me, it's happening all over again."

Sarah doesn't say anything so I continue, assuming that's what she wants me to do, saying "I never dreamed I'd have a chance with you. I just knew I had to talk to you, that's it. I figured you'd probably look right through me like all the other girls, but I had to at least try."

A plump drop of rain falls onto my shoulder. I swear I hear it sizzle. I run my hands through the grass in the thick, muggy silence that follows. This isn't easy for me.

All of a sudden the sky opens up and the rain comes down in sheets. I sit up and look at Sarah. The drops roll off her eyelashes and down her cheeks, soaking her clothes. I laugh briefly, until I see her expression. There's this intensity on her face that I've never seen before. Suddenly she's not the only one breathing heavier than usual. *What are you thinking?* I want to ask her, but I can't. Her expression has rendered me useless.

She moves closer and lifts a hand to my face. "I love you," she whispers, her breath warm in my ear. The air around us hums with sexual tension. Her fingertips trace my jawbone then her lips brush mine with a tantalizing slowness. I taste the rain on her lips. I watch her eyes, hungry for me, and I feel myself losing control.

My shirt clings to my chest. "Kiss me," I plead. She pulls my face to hers and her mouth crushes mine. We both let go, grabbing and kissing and tugging at clothes in desperation. Sarah peels off my shirt and it lands on the grass with a splat. Then she puts a hand on my chest and forces me onto my back. Rain pelts my face until she climbs over me, straddling me and looking at me in a pulse-hammering way. She pins my hands behind my head and kisses me harder. I'm cross-eyed with lust.

Twelve plus twelve equals twenty-four. Twelve times twelve equals a hundred forty-four. No, harder. Twelve time thirty-six is...four-thirty-two. Four-thirty-two plus three-seventy-five is...ahh...not working! I wrap my arms around her and pull her closer. "I love you, Sarah," I whisper, gasping for breath. "I want you so bad it hurts," I breathe as I try to pull up her shirt, heavy with rain on my chest.

She hesitantly lifts her arms and I pull the wet shirt over her head. When I see what's underneath my mouth falls open. I stare at her in awe. Taut stomach. Perfect breasts. She looks like one of the girls in my father's dirty magazines.

"You're so beautiful," I tell her.

"Thank you," she replies with a crooked smile. She's self-conscious, but her vulnerability's sexy. The knot in her hair falls out and her hair tumbles onto my chest, wet and sticky with rain. I run my hands over her warm skin. I breathe her in. I pull her on top of me and bring her mouth to mine.

Sarah kisses me back, but not like before. She keeps one hand grounded this time. When I reach for the buckle on her jeans I feel her shaking.

"Hey, what's wrong?" I ask, letting my breathing return to normal. Sarah rolls off my chest. She clutches her shirt and continues to shake. She won't look at me.

The frenzy subsides and it hits me like a ton of bricks. "I'm sorry. I'm so sorry. I'm an idiot." I reach for her hand. Every muscle in my body wants to pull her back, but I exercise incredible restraint.

"I'm getting better." She says softly. "I trust you, I do. But I still have my convictions, you know?" It's a watered down protest but she makes it nonetheless.

She hugs her knees, rocking gently back and forth. "Trust me, I want this as much as you do, I'm just not ready. I can't."

I think I know what she's saying. Religion, right? I try to hold onto it, I really do, but there's a pain down under that's hard to ignore. I close my eyes, then I reply in strained tone, "Never feel bad for having convictions. We'll wait until you're ready. That's the way I want it." I try to sit up and realize I can't move just yet. "Give me a minute," I plead as I return to my back, taking deep breaths and trying to do long division. "I love you," I remind her as I curse my pheromone-riddled body, and the crippling charge that's coursing through it.

"Thank you," she says sweetly, kissing my cheek. I feel myself smile. The rain has slowed to a cool drizzle, but I'm thankful for it. I keep my eyes closed and let it wash over me.

While I'm lying there, paralyzed, I hear a belt buckle chink. I feel something warm slip down the front of my jeans and I hear a breathless "oh" escape Sarah's lips. Next thing I know I'm writhing in pleasure. There's this toe curling sensation as my heart finds its way in my ears. The dizziness, the shortness of breath, the volley of colors behind my lids as my eyes roll back in my head. I grab at the ground with both hands.

All it takes is a minute. While I plummet, my mind opens up like a sky and there she is. I see her on the beach. Crying. Kissing in the animal shelter. Lying together in the cold and watching her smile. Her achingly beautiful body. It all comes at me so fast. I cry out for her.

I feel her eyes on me as I flop around like a fish out of water, trying to deal with the aftermath. I try to say something and then stop. I release a contented sigh. Out of the corner of my eyes I see her wipe her hands on the wet grass. "Sorry," I mumble, on the brink of unconsciousness. She lies down beside me, wide-eyed and glowing and lays her arm across my bare chest.

"My angel," I murmur, starting to think about the mess I've caused. I squirm, drenched and uncomfortable, and at the same time still quite comfortable. I blink a few times, trying to fight the exhaustion. I want to thank her, to tell her I love her more than she could possibly know. I touch her hand. But all that comes out is a muffled goodnight.

CHAPTER 23

I hate mosquitoes. They're one of the worst things about sleeping outside in the summer. I'm reminded of this when I wake up on the esplanade to a buzzing swarm of mosquitoes in my face. I swat them away and sit up, scratching the bites. I'm always itchy. It's one of the many things I've learned to live with here.

Aside from the bugs, it's a beautiful morning. The air's warm and fragrant, and the river looks like peach-colored glass. I let out a massive yawn.

I look over at Sarah, snoring softly beside me in a tangle of blankets. I watch her sleep for a few moments, then I brush the hair out of her face. She stirs gently and rolls over.

I decide to take a walk. I wander over to the water fountain, past the cannon replica and the statue of the Pops conductor, only to find myself cross-legged on the dock. A gentle breeze blows through, shaking leaves to the ground. I stare out at the river with my thoughts. I think about the article we saw in The Boston Globe about the charred dead body that washed up to shore. The statement from the Boston Police saying they were going to do everything they could to identify the body and make sure justice was served.

There was nothing after that. No one came forward to ID the remains, no one filed a missing persons report that matched his description. Their "priority case" fell to the bottom of the list. I just wanted to do right by my friend. I didn't know it would end up in more rejection and humiliation for him. I wanted to tell police who he was, and what a great person he'd been, but Sarah convinced me otherwise. She said it would only lead to speculation about his death. They'd start an investigation and they'd think I killed him, and it wouldn't do anyone any good. She said Liam knows I love him, and that he loves me, which is why he wouldn't want me to.

"Hey buddy," I murmur foolishly at the water. "I hope things are going better for you up there." I scope out the area for eavesdroppers. It's too early, even for runners. I return to my one-sided conversation. "I'm scared Sarah's going to leave me. I just have this feeling." My heart aches at the thought. "She doesn't belong here. *I* belong here. And she keeps talking about her aunt. I don't know what to do. I don't think I could live through that, losing another best friend." I get no response from Liam. Crickets fill the silence that follows. I scratch my nose and sigh.

The river mirrors the sunrise in the east. I skip a couple rocks, watching the ripples spread like fire across the surface. A duck smiles at me as it glides by. His little legs go at full speed. Quack, quack. He dunks his head and ruffles his feathers. He looks at me hopefully, to which I reply, "Sorry buddy, no food for you." He tilts his head, like he understands, and eventually resorts to diving for his own breakfast.

I get to my feet. Sarah must be up by now. I step off the dock and the cluster of seagulls perched alongside me take off, flapping north. I jog back to camp. When Sarah hears my footsteps, she calls my name.

"It's me!" I shout, putting her mind at ease as I round the corner. She props her head on her hand and smiles.

"Morning," she says in a raspy whisper.

"Good morning."

"How long have you been up?" She asks.

"Not long." I bend over and kiss her lips. She grabs my chin, stretching closer.

"What do you want to do today?" Sarah asks. "I was thinking maybe we could work the same side of town. I don't feel like being away from you today."

"Actually, I had another idea. I was thinking maybe we could get some food and go to the park."

"A picnic!" She trills.

"Yeah, I guess so," I answer with a grin. "We have a couple dollars left over from yesterday, so I was thinking we could go to the grocery store and comb the clearance cart. What do you think?"

"I love it!"

"Ok then. It's a date."

CHAPTER 24

We approach the Shaw's on Huntington Avenue, hopeful about what our three dollars and seventy-two cents will buy us. We go straight to the back of the store, by the eggs and the cream cheese, to the cart of rejects. We paw through the brown speckled bananas, the dented canned goods, and an array of baking mixes with expired labels. Eventually we settle on a couple bruised apples, some deli cheese on a blue Styrofoam tray, and two loose cans of generic brand soda. Sarah points to a bag of sour candies branded in Chinese writing. I toss it in the basket. It's only fifty cents.

I carry our basket to the checkout and we get in line behind an elderly couple. The old man clutches his wife protectively, stabilizing himself with a cane in the other hand. "Aren't they the cutest?" Sarah asks. I watch them interact with each another. They're not from around here, that's for sure.

The old woman's wearing a purple sweater with a cocker spaniel on it. She can't stop smiling. She calls the cashier honey and talks about her grandson like he's the light of her life. People around here don't make chit-chat with cashiers.

"He has a dwelling in the city, and all he has in his cupboards are condiments and tonic! Can you believe that? I told him we'd pick up a few things," she says, pulling out her wallet with unsteady hands. The cashier starts bagging their groceries. It's mostly canned goods and pasta, and a box of powdered milk. "He goes to Wentworth," She adds proudly.

"Where are you coming from?" The girl behind the counter asks.

"Maine." The husband answers, then starts coughing into a handkerchief.

His wife continues. "We took the train here. It was just wonderful."

"And expensive," the man says with a scowl. "We don't get our next social security check for two weeks."

She waves him away. "Oh you shush. We do just fine. We've never gone hungry before."

"Where in Maine are you from?" Sarah asks.

The white-haired woman turns around and smiles. "Oh, hi dear. We're from Bangor. Have you heard of it?"

Sarah grabs my arm. "You're from Bangor? I grew up there!"

"You don't say! What a small world. What's your father's name, maybe we know your family?"

I rub Sarah's back with my free hand. She smiles at the woman and says in a small voice, "My mother's name was Teresa Angelo. Did you know her?" She asks, hopeful, entwining her fingers with mine.

"No, sweetie, I didn't. But I bet she was a wonderful woman." She reaches out and squeezes her other hand. She's inconspicuous about it, but I catch her looking us over. There's compassion in her eyes. "My, you look just like my grandson." She says, patting my arm. "Doesn't he, Ed?"

Her husband shuffles forward with his cane. "Come on El, we've got to get going."

"Oh all right." She closes her purse and reaches for his arm. They move very slowly. We put our food on the belt and the cashier rings everything through. El turns around. "It was very nice meeting you both. You seem like nice kids. Good luck to you."

"Thank you," we reply in unison. Sarah adds, "You two make a cute couple."

"God bless you child. We've been married fifty-one years this past April. It hasn't always been easy, that's for sure. But

I love the old man."

"That's amazing. Congratulations!" Sarah smiles at me lovingly. "Isn't that amazing?" She's absolutely glowing.

"Yeah, that's—"

"Your total is five dollars and twenty-seven cents."

"Wait. Five dollars?" I repeat. "I thought it was less than that. We added up the stickers. All of this was on clearance, fifty percent off the lowest price." My stomach sinks. We don't have enough to cover the bill. "Did you double count something?" I ask.

She checks the tape. "No, I don't think so. It doesn't look like the soda was on sale. Did you factor in tax?"

"I don't know..."

"It's ok," Sarah chimes in. "We don't need it. We can eat on the esplanade, use the water fountains. Or we can get rid of the candies."

"But what about the picnic in the park? You wanted the candy."

"I know, but—"

The old woman clears her throat. "Honey, please. Will you let us pay the difference?"

"Oh no, we couldn't ask you to do that," Sarah replies sweetly. "We don't need it, really."

"But I insist." She takes a small wad of cash out of her wallet and peels off a few bills. "Here you go, that should cover it. And keep the change."

Sarah hesitantly accepts the money. "Thank you so much. That was very kind of you," she says as she puts our three dollars on top. She hands the money to the cashier, who promptly cashes us out.

"You're welcome, sweetie. I wish I could do more." She scrawls something on a piece of paper. "Here. You take this. If you're ever in Maine, or you need a place to stay, we have a basement apartment you could stay in free of charge until you get on your feet. You just call us anytime and we'll arrange it." Her husband perks an eyebrow, as if to say, we didn't talk about this. But there's pride in his eyes. I can see it.

I take the sheet of paper. It says Eleanor Goodwin, and it has a phone number written in black ink. "Thank you." I don't know what else to say. I'm touched.

I loop the grocery bag over my wrist and put my hand on Sarah's lower back. We follow the Goodwins out of the store, holding the door for them and helping them with their bags. When we get outside in the sunshine we go our separate ways.

"I liked them," Sarah says when we're alone. "Can you believe it? Fifty one years. They were cute. And they looked so happy!" She grabs my arm with a gleeful expression.

"Yeah, they were great," I respond, distracted, watching the cars go by. We cross the street in front of a duck tour vehicle. Big mistake. The driver shouts something over his intercom, triggering a knee-jerk response from the passengers. They hang their arms out the windows and quack at us. I hide my face and hurry Sarah along.

We approach the familiar gates of the Public Garden. The grass is trimmed short like a crew cut and it smells like summer. We walk around, admiring the fountains, tulips, and crab apple trees. Sarah points out a family of water bugs swimming in the pond. "Ooh, look at the swan boats! Do you think they're free?"

"Probably not," I respond, eyeing the long boat with a swan shell at the stern. "But we can ask."

She jogs ahead and twirls around, so she's facing me again. "That's ok," she says as she does another spin. She shuffles over to the footbridge and leans over the railing. "Do you want to go to the common and eat our lunch? There's a little more privacy over there." We look across the street at the massive expanse of green. There are dogs, sunbathers, and frisbee throwers, but it's a lot spottier than it is in the garden. Sarah knows I'm not big on crowds.

"That would be good."

"Good!" She says with a toothy grin. I watch her spaz out again, bouncing around like a pinball. She can't stop smiling.

We find a grassy spot on the common to sit down. Sarah pulls out the food and displays it on top of our shopping bag.

I chomp down my apple in four massive bites, practically swallowing the core. Sarah picks delicately at the cellophane on the cheese.

I crack open my soda and shoo away a begging pigeon. He ignores my attempts. His feathers are puffed out and his beady eyes are staring at me, examining me. I cluck at him, feeling foolish. He coos back.

"It likes you," Sarah says with a giggle. She sits back on her knees and throws him a small piece of cheese. He eats like he's never eaten before. He tilts his head and jumps a few steps closer, still staring.

"Look out!" A frisbee lands beside us, and the pigeon flies away.

"Odd little bird," Sarah utters, handing me the rest of the cheese. She lies across my legs with her hair fanned out on my lap. I can't take my eyes off her. She's tanner now, and stamped with freckles from a summer's worth of sun. She starts humming.

Sarah's oblivious to my thoughts because she's caught up in her own. She looks up at me thoughtfully and asks, "Do you think we'll be together in fifty years?"

"I hope so," is my automatic response.

Her cheeks redden. After a short pause she says, "Me too."

It's at that moment that everything clicks into place. I know how to make her stay. I'll marry her. I deserve to be happy too, don't I? I'm ashamed by my selfishness but that doesn't mean I have the will to stop. I'll make up for it. I'll vow to protect her, and take care of her, and to always be a good husband. I know she can do better, but if I can make her happy, then that makes it ok. Right?

My heart beats fast as I anticipate what I'm about to do. I lean down and kiss her lips, lingering for a while. Sarah looks taken back. "What was that for?" She asks.

"Marry me."

"What?" She bolts upright with an expression of disbelief. I take both of her hands in mine.

"Please marry me. No one's ever loved anyone as much as

I love you, and I can't imagine my life without you in it." I get to my feet and then drop to one knee so I'm eye level with her. My voice gets low and husky, very serious, when I say, "Sarah Angelo, will you marry me?"

In the stretch of silence that follows, her eyes fill with tears. I don't know what she's thinking. My hands are clammy. I'm dizzy. I may have just ruined everything. I get to my feet again.

"Wait, where are you going?" She asks, as the tears spill over and roll down her cheeks. She gets up and grabs my arm.

"I uh—I don't know," I respond sullenly.

"Charlie, look at me." She says with a breathless laugh, taking my face in her hands. I slowly raise my eyes to meet hers. She's smiling. Beaming actually. And the piercing pleasure I get from this is almost too much to handle.

"My answer's yes. Of course I'll marry you!" she exclaims with tears in her eyes.

"Really?" I ask like a fool. I need reassurance. Sarah nods her head fervently until it finally sinks in. She looks so happy.

"Woo hoo!" I shout, lifting her off the ground and spinning her around. I put her down and we kiss like it's the last time we'll ever see each other. *She said yes.* I want to shout it out loud, tell everyone I know. I see a flashback of my parents. My mom, standing there pointing at me like an insect. "You'll never be good enough for anyone," she'd say, while my father whole-heartedly agreed. Well they were wrong. There is someone that wants me, and she's perfect. She's sweet and smart and beautiful and they'll never get the chance to meet her.

I brush back her hair. "We're getting married," I whisper, leaning my forehead against hers. I take her left hand in mine. I graze my thumb over her knuckles and my heart sinks.

"I'm sorry I don't have a ring for you," I apologize, remembering the one my mom wore on her left hand. She worshiped that thing. And yet, the diamond was no bigger than a crumb.

"Don't be sorry. It's you I want, not the ring. Besides, I

wouldn't feel right wearing a diamond with all that goes on in Africa." She kisses my hand. "It's more symbolic anyway, and I have this," she says touching the shell hanging from her neck.

"Yeah, but I want people to know. I want the whole world to know. How about this?" I suggest, taking the twist tie off our candy. "It might work for now."

I secure the wiry twist of green paper around her ring finger. She extends her left her arm to admire it. "I love it!" She pronounces, angling her hand in different directions so its imaginary facets catch the light.

"I'm glad you like it. It was *very* expensive," I say with a chuckle.

She gets on her tiptoes and kisses me. "Let's get married."
 "Right now?" I ask.

She plays with my fingers. "Maybe."

"Ok."

She looks at me in surprise. "Really?"

"Yeah."

"Are you sure?" She asks.

"I've never been more sure of anything in my life." I state plainly.

Sarah jumps up and wraps her legs around me. "Me too," she breathes. I hug her tight, feeling happy, suppressing the part of me that knows better.

CHAPTER 25

The sun beats down, heating the pavement like a cook top. With worn soles, it's like walking on fire. Today I don't care. I love the smell of warm concrete in the summer. We pass a crew of construction workers who feel the need to hoot and holler at Sarah. *I smile at them.* That's a first.

It's Sam that finally brings me down from cloud nine. When we get to him I see his face is red and blistered. There's dried blood smeared over his left eye. Despite his pain, he smiles when he sees us. Sasha's ears perk up and her tail starts to wag. Without a word, she knows it's us.

"What happened, Sam? Did someone hurt you? If it's Kain, I swear to God, I'm going to—"

"Charlie, stop." Sarah drops my arm and kneels beside him. She examines the cut with sympathy and kisses Sasha on the nose. She takes Sam's empty water bottle and jogs over to the library entrance. "I'll be right back!" She shouts, before ducking inside.

"Here. Take this," I offer, pulling the remnants of our picnic lunch out of my pack. "The candy isn't very good, but don't tell Sarah I said that." He laughs weakly.

After I've stared at him for an uncomfortably long period of time he says, "sunburn," pointing to the peeling red skin.

"And the gash over your eye?" I question abruptly.

"Wrong place at the wrong time." He gives me a look that says *that's all you're getting out of me, sonny.* I begrudgingly let it go.

We sit in awkward silence until Sarah comes back with the water. She gives the first sip to Sam, and then daps a little on his blanket. "There you go, we'll just wash this up a little…" Sam winces and waves her away. Sasha whines and licks his hand.

"Sasha needs some," he interrupts, refusing treatment until she's been cared for.

"Sorry about that, Sash," Sarah says as she pours water onto her tongue. She laps it up with heartbreaking urgency.

"There's somethin' goin' on with you too," Sam muses, looking us over. "Sasha can feel it, can't ya girl?" He pats her back gently and her tail wags in agreement. Sam opens his mouth like a baby and Sarah gives him more water.

I look at Sarah with a diffident expression. "I'm not so sure now's the best time—"

"We're engaged!" Sarah blurts out. I grit my teeth, smiling reluctantly as I wait for Sam's reaction.

"How about that!" He hoots, clapping his hands and setting Sasha into a howling fit. "I knew you two were gonna make it. That's great news." His smile is genuine. "When?" Sarah tells him right away.

"Sash and I were like that. Once we got the idea in our heads, that was it. We didn't have two nickels to rub together but boy was it a celebration." He laughs. "We had our shindig at the church. It was friends, family, outdoor barbeque, and one heck of a choir. For two teenagers in a small town, it was all we could afford."

"That sounds nice," Sarah cuts in. "And expensive. Luckily we're getting married by a minister, just the two of us."

"It doesn't matter. Ours was pot luck. I'm talkin' the marriage license, certificate, fee for the church," he explains, clearing his throat. Sarah doesn't seem as disappointed by this as I am. She hands Sam the water.

"Well, we're going to City Hall to check it out," she tells him cheerfully. "Hopefully it's not that much."

Sam nods. "I'm happy for you both. If you ever need marriage advice, you let us know."

"We will!" Sarah croons. "Thank you, Sam." She gives him a hug, careful not to touch his burns. His left arm reaches for her back unbearably slowly.

When Sarah pulls away she hesitates. "Do you want us to buy you some sunscreen?" She asks reluctantly. My heart stops. Sasha looks at her and licks her chops.

"No, no. You'll need that money for bigger things. I'll be fine." He scrubs Sasha's neck and tells Sarah, "You two better get going. There's a waiting period, you know." His words are rough like sandpaper.

"A waiting period?" I ask.

He smirks and answers, "Yeah, but it's worth the wait. You'll see."

CHAPTER 26

Sarah and I approach the massive architectural oddity that is City Hall. It looks like a block of faded gray honeycomb. Sarah says it's made of corduroy concrete. Whatever it is, it's pretty cool.

I take a deep breath and head for the entrance. Sarah touches my arm, pulling me back. "Before we go in, I have to tell you something." She says.

I fear the worst.

"I saw Cory in the library, sleeping in the stacks." She pauses. "She told me Ethel died last week."

"How?" I ask.

"Natural causes I guess. But Cory said something about a car accident, too, so who knows. It's so sad."

It is. Ethel was a legend around here. It will be weird without the eccentric lady with the cart full of junk cruising around. At least Liam will be happy to see her, if that's really how it works.

I wait for the ok from Sarah to go inside. I'm not sure what the appropriate grieving period is for an elderly woman. A cohabiter. A friend. I feel bad, but compared to the loss of Liam, this is a mere blip on my emotional radar. I'm getting used to people dying.

Sarah gives me a hug and apologizes. "I know how close you were," she says, and I'm puzzled, but I play along.

"It's ok. She's in a better place now." I know saying this

will make Sarah happy.

"You're exactly right," she agrees as she takes my hands in hers. "They say when one life ends, another one begins, right?"

"I guess."

"Well, in honor of Ethel, maybe we should do this, start our new life together."

"To Ethel," I say, reaching for the door.

~ ~ ~

We walk blindly down a series of hallways, until we find someone who can help us. Sarah does all the talking. She tells the man behind the window we'd like to purchase a marriage license. In stark contrast to her excitement, the guy has the personality of a mannequin. He's wearing horned rim glasses, and his expression is a mixture of disinterest and sheer boredom. He slides a brochure at Sarah. From behind her, I rest my chin on her shoulder so I can read it. When I see the numbers my heart sinks to the ground.

Poor people can't get married.

"Fifty dollars for the license and twelve for the certificate?" Sarah asks sadly.

"Another seventy-five if you use our Justice of the Peace," he pitches dryly.

"But we can't afford that," she squeaks, putting both of her hands on the desk.

"I'm sorry," he answers like an automated machine. I want to tell him this is important to us, that this is our life. *Show some God damn emotion.* For Sarah's sake, I keep quiet.

Sarah turns around and looks at me hopelessly. When she sees my face, her eyes widen. "Charlie, calm down. We'll figure it out. We'll save, we'll do something," she mumbles, her voice cracking as her eyes fill with tears.

"You can check out other cities," the robot interrupts. When Sarah turns around, his face softens. "Boston's prices are really high compared to some of the surrounding towns.

Do you have your heart set on getting married here?"

Sarah shakes her head, wiping her eyes with the back of her hand. I wrap my arms around her. "How much lower are we talking?" I ask.

"Maybe thirty-five instead of fifty. The certificate costs about the same everywhere."

I swallow the lump in my throat. We would have to starve ourselves for weeks to come up with that kind of money. "We can save and come back," I lie, rubbing Sarah's arm for reassurance.

She looks at me with sad eyes and says, "But I wanted to marry you today."

"That's not possible anyway," the kid cuts in. "You fill out the application and then you wait, usually three to four days. There's a three day minimum." He explains. He's starting to look annoyed, like we're wasting his time. A line is forming behind us.

"Let's go, sweetheart." I push gently as I walk her out of line. The couple behind us sees her tear-stained cheeks and looks at the ground. Everyone else looks bored. Impatient. I forget this is just another day for them. They probably have some well-compensated, highly mundane task to get back to.

I turn to Sarah. "We'll figure it out, right?" She nods. "We could ask one of the ladies at the Alliance? I bet they'd give us the money," I suggest, already knowing her answer.

"We're not asking them. They volunteer for a living. They don't have much more than we do," she adds. She's probably right. We found out the other day that Ruth lives in subsidized housing in Dorchester. I had no idea. I thought they volunteered because they didn't need the money. Then again, look at us I suppose.

I hide my crushing disappointment from Sarah. The look on her face only makes it worse. We find our way outside, into the cheery sunshine of what could have been the perfect day. I kick myself a thousand times for getting my hopes up. It serves me right. After all that's happened, I should have known.

CHAPTER 27

I wanted to do something fun to take Sarah's mind off what happened at City Hall. But after two weeks of searching, I haven't come up with a thing. Well, that's not true. I've had plenty of ideas, but none of which I can afford.

I'm jogging toward the Garden, racking my brain, when I see the first poster. Then the crowds. My stomach seizes and I slow to a walk. People are pouring out of the train station like ants, making their way toward the river. What's an India Day Festival? The poster says Anniversary of Independence. *Event takes place at the Hatch Memorial Shell, Sunday, August 8th, from 4-9 PM. Free admission.* I'm listening. *Come see Indian culture...bollywood beats...bharatnatyam, kuchipudi, and bhangra dances ...food from the city's best five Indian restaurants...free medical checks, games for children.* It definitely has potential. Sarah said she always wanted to travel, to see new places and cultures, so this could be perfect.

I follow everyone to the Esplanade, where a massive crowd awaits the festivities. The vendors are starting to set up behind them. I ask the man beside me for the time. "Eight o'clock," he says, and that's A.M. This thing starts at 4? This must be quite the show.

I watch a balding Indian man lay down a blanket for his wife and two children. His wife's holding a screaming baby, trying to calm her down. The other child tugs at her leg. All I hear is the screaming. Someone bumps into me and my anxiety flares. I try to keep it in check, closing my eyes and taking deep breaths. I want to do this for Sarah. Unfortunately, it's always harder when she's not here.

I take a step back, testing my ability to keep it together. I count to ten before I decide to leave. I jog away from the mass of people, following the bike trail down the river until the buzz of excitement fades away. Out here I can hear myself think.

I stop running when I get to the old boathouse with peeling white paint. It's a little cooler today, for August at least. It feels nice. I walk to the dock and lean on the railing. There's a lot of boat traffic, plugging up the Charles with people going to the festival.

"I can do this," I say aloud, trying to psych myself up. I picture the smile on Sarah's face and it's a no-brainer. I'll do anything for her. But first thing's first. I move to the left of the boathouse, where it's shady, and I remove all of my clothes. I smell sour.

I'm wound tight, like a spring ready to uncoil. I often feel this way. I take a deep breath, filling my lungs with air. Like a balloon I release it. *So many people*, I think to myself. Then I stop thinking. I start sprinting toward the water as fast as I can. I plug all of my orifices and cannonball in, not knowing how deep the water is. The initial plunge is shockingly cold. I flail my arms in an attempt to swim when I can't find my footing. It's not working, I panic, but I know better than to open my eyes. I keep everything closed tight. I'm both reassured and embarrassed when my toes touch down on the muck at the bottom.

I submerge myself one more time, trying to scrub everything clean with the murky brown water. A few minutes later I pop up and spit until I'm blue in the face. I want to make sure I don't swallow anything. Been there, done that, and it wasn't pretty. I was sick for two days.

I shake the water out of my hair and look up, feeling exhilarated. That's when something catches my eye. The stares. People are watching me from their boats with a mixture of interest and horror. They're sunning, eating, drinking beer and watching the homeless kid bathe. Something about this angers me to no end. I lift my arm and wave until they look away. Then I flip them off and walk leisurely to the shore to get my clothes.

CHAPTER 28

I watch Sarah out of the corner of my eye. She's completely absorbed in the show. I casually drape my arm over her shoulders and she leans against me, barely missing a beat. It's pretty incredible. A big orange, white, and green-striped flag hangs center stage, and there's a woman singing underneath it. Her voice is nasally and high pitched. It's a kind of moaning that penetrates the soul. She's accompanied by an orchestra of small drums and wooden flutes and violins. Together they create this drony, whiny sound that, in an odd way, I can relate to. I close my eyes.

A new wave of dancers pour onto the stage. Some are old, some are young, and they're all dressed in bright colors. Together they look like a bouquet of flowers. They start clapping and stomping their bare feet, twirling and jumping and gyrating their hips around stage. Whenever they flail their arms, you hear jingling jewelry, making music of its own.

A group of men dressed in different combinations of red and gold join them onstage. They're wearing turbans and carrying sticks. The dance gets faster, the music speeds up. It's a sea of black hair and russet skin, moving in complete and utter synchronicity.

~~~

The performers stop for a short break and everyone floods

the restrooms. "Are you having fun?" I ask idly, playing with a lock of Sarah's hair. She looks at me, wearing my favorite smile. She leans in and kisses my cheek.

"There aren't even words to describe how much fun I'm having. Thank you," she says graciously. "Are you?"

I nod, truly meaning it.

"I'm sorry about the crowds," she adds, getting to her feet. I stand up with her.

"It's ok. It's worth it to see you this happy. Plus, I've never seen anything like this before."

"I can't believe you've been here four years and never seen this."

"Almost five now." I clarify. The realization shocks me. I don't know whether to feel sorry for myself, or proud that I survived five years on the streets.

We stretch our legs and wait for the bathroom crowd to disperse. It's an idyllic day for this. The sky's bright and clear, the sun's shining, and the humidity's low. You can't ask for any better than that.

We saunter in the direction of the stalls. There's an element of torture that comes with this place and all the delicious smells. The spiciness of the soups, chicken kebabs, basmati rice. It's too much to handle. I turn from the food to Sarah. She's staring at a group of kids with this dreamy expression on her face. All they're doing is running around in circles, playing tag. Yet, she's oblivious to everything else around her. This is nothing compared to the way she looked at that Indian baby earlier. She was cooing and blowing kisses from over ten yards away. I sigh. It wouldn't be fair to bring one of those into our world.

Sarah and I part ways when we reach the back of the bathroom lines. The men's line is much shorter, so I'm at the door in minutes. The guy behind me says something about the weather. I agree, feeling confused because people never talk to me without Sarah.

"Oh, you're up," he says jovially, pointing to the entrance.

"Thanks," I respond. On my way in I do a half spin to look

at him, but I accidentally bump into someone before I get a good look.

"Watch where you're going, asshole!" He shouts as he brushes himself off. He's tall and tan and scowling at me like I just ran over his dog. "These are new clothes," he spits rudely, examining me like a bug that needs to be squashed. He's wearing khaki shorts, a pink shirt and flip-flops. I don't see what the big deal is.

"Easy down," I respond.

"The shirt alone cost more than your life savings." He voices maliciously, blocking my way. He stands tall and tries to intimidate me. He is taller, but not by much.

My breathing accelerates and I clench my teeth. "I'm not going to fight you, I just want to use the bathroom." It takes an act of God to say it. "Move out of my way," I command.

He starts to come closer. Before I can do anything, the guy behind me drives an open palm into his chest, sending him back a few feet. "Stop being a pompous douche and let the man do his business." He snaps, then adds firmly, "You were checking yourself out in the mirror on the way out. It's your fault he bumped into you, so get over it."

I turn around. The guy looks familiar, but I can't quite place him. I give him a nod and turn back to the guy in the pink shirt, glaring him down until he walks away. What kind of a guy wears pink, anyway?

"Thanks man. Fights seem to find me when my girlfriend's not around. Fiancé now, actually," I remember with a blissful jolt.

"Congratulations. I just got married myself," he says as he unzips and starts pissing in the urinal next to mine. He holds up his left hand and touches the ring with his thumb. "Ball and chain," he adds jokingly.

"Congratulations." I try not to let the envy get to me. He seems like a nice enough guy and I don't want to ruin it. He's talking to me like an equal, a friend even. That's a first from someone like him. He's in his late twenties, he's likeable, he dresses well, and he certainly doesn't have to be talking to a bum like me.

We shake off and make our way to the sinks. "So you're a Red Sox fan?" I ask, pointing to his hat and trying to keep the conversation going. I never do that. But with him it feels different, easy somehow.

"Oh yeah, huge fan. I've been going to games with my dad since I was four."

"I went to a game with my grandpa back in the nineties."

"Oh yeah? They've come a long way since then. Two World Series, can you believe it?" I shake my head.

While we wash our hands he rambles on about the season, the players, the prospective trades on the forefront. I soak it up like a sponge. Until now, I didn't realize how much I've missed this male interaction. How much I miss Liam.

"My name's Phil, by the way. Phil Ferrari." He states as he extends a damp hand. Even his name is cool.

"I'm Charlie," I say as we shake hands.

"Well, thanks for letting me talk your ear off, Charlie. Enjoy the show," he says with a tip of his cap.

"You too," I reply sadly, following him back into the sun.

CHAPTER 29

I meet Sarah outside the bathroom twenty minutes later. She says she's sorry for making me wait so long. "The ladies' room was a circus," she explains. Judging by the trail of toilet paper outside the door, I believe her.

"Don't be sorry. It's not your fault."

"I know, but you had to wait for me, alone, with all of these people."

"It's ok. I met a guy in there and we talked about the Red Sox for a while," I detail, taking her hand as we walk back to our seats. I don't tell her about the almost-fight.

"Really? That's great. I met a girl in the ladies' room, too. She was Indian, and really beautiful. She just got married, actually. We talked about our engagement and how expensive everything is. Her ring was the size of my fist!" She feigns excitement, but the undertone of sadness breaks my heart. I don't say anything in response. I don't know what to say. Instead, I just nod and smile, like she's talking about something else.

"You know what else she said?" She asks me.

"What?"

"That a marriage license in Lawrence only costs fifteen dollars."

Now she has my attention. "How does she know that?"

"She lives there. They got married there. How much would it cost to take a train to Lawrence?" She asks, sounding hopeful.

"I don't know. I'm not even sure the commuter rail goes there. If it did, it would probably be another five or so bucks...each. Now we're up to twenty five."

"But we already have ten, so that's more doable," she reasons, "and if we can at least get married, we can worry about the certificate later. Maybe we can work there for a few days?"

The light bulb flickers on in my head. "Or, we could bum a ride with your friend, and save some money," I suggest, feeling like a friggin' genius.

"I guess we could ask Karuna." While she considers this, her face transforms with guilt. "I mean, I don't want to. But I really want this. And maybe five dollars isn't so much for her?" She justifies. She chews on her fingernail, mulling it over. "Ok, she finally concedes. Let's do it."

We get water from the fountain before going to concessions. Sarah's mouth is dry. Apparently mine is too, because I lap it up like a stray animal. No sight of her over here. She doesn't appear to be sitting down, either, although it's mass chaos on the ground. People everywhere. We eventually find Sarah's friend between the carts for Kashmir and Cafe of India, trying to decide what to order. Incidentally, she's holding hands with Phil.

"Look honey, it's the girl I was telling you about." Karuna exclaims as she tugs his arm. "Hi Sarah!"

"Hi," she responds softly. She feels pretty bad, I can tell. I squeeze her hand for moral support.

"Charlie, nice to see you," Phil acknowledges with a nod. I nod back politely.

"You two know each other?" The girls ask in unison. "This is the Red Sox guy?" Sarah whispers. I confirm with another nod, feeling embarrassed.

"It's ok, he was talking about you, too," Karuna says with a breathless laugh. A flicker of pity crosses her face. I can wager a guess on what he said. *I met this really stand-up homeless guy in the bathroom. He was so young, and he didn't have two nickels to rub together. It's a damn shame.*

"No, no. It was all good," she clarifies when she sees my face. She winks, and I affix my eyes on my feet. Sarah was right. She is beautiful. She's hard-to-look-at pretty, like Sarah, except they look nothing alike. Karuna has big brown eyes and a nose ring. Her hair's pulled back in a dark twist at the nape of her neck.

"What a small world," she says, as she pulls the enormous sunglasses off her head and slides them onto her face. She has a hint of an accent, but it's barely detectible. "My Phil met Charlie, I met Sarah. Maybe it was fate meeting you today. I believe in that sort of thing," she says, looking at her husband. She kisses him and leaves a crimson-colored lipstick print on his cheek. Sarah giggles, and Karuna wipes it off with her hand.

Maybe it is, I think to myself.

"So this is the lucky bride-to-be?" Phil asks, pointing at Sarah.

"Oh yeah, sorry. This is my fiancé, Sarah. Sarah, Phil," I introduce. Fiancé. It rolls off the tongue nicely. I can tell Sarah thinks the same thing. She's pink with pride.

"It's a pleasure to meet you, Sarah," he says, shaking her hand. She looks at him but doesn't seem to notice how handsome he is. This pleases me.

"This is my wife, Karuna. Babe, this is Charlie, the guy I stopped from getting whooped in the bathroom," he says with a chuckle. I do a cutting motion across my throat and he laughs even harder.

"What's that now?" Sarah asks, casting a disapproving look in my direction.

"So who's hungry?" Phil bellows.

~~~

Phil insists on buying us dinner. We're so hungry we can't possibly refuse. Sarah gets the mulligatawny soup, with naan and coconut sorbet, and I order meat samosas and this rice dish I can't pronounce, that has shrimp, nuts, and Indian spices. It's quite possibly the best meal I've had in my twenty-one years of existence.

I consider the possibility that I'm in love with our new friends. We spend the rest of the evening talking to them, and I don't want it to end. They're both nice, down to earth people, and I want to ask them to stay, to come live on the streets with us. But I know that's not how it works. It's not like asking a neighbor over for dinner. We're just grateful they made us feel like human beings for a few hours. It means more than either one of them will ever know.

It's getting late now. Karuna yawns and rests her head on Phil's shoulder. We watch the maintenance crew sweep off the stage, sending colorful confetti swirling to the ground below. The sun sets over the river and Sarah and I know what we have to do.

"We have a favor to ask," I blurt out before we lose the courage.

"Anything," Karuna responds lazily.

"We need a ride to Lawrence, and we were hoping maybe we could catch one with you," I explain, preparing to be shot down.

She sits up taller, with a puzzled expression on her face. "Of course you can," she answers, "but why do you need a ride to Lawrence?"

Sarah tells her…everything. She tells her about the picnic in the park, the proposal, our trip to city hall. By the time she's done explaining, Karuna's eyes are wet with tears.

"Of course you can, sweetie. We're going to give you whatever you need."

"Oh no, we don't need anything, just a ride to the town hall," she clarifies. "We can take care of everything else from there."

"Don't be silly," she says in response. "You can stay with us tonight, and we'll introduce you to the minister in the morning." Sarah's eyes widen. "Oh, I'm sorry," Karuna apologizes, "that was presumptuous of me. The town hall has a fine justice of the peace if you don't have a religious affiliation."

"No, no, a minister would be perfect!" Sarah tells her. "Is he expensive?" She asks hesitantly.

"Oh no, Mr. Starbuck? He won't charge you a dime, trust me. He and his wife are very generous people, and they're always looking for a worthy cause."

A worthy cause? Her words sting. It still doesn't change the end result, that they're helping us get married, but it sucks to be someone's charity case. I look to Sarah for sympathy, but she's beaming, absolutely glowing. That's when it hits me. This could actually happen for us. And before I know it, I'm smiling too.

CHAPTER 30

Sarah and I sit unusually close together in the back seat of Phil's Saab, watching the desolate townscape go by. I peer out the sunroof into the darkness. There are a lot more stars out here. Karuna and Phil talk quietly in the front seat, while U2 pours out of the speakers. Sarah stares out the window, taking it all in.

We cross a long bridge and I see signage that indicates we're in Lawrence. Phil points out the massive mills and clock and bell towers lining the Merrimack River, and tells us that Lawrence was one of the first industrial cities in the US. Karuna shows us the Great Stone Dam, a powerful cascade spanning the width of the river. Even in the dark it's breathtaking. Sarah gushes about it too, and says she loves waterfalls. I get an idea for our honeymoon.

We pass a cinema, a pizza place, stores and apartment buildings on what looks like a main street, decorated with old, hanging wooden markers and glowing Pepsi signs. The area's getting more residential now. "Just a few more minutes," Karuna tells us. I glance at the clock on the dash. The florescent blue display says ten o'clock. No wonder I'm so tired.

We turn into a cozy, tree-lined neighborhood with beautiful old houses and a cul de sac. Phil pulls into the driveway of a white cape. It has blue shutters and overgrown flower boxes. It looks like something you'd find on an advertisement for oceanfront property.

"This is your house?" Sarah chirps, floating around the yard like a ballerina.

"It's nice," I comment, trying to share her enthusiasm, but at the same time, utterly consumed by envy. I grab our bags from the car.

"Yup, this is it. I'm glad you like it," Karuna says proudly when we join her at the front door. "Phil, what are you doing?" She asks impatiently. He's elbow-deep in the glove box, fishing for something.

"Nothing," he replies with irritation. I don't know why they're so upset, but the tension makes me uncomfortable.

"Do you really need that now?" She asks, tapping her foot on the front step. "Come on honey, I'm cold," she whines. Without answering, Phil shuts the box and slams the door. He holds his keys over his left shoulder and hits something on the keychain. The car beeps twice and flashes its lights.

Phil fumbles with his keys in the dark, grumbling under his breath until he eventually frees the front door. I don't know what's going on here. I don't understand why Karuna's so cold. Granted, it's not eighty degrees anymore, but it has to be at least sixty-five. I look over at Sarah. She's not shivering. I guess we're tougher than suburban folk. I ponder this with a grin, reaching for Sarah's hand before we cross the threshold.

"Please excuse the mess," Karuna exclaims as we step into their perfectly immaculate home. All signs of agitation are gone. "I didn't know we'd be having guests."

The front door opens into a passageway between the kitchen and living room, at the base of a flight of carpeted stairs. "All of this carpet will come up eventually," she explains, making a sweeping motion around the room. "It's just awful. I think that's why it smells musty in here."

"Oh I think it smells wonderful," Sarah cries. "All I smell is candles," she says as she inhales deeply. I smell Indian food, but I don't say that for fear of sounding racist, or like I'm stereotyping, or whatever.

"Thanks, Sarah, you're too sweet. Can I get you guys some

tea?"

"No thanks," I respond, stifling a yawn. I don't suppose we'll be up much longer. I meander around the house, taking it all in. There are vases, and figurines, and a china cabinet full of gold-plated dishes and crystal. Everywhere you look there are framed photos and candles in different shapes and sizes. There's a large hanging rug in the living room that's pretty cool, and various Indian artifacts strewn around the house. It's a mansion compared to the little junk box I grew up in. But it still only takes a few minutes to finish the tour.

"Thank you so much for showing us around. You have a beautiful home," Sarah says politely.

"You haven't seen your room yet," Phil tells us, motioning toward a closed-off bedroom on the first floor. He opens the door to reveal a massive four-post bed with a quilted bedspread. It looks like a cranberry threw up in here. The bedding, the curtains, the candles on the bureau, they're all cranberry red. But something about it is cozy, and warm. I like it.

I walk over to the bed and touch it. It's so soft. My eyelids are heavy just looking at it. Sarah sits on the edge and bounces a couple times. She looks like a kid at the playground, having the time of her life. She throws her head back and laughs. Phil laughs too, but Karuna gets choked up. She fakes a cough and covers her mouth, trying to hide it. I pretend not to notice. Instead, I slip off my shoes and crawl up there with Sarah. There are so many pillows. "May I?" I ask before defacing them with my grimy hands.

"Of course," Phil responds, and then whispers something calming to his wife. I lay down and there's only one word to describe it: heaven. It's like sleeping on clouds. Sarah crawls into the nook under my arm and I tuck my legs behind hers. I'm so happy right now it hurts. I haven't been this comfortable in...well, ever.

"We'll let you two go to bed," Karuna says, more to her husband than us. "Do you need pjs or anything?"

To be honest, I forgot there was such a thing.

"No thank you. You've already done too much," Sarah mumbles, quickly succumbing to sleep.

"Thank you," I echo, feeling myself do the same.

"You're welcome," she responds softly, wanting to say more. "You can sleep under the covers, you know," she suggests, holding onto my consciousness until Phil herds her out of the room.

"Let them be," he tells her as he turns off the light.

The room goes black. No city lights, no traffic, no screaming, no keeping one eye open. We're safe here. I hear the door click shut and for the first time in a long time, my mind is at peace.

CHAPTER 31

I wake up to an orchestra of sounds: clanging dishes in the kitchen, the shower running, a pot of water whistling on the stove. Domestic bliss, I think to myself with a sigh. It's six fifteen and I'm wide awake. Maybe Sarah will wake up soon. Although, I really have to pee...

I slip out of the room and pad down the hallway in the dark. There's light coming from the kitchen but I sneak by. Phil's using the bathroom upstairs so I'm all set to use this one. I duck in quietly and do my business. While I wash my hands, I eye all the sprays and creams and washes arranged neatly in the filing cabinet above the sink. What are they all for? I pop the cap off one of them and smell it. It smells fruity. When I go to put the tube away, I spot an orange bottle with a white Rx label. I pick it up and shake it. It's full of pills. The label says 10 milligrams of Ambien. *Take one tablet at bedtime as needed for sleep.* They need help sleeping in a bed like that? It doesn't make sense. I put the pills back on the shelf, beside another orange bottle with a similar label. It says Prozac. My mom used to take that! I thought that was for people with depression. I shut the mirror and shake my head. I guess things aren't always as rosy as they seem.

I exit the bathroom, feeling bad about snooping. I forget what it's like to have a home, a place to store medicine and food and all your stuff. I peak into the kitchen on my way out. Karuna's there, unloading the dishwasher and simultaneously stirring sugar into her tea. Her hair's down today. It's long and straight and it swishes when she moves. She's all dressed up, too, in a pencil skirt and high heels. She looks nice.

"Good morning, Charlie," she says as she bumps the dishwasher door shut with her hip.

Dammit. She must have seen my shadow.

"Good morning," I reply, blushing profusely. "I wasn't spying or anything, I just couldn't sleep."

"I didn't think you were," she says sweetly. She breezes to the refrigerator to get some milk. "Can I get you some breakfast?"

"Maybe I should wait for Sarah," I suggest, looking around. My stomach growls back at me.

"Don't be silly. You can eat with her again later," she reasons as she starts lining up cereal boxes on the counter. That does sound awfully tempting.

Phil enters the room wearing jeans and a striped polo shirt, the picture of comfort. "Morning, honey," he says tiredly as he kisses her cheek. "Did you sleep well Charlie?" He asks, rubbing his eyes.

"Oh yeah, I slept like a rock." I respond, stifling a yawn to discredit my story. "No, really. I slept like a corpse. I didn't move all night."

"Good to hear," he says with a thumbs up. He flips open the morning paper and turns to Karuna. "Let me guess. Egg Beaters, wheat toast, Earl Grey with two sugars and a splash of milk?"

She laughs and says, "I'm such a creature of habit," more to me than Phil. "Sometimes I feel like a hamster, going around in one of those wheels." She makes a circular motion with her finger, then pulls the wheat bread out of the breadbox over the fridge. Phil puts down the paper and gets the coffee machine going while Karuna makes her eggs. The two of them move around like a well-oiled machine—cupboards clanging, bodies crossing, dishes set and cups filled, all in one seamless motion. You can tell they've done this before.

Phil and I eat cereal and english muffins with honey, while Karuna eats her mushy, florescent yellow eggs. Phil reads the headlines in sports, and I listen attentively, pretending I follow it daily like he does. I stare off into the dark hallway. I hope Sarah wakes up soon. It's not the same without her here.

Halfway through my second bowl of cereal, I hear the door open. I excuse myself from the table and run to meet her in the hall. "Why dinnit jou wake me?" She asks, blinking into the light.

"I wanted to let you sleep," I answer, suspecting that I did something wrong.

"Ok," she says groggily, resting her head on my chest. She mumbles something into my shirt. I hug her and breathe her in, without the slightest idea of what she's talking about.

~~~

I continue eating with Sarah while Karuna wipes the counters with a dishtowel. She tells us Phil works from home, so he can take us over to meet Minister Starbuck after breakfast. "They're usually up pretty early," she says. "I, on the other hand, have a long commute, so I have to get going." She makes a sad face and Phil throws her the keys.

"I'm sorry about that," Sarah murmurs between bites. "Have a wonderful day at work."

Karuna smiles. "Thank you. I'm anxious to see how everything works out with you two. It was a pleasure meeting you both."

"The pleasure's all ours!" Sarah exclaims. "Thank you so much for letting us stay in your home." Sarah has morphed into her usual chipper self. She and Karuna hug, and I sit there uncomfortably.

"Bye Charlie."

"Bye," I respond shyly, with my eyes on the plate. "Thank you, for letting us stay here and everything."

"Sure!" Karuna slips out the door and within seconds, we hear the car fire up and drive away. I'll probably never see her again, I consider emotionlessly.

"So what do you do from home?" I ask Phil, now that Karuna's gone. I sensed some tension there, because he gets to work from home and she has a long drive.

"IT consultant, for a company out of California," he says matter-of-factly. "It's a money job if you're a nerdy techy like me. You like computers, Charlie?"

"I never had one, really. We used them at school but only to do research projects and stuff. I never got to surf the net or play games or anything like that." I tell him.

"Well that needs to change..."

"What?"

"Ever heard of World of Warcraft?" He asks as he clears the dishes from the table. I tell him no. "Want to be enlightened?"

"Sure," I answer, feeling excited.

Phil leads us upstairs, into his office, where there's a huge cherry desk, a rolling leather chair, and a laptop hooked up to a giant monitor. There are papers everywhere. Phil slides them all to one corner of the desk and tells me to sit down.

"What about Sarah?"

"I'm fine," she says with a laugh. "Sit down, play!"

"Ok. What do I do now?" I ask, turning to Phil, bouncing lightly in my seat.

Phil leans over me and starts the game. "Ok, so first you have to create your character. Basically, there are two factions, the Horde and the Alliance, and you pick races and classes based on the one you choose."

"What's the difference?"

"Not much really, except the races you choose from, and the people you talk to. Each faction is like a big team, and you can only talk to other players in your faction."

"Talk to other players?"

"Yeah, other people playing the game. We're all playing on the same server so we can interact with each other. Fight, team, chat, that sort of thing."

"Cool," I add matter-of-factly, hiding my confusion. *How is that possible?*

"Ok, so take your pick," Phil instructs.

I turn to Sarah. "What are you going to pick?" I ask. I want to make sure we're on the same team.

"You pick whatever you want, and I'll pick the same," she answers.

"Ok." I bite my bottom lip and select the Alliance faction. I never was good with choices. Lucky for me, when your home is a zip code, there aren't a whole lot of choices to make. The soup kitchen that's serving that day, the corner that's least crowded, the clothes on your back.

"Now you choose your race. In the Alliance there are dwarves, gnomes, elves, draenei, and humans."

"I don't want to be a human," I interject with alarming speed. "I want to be something else."

I examine all of the characters on the screen. I know dwarves, gnomes, elves. Not dranaenei. I reluctantly pick the gnome. He's smiling, as if to say *I know something you don't know.* There's something oddly appealing about that.

We go to the next screen where I pick my class. I click on the warrior without hesitation. "Now what do I do?" I ask.

"Start walking. Look for quest givers, find your teammates, kill monsters..."

Phil warns me about giant moths and six-legged crocodiles and fire-breathing dragons. I'm jittery with excitement. My gnome inches forward. He tells me as you advance, you unlock more regions: swamps, deserts, cities. It's like an alternate life. I quickly understand the appeal of video games.

~~~

"Shit, we've been playing for three hours," Phil exclaims, running a hand through his hair and making the pieces stand up.

"Wait, just let me finish this game," Sarah pleads, hunched over the keyboard like a hedgehog, clicking away on the mouse. She has this intense look on her face. I lean over her shoulder with one arm on the desk, coaching her and giggling like a little girl. Sarah chose the Draenei Priest, a healer, which is fitting for her. She's really bad, though. Absolutely terrible. Phil said she's the worst player he's ever seen. She walks into buildings and drops her weapons. It's hysterical.

Phil clears his throat. "Ok, but after this game we have to go see Reverend Starbuck. Karuna would kill me if she knew I was playing hooky to teach you guys video games."

I turn away from the monitor so I can see if he's serious or not. I can tell by his deadpan expression that he is. I sigh. Despite my crushing disappointment, I peel myself away from the land of dragons and wizards and medieval weaponry. Back to the life of Charlie. Not that a carpeted office with bright yellow walls is the worst place to be, I consider optimistically.

I look at Sarah, completely engrossed in combat. It's like taking candy away from a child. I place my hand on her shoulder, then bend down and whisper, "We should probably get going." She whimpers and shies away from my touch. This is the worst.

Phil gives me a look and clears his throat again. Ok, change of tactics. "We're getting married though. We have to go meet the minister."

"Uh huh," she murmurs, ignoring me.

I drop my face so it's level with hers and pull out the big guns. In the saddest voice I can muster I ask, "Don't you want to marry me?"

She snaps her head to the left and sighs. "Not fair," she says as she exits the game. "Of course I want to marry you, silly."

Sarah gets up and Phil takes her chair. "Wanna see my guy?" He asks, loading the game again.

"Sure," we reply in unison. Sneaky move.

Come to find out, Phil's an Orc Warlock in the Horde faction. His character has a robe and a magic stick and a shitload of spells, armor, weapons, honor points. You name it, he's got it. And his friend list is over a hundred people long. Phil plays the modest card, but he's not fooling anyone. He runs the pointer over his stash, as if trying to decide which one to use. He's in a jungle, for crying out loud. Nothing's around.

All of a sudden, this busty creature with long hair comes out of the woodwork. A conversation bubble pops up and she says, "Hey baby, wanna trade potions?" Her name's Natalie. She's on his friend list.

Phil grins and types something back. Sarah and I eye each other uncomfortably. They converse back and forth for a while. I keep my eyes off the screen because it's none of my business. Sarah watches with a disappointed expression. Phil continues typing, lost in his own world and grinning from ear to ear.

"Natalie's on my team," he explains quickly. "I group with her a lot on quests."

"Cool," I respond casually. Sarah turns away.

"She's really good, actually. She's a hunter." He says.

"I bet she is." Sarah says under her breath. I nudge her, telling her to stop.

Phil rolls his chair around and looks at us. "What? It's just a game. We slay make believe monsters, go on imaginary missions. Why are you looking at me like that?"

"We're not," I interrupt, pulling Sarah toward me. "You're right, it's just a game."

"Does your wife know she talks to you like that?" Sarah asks. "How often do you play this game?"

"Sarah, stop—"

"Don't judge me." He says, forcing a laugh as he shuts his laptop without closing out of the game. "I'm a good husband. Besides, what do you know about marriage? You don't have a mortgage, bills, a car payment. You don't have a high maintenance wife, or a sixty hour a week job. Your in-laws aren't crawling up your ass, looking for grandchildren. It's not easy," he adds, getting up from his chair. He keeps his voice even the entire time. He doesn't sound mad, or even accusatory. Just tired.

I look at Sarah, waiting for a response. Her face tenses and her bottom lip quivers, but she says nothing. I want to chime in, tell him to go fuck himself, that I'd give my right nut to have all those things, that he has NO idea what it's like living on the streets. But deep down I have to believe that Phil's a good guy. He treated us like friends, welcomed us into his home. He's helping us get married. I'm willing to eat my pride for that.

"It's probably time to go." Phil says quietly.

"Good idea," I agree, as I follow him to the front door.

CHAPTER 32

There's only one way to put it. The minister's house is a mansion. It's the mammoth colonial three houses down from Phil and Karuna's, and it's the one house on the block that really stands out.

"This is where he lives?" I ask in awe. I had no idea the clergy got paid so well. I thought it was one step up from community service.

"Yup. Steve, his wife Sandra, and their daughter Cara. They're the sweetest family you'll ever meet."

"Thank you, Phil," Sarah says apologetically, looking him in the eyes.

"No worries," he says with one of his hundred watt smiles. I watch Sarah soften under its force. "I hope everything works out for you two." He adds. The finality of it tells me we're on our own from here on out.

We climb an elegant slate staircase leading to the front porch. Phil rings the doorbell and we wait. It's extremely hot today, probably in the nineties if I were to guess. I swat at the mosquito circling my head and ponder the realities of the situation. What if they don't like us? Or they think we're too young? Or they can tell I'm conflicted about religion? I'm suddenly seized with doubt. Before I can dwell on it any longer, I hear a woman's voice and the scuffle of nails on hardwood approaching the front door. "I'm coming!" She says. I reach for Sarah's hand. Something slides into the door with a thud and starts barking. "Oh shush you," the woman hisses on the other side.

A sturdy woman with pale skin opens the door. She has short brown hair and a kind face, worn and wrinkled with age. "Well hello there," she says warmly. "You must be Sarah and Charlie."

"Yes, Ma'am," I reply nervously.

"Well I'm Sandra, Sandy for short. It's a pleasure to meet you both."

"The pleasure's all ours," Sarah says sweetly, her voice shaky with nerves. I feel like we're on an interview.

"Karuna called me this morning and explained the situation," she tells us, smiling, sprouting crows feet at the corners of her eyes. "It's a touching story." There's a long pause as she looks off into space. Then she leans on the doorknob and says casually, "We'd be more than happy to help you." My stomach soars. Just like that?

"Hello Phillip," Sandy says as an afterthought, pulling him in for a hug. "How's everything going with you?"

While they talk, the fluffy white dog cowering behind the door eyes us nervously. He's a cute little guy, hardly bigger than a football. I picture myself punting him across the yard. While I laugh at the thought silently, Sarah makes a fuss and waves at it, and the little dog storms our feet, wagging its tail and barking up a storm.

"Don't mind Cotton, he's as harmless as a housefly!" Sandy exclaims.

"Fitting name," I think aloud.

"My daughter named him when she was in kindergarten. Pretty creative if you ask me," she says proudly. "Cotton's an old boy now." She pauses to do the math. "He's almost ten, actually. My, how time flies. Cara's going to be a sophomore in high school. I'm sure you'll get to meet her in a few hours, when she gets home from church camp."

"I'd like that," Sarah replies.

"She's going through a rebellious stage. You know teenagers. But she has a big heart. She just feels misplaced."

"That's very normal, trust me," Sarah reassures.

"I don't think she has many friends. Maybe you could talk to her? You're around her age. She might listen to you."

"I'd be more than happy to."

"You can too," she says pointing at me. "She thinks she's un-dateable for some reason. I guess the boys ignore her at school, call her freaky or something like that."

"I can try." I bend down to pet Cotton. "But I'm not good with girls either," I tease, looking to Sarah for confirmation. She shrugs her shoulders and Sandy laughs.

"I'm sure you'll do fine. Although, my daughter can be quite intimidating."

All girls are intimidating to me. Cotton licks my arm, drawing my attention away from the conversation. I'm surprised he likes dirty, sweaty things. I guess he is a dog. I run my hand along his back. His fur's thick and course, like wool, but it's spun in tight curls. He seems to enjoy being scrubbed. I scratch behind his ears and he flops on his back, inviting me to rub his belly.

"He likes you," Sandy points out.

"Charlie's good with animals," Sarah boasts. "We volunteer at an animal shelter once a week and all the animals there just love him."

Sandy looks pleased. "Well aren't you nice. Now I can see why Phil and Karuna brought you home," she utters, placing a hand on her hip. Sarah smiles, blushing slightly. Her cheeks are already flushed from the heat. I notice how uncomfortable she is. She pulls up her sleeves and wipes her forehead with the back of her hand.

"Oh sweetie, you must be sweating in that!" Sandy recognizes at the same time I do. She starts talking a mile a minute, her voice smooth as honey. "Let me get you something to wear. Cara's a little bigger than you, but I have a bag of her old clothes that may fit. We have the AC on in the house, and Steve should be home any minute, so he can help me with the pool filter. Get you all cooled off. He just stepped out to run a couple errands."

Sandy invites us inside for lemonade. Phil politely declines and heads back home. Sarah and I follow her down the hallway to the back of the house. We enter a wide open space, housing the kitchen and living room. The room has cathedral ceilings with skylights, and this old brick fireplace. The staircase is the coolest part. It starts on the right side of the room, where the living room breaks away from the kitchen, and it twists into another hallway over our heads. The railings look ancient.

"You have a beautiful home," Sarah remarks. She has always been better than me with niceties.

"Thank you, dear," she says, stopping in the kitchen.

"How old is this place?" I ask, looking around. Sandra pulls a pitcher with floating lemon slices from the fridge.

"Built in 1902," she answers as she sets it on the island. She takes two tall glasses out of the cupboard and fills them with lemonade. "Take a seat." She motions to two bar stools on the backside of the island.

We sit down and drink our lemonades while Sandy gets Sarah some new clothes. "Can you believe this place?" Sarah asks me. I shake my head.

"I feel like we're in a movie or something," she chirps.

"Tell me about it." I mumble, crunching on ice.

She sucks on one of the lemons, puckering her lips and making a face.

"Very cute," I say with a chuckle.

She plunks the rind back into her glass, sending the ice cubes into a vortex. "I know," she says smugly, licking her fingers. She breaks into a fit of giggles as the reverend enters the kitchen. When she sees him she chokes back her laughter and jumps out of her chair. The man places a bag of groceries on the counter and shakes her hand.

"Steve Starbuck. Nice to meet ya," he mutters lightly, looking around for his wife.

I get up to do my introduction. Before I get a chance, Sandy comes down the stairs carrying a neatly folded pile of clothes. "What did you do in here, Steve? One minute they're laughing, the next it's like a funeral procession," she jokes, handing off the clothes to her husband.

"What can I say? I have a gift." He responds with a laugh. He loosens the collar on his starched, short-sleeve button up shirt. There are sweat stains under the arms.

"I guess so," she says warmly, placing a hand on my shoulder. "So I see you've already met Sarah and Charlie?" I wave when she says my name.

"Yes I have. It's a pleasure." He nods and looks down at the pile of clothes in his arms. "So you'd like me to marry you in the Green Street Church, I hear?"

"That would be wonderful, Reverend." Sarah fiddles with her lemonade glass.

"Please, call me Steve."

"What have you done to these kids?" Sandy asks. She takes Sarah's shoulders and gives them a little shake. "Don't be intimidated by him, sweetie. He's a big teddy bear."

He sort of resembles a teddy bear, actually. Soft in the middle, fuzzy gray hair, button nose.

"I didn't think these fit Cara anymore." Steve says inquisitively, lifting the pile in his arms.

"Oh, those are for Sarah," Sandy says, transferring the clothes. "I've been meaning to bring them to the Salvation Army but I keep forgetting. I guess there was a reason."

I eye the pile. It looks like shorts and a tank-top, but I don't know if they're going to fit. Even folded, they look big.

"Thank you so much," Sarah says appreciatively.

"You're welcome, sweetie. Let me show you to the bathroom. Come with me."

"Can Charlie come?" Her question prompts a motherly glance from Sandy.

"Can he wait outside the door, I mean, in case I need help. No funny business, I promise."

"All right. I suppose, but you're getting separate bedrooms tonight, I'm telling you that up front." Steve smiles, amused by his wife's words.

"Tonight?" I ask.

"Do you have anywhere to go? It takes three days to process a marriage license, and I wouldn't be able to sleep at night if I knew you two were camping out under the stars."

"No, I guess not. But we wouldn't want to impose—"

"Nonsense. I don't want to hear another word. You'd be doing us a favor. You can watch Cotton while I'm at work tomorrow. I'm at Children's Hospital all day, and Steve has a seminar in Cambridge."

"Sandy's a traveling nurse. A floater," Steve clarifies. "They use her at the Children's Hospital quite a bit."

"Speaking of being used, I could sure use a swim. Hun, you want to help me clean out the filter real quick?" Sandy turns to us. "I'm sorry, you don't mind, do you? I know you want to get to town hall, but lunch is the worst time of day. It's a zoo in there," she says, waving the thought away.

Sarah's face lights up. "You have a pool?" She must have missed the earlier reference.

"Yes, ma'am. How would you feel about a quick swim and some lunch before we go?"

"Are you kidding, that would be perfect!" She turns to me. "Wouldn't that be perfect, Charlie?" Despite my overwhelming fear of ending up face down at the bottom of the pool, Sarah's so excited I can't possibly say no.

CHAPTER 33

Mr. Starbuck lets me borrow one of his swim suits. It's blue and baggy, with these god-awful gold stripes, but it feels much better than wearing jeans. Sarah's wearing one of Cara's racing suits from a couple years ago. I guess their daughter used to swim in middle school or something. Despite the generous coverage of a one-piece Speedo, it's form fitting and Sarah looks really good in it. I tell her this when she comes out of the bathroom. She covers herself with a towel.

"I feel embarrassed. I haven't worn a bathing suit in a while."

"You look beautiful. You always do."

"Really?"

"Of course you do."

Sarah finally registers my swim suit. She looks me up and down and her eyes widen.

"Pretty bad, huh?"

"Shut up. You're all tan and muscular." She touches her stomach. "I have the muscle tone of a veal."

I laugh out loud. "Ok, crazy. Let's go."

As instructed, the two of us walk through the living room, out the French doors, and into the sunroom. From there, the backyard comes into view. My mouth falls open.

The yard is enormous. And perfectly groomed. And the pool's a sparkling, crystal blue ocean in the middle of it. It's like a resort. It's a landscaped golf course with fountains and gazebos and an Olympic-sized pool.

"Oh my," Sarah breathes. "I feel like orphan Annie."

"I feel like I'm in a Sandals commercial."

Sarah laughs. "You remember those?"

"They were on all the time when I was younger. My mom used to throw beer cans at the TV," I remember with a chuckle. Sarah looks at me curiously. "TV is one thing my parents didn't scrimp on." I explain. "Good food, yes. Soap operas and sports, never."

Sarah gets on her tip toes and kisses me. "I love you."

I experience that familiar rush of joy. "I love you, too."

We walk outside, over to Sandra, who's standing by the pool in a big black suit. Her cleavage spills out the top. She skims a cluster of leaves off the surface and dumps them in what appears to be a compost bin. "Hello there," she greets us jovially.

"Hi!" Sarah exclaims.

"You look cooler, so that's good."

"I am, thank you so much. Your yard is amazing!" She exclaims, tightening the towel around her waist.

"Thank you." She chucks another basket of leaves. "You two should go in. It's clean for the most part, I'm just waiting for Steve."

"Thanks," Sarah says before looking at me, then turning back to Sandy. "Hey, do you have any flotation devices, by any chance? Noodles or tubes or anything like that?" My face turns fiery red.

"I think we have some in the garage. Let me check."

"Thanks. I'm not the best swimmer, that's all," she lies, covering for her aquatically-challenged fiancé. I cast an appreciative glance her way.

While Sandy's in the garage, Sarah drops her towel and walks over to the diving board at the back of the pool. "What are you doing?" I ask nervously.

"Watch this!" She gets up on the board and bounces a few times, then launches herself into the air, does a front flip, and slices into the water like a knife.

"Not the best swimmer, huh?" I say, cocking an eyebrow. "Show-off." She giggles and swims to the other end of the pool. She's so graceful, slithering through the water like a fish. "Maybe you can teach me?" I suggest.

"What?" She asks, shaking the water out of her ears.

"Teach me to swim," I whisper, not wanting anyone else to hear.

"I can't hear you. Come here," she says, waving me closer.

I walk over to the edge of the pool and bend down so she can hear me. She stretches her neck to kiss me. I meet her halfway. Before I know what's happening, her hands are on my hips and I'm tumbling head first into the pool.

I find my way to the surface, flailing and spitting water. Sarah's grinning wildly. I lift her out of the water and toss her into the deep end. She squeals and kicks her legs before landing with a splash, sending waves over the sides of the pool. She gives me a challenging look and kicks her way back to me. It's like watching a mermaid.

"Yes, I'll teach you how to swim," she agrees when she pops out of the water. She looks proud of herself.

"What? I can't hear you," I tease, pulling her closer. I tuck a sopping strand of loose hair behind her ear. The only sound around us is the hum of the pool filter as it churns through the remaining sediment in the pool. No street noise, no car horns. It's nice.

The silence is quickly broken by Cotton's high-pitched yapping. "Hi kids!" Steve calls from the back door, warning us of his approach. I instantly release Sarah and she swims to the edge of the pool. Cotton scurries over to her, barking and dancing in circles, but never getting too close. "He's scared of the water," Steve tells us as he removes his sandals. "He fell in once."

"Aw, poor baby." Sarah holds out her hand to sniff. Cotton inches toward it, then laps the chlorine off her fingers.

Sandy rounds the corner, carrying these colorful, fingerlike sponges. "I couldn't find the float," she tells us, "and the blue inner tube had a hole in it." She says, looking at her husband.

"That's ok." Sarah answers. "These are perfect, thank you so much!"

"You're very welcome, sweetie." Sandy tosses the peculiar sponges in the pool.

"They're noodles," Sarah explains, sensing my confusion. "Try one." I watch her wrap one around her back and under her arms, then another under her legs. She bobs in place like a buoy. I take a green one from the pile and thread it through my arms. I hesitantly lift my feet off the bottom of the pool, touching back down for a second and trying again. "You're not going to drown. I gotcha," Sarah teases. "You know, for someone so tough, you're a bit of a sissy," she says with a chuckle.

I glare at her smiling face. "You're really enjoying this, aren't you?" She sticks out her tongue. "Ok, here we go." I take a deep breath. "One...two...three." I throw all of my weight forward, sinking into the noodle, hanging on for dear life. My head stays above the surface, which I take as a good sign. I start kicking to keep my legs afloat.

"Good. There you go!" Sarah encourages, swimming beside me as I veer awkwardly towards the deep end. I sneak a quick peek at the adults. They're treading water near the stairs, trying to give us our space. All I can do is hope they're oblivious to the situation.

"Isn't it the best feeling?" Sarah asks. "I imagine this is what it's like to float in space. To be weightless, free." She slinks over to the ladder and dunks her head underwater again.

It does feel pretty incredible, now that I think about it. Gliding around without resistance, feeling the water around me, like a cool breath of fresh air. The smell of chlorine is heavy in the air as I breathe in the humidity. This is hands down the cleanest I've ever felt.

"Want to try it without the float?" Sarah asks me. "All you have to do is paddle and kick like crazy. I won't let anything happen to you."

"No offense, but I don't think you could pull me out of here, muscles."

"Sure I could. Come on." She signals toward the middle of the pool, where she regains her footing on the bottom. I reluctantly follow, feeling nervous about what I'm getting myself into. I swim over to her and stand up, keeping the noodle firmly positioned against my chest. "Ok, now lose this," she says, tugging the florescent green float out of my grasp. I stand there feeling extremely vulnerable. I'm torn between wanting to keep my pride intact, and keeping the water out of lungs. "Now put your arm around my neck, like this, and hang off me. I'm going to lift your legs and carry you." I flash her a disbelieving look. "Do you trust me?" She asks confidently.

"Yes."

"Then lean on me and lift your legs." She instructs.

"I don't want to hurt you. I'm a heavy dude."

"You won't."

"Fine, you asked for it," I caution. I wrap both arms around her neck for stability, and I lean on her with all my weight. She swiftly scoops my legs out from under me. I close my eyes, expecting to be sucked under, to get a mouthful of chlorine. But instead, I open them to find myself slung across her arms, being cradled like a child. She's holding me up.

"See? I told you I wouldn't let you drown," she says in a smug tone, kissing me on the cheek. "I'm just *that* strong." I laugh, trying to hide my relief.

She walks me around the shallow end, careful not to get too close to the Starbucks. She spins around, dragging me through the water, and I try to relax, I really do. But when she stops, there are red marks on her shoulders from where my fingers had been gripping her too tight.

"Charlie?" Sarah puts me down.

"I'm so sorry about that, I didn't—"

"Why are you so petrified of the water?"

"I'm not," I respond, acting surprised by her accusation. "I bathe in the Charles all the time."

"You know what I mean. Deep water, swimming. You're not afraid of anything else, but this makes you freak out, and

I'm just curious as to why."

"I'm not freaking out," I snap, finding myself on the defensive.

"Sorry," she apologizes. Then she does the side-stroke to get away from me.

"Wait," I plead, reaching for her. "You're right. There is a reason." Sarah stops. "When I was a kid, real little, they built this local pool near our house." I keep my head down. "I remember thinking it was going to the best thing since fried dough. I was so excited when my mom said she was taking me there. But then we got there and it wasn't fun at all. My mother dunked me until I was sick, and she threw me in the deep end so I'd learn to swim, but I didn't. I just choked on water and sank straight to the bottom. She screamed at me and said it was because I was so fat. Even at three or four I was big.

Anyway, that night my dad came home drunk and she told him about our day at the pool. He took me down there himself, picked me up by the neck, and threw me in. Keep in mind it was nine o'clock at night and pitch dark, no one around. He just threw me in and left." Sarah sucks in her breath.

"What happened?" She asks with a scowl on her face.

"Luckily one of the maintenance guys forgot his bag or something, so he walked through the yard to get it, snapped on the light and saw me there. Lucky for me he knew CPR. It was one very fortunate coincidence."

"That doesn't sound like a coincidence to me," she adds hastily. "Did your dad ever get caught?"

"No," I reply sullenly. "The police brought me home and my parents were ecstatic, or least pretended to be. They said I'd wandered away from home and no one could find me. 'He must have fallen in,' was what they kept saying." I watch the scene unravel like an old video reel. "I remember standing there with a towel wrapped around me. I had these doting parents hugging and kissing me like they really cared. Like they were actually happy to see me." I stand there silent for a bloated minute. "It was one of the happiest moments in my life to that point," I mutter sadly.

Sarah looks like she smelled something sour. "I'd like to have a serious talk with your parents," she says sternly. She hops over and gives me a hug.

"First of all, I would never let you do that," I answer abruptly, "and second, I don't even consider them my parents anymore." I slap the surface of the water with the palm of my hand. "When we get married, I'd rather take your name."

"But Hope is a nice last name," she argues.

"I don't want it anymore."

She goes to say something, and then stops. "Ok," she agrees.

"Ok."

Her face looks pensive for a moment. "I hope you know I'd never do anything like that. I'd never hurt you, I promise."

I toss the floatie into the deep end. "I know."

CHAPTER 34

Sarah starts me off on the edge of the pool, where I hang on and kick to keep my bottom half afloat. After I'm comfortable with that she tells me it's time to paddle. She comes beside me and slips her arms under my stomach. "We already know I can hold you up, so that's what I'm going to do. Worst case scenario, the bottom's four feet down. So I want you to push off the wall and start paddling your arms like this." She lets go of my stomach and shows me. I can't help but laugh. She laughs too. I'm going to look ridiculous.

"Ok, let's do this," I exclaim, taking one last breath. Sarah gets in position and I push off the wall, paddling like a moron as I slowly sink below the surface.

"Keep kicking!" She instructs, struggling to hold me up. *Oh, right.* I resume kicking and like a buoy I surge upward and onward, back toward the wall. I reach for it and Sarah stops me. "Keep going," she says as she angles my body toward the deep end. Before I have time to panic, she forms a giant arc with me, leading me back to the shallow end. I swim, slapping and splashing my way around the pool like a dog. My neck muscles hurt from stretching to keep my head above the water.

"You're doing it!" Sarah calls from behind me. She sounds far away. I crane my neck to see her but she's not there anymore. I'm doing this on my own.

"Keep going, you're doing great!" She cheers like a soccer

mom routing for her five year old kid. To my chagrin, Sandy and Steve join in. I'm surrounded by clapping and ridiculous praise as I make the home stretch to the stairs. My cheeks burn hot with embarrassment. I stop paddling when my knees scrape against the bottom step. I flop onto it, panting heavily and wondering why I'm so tired. I can run for an hour, but I can barely do one lap around the pool. Go figure.

Sarah rushes toward me. She wraps her arms around my neck and pushes me into the side of the pool. She kisses me, briefly, but it's distracting. I forget there are adults nearby as I kiss her back.

"Ahem, gross," a female voice spews sarcastically. There's a girl standing by the pool, dressed in black. Sarah and I scramble away from each other, thoroughly embarrassed. She looks down on us with disgust.

"Hi sweetie, you're home early," Sandy says, climbing out of the pool.

"I came home for lunch." She states plainly.

"Why didn't you eat with the other kids at camp?"

"Because I didn't feel like it. What's with the fifty questions?" She barks.

"No fifty questions," Sandy says calmly, "just happy you're home." She turns to us. "In case you haven't figured it out, this is my lovely daughter, Cara. Cara, this is Sarah, and Charlie. They'll be staying with us for a few days."

"It's a pleasure to meet you," Sarah says sweetly.

"Hey." I add awkwardly.

"Hi," she says gruffly, avoiding eye contact. She looks annoyed. "Why do we always have to house people here? It's not fair. No one ever asks me if I'm ok with it."

I can definitely see what Sandy means about her daughter. She's a real treat. Even her appearance screams difficult. She's a bigger girl with pale skin and purple hair. Her eyes are outlined with a generous application of black make-up, and she has three piercings in each ear, a string of bangle bracelets, and about ten rings on each hand. I'm surprised they let her wear all of that at church camp.

"Enough." Steve says firmly, flashing his daughter a warning glance. She rolls her eyes.

"I'll go make lunch," Sandy offers, trying to break the tension. "Are ham and cheese sandwiches ok?"

"That sounds delicious!" Sarah exclaims. Cara sighs loudly. Despite Sandy's request, I don't think we're going to crack this one.

~~~

We drip dry at the picnic table while we eat the ham and cheese sandwiches Sandy prepared. There's something to be said about the feeling you get when you first come out of the water and you're wrapped in a towel, sitting in the sun. It's different than the sopping wet feeling of sand-caked jeans at the beach. I feel so clean.

Sandy tells Cara that her father's going to marry us in a few days. "Mmm hmm," she mumbles in response, taking a bite of her sandwich and washing it down with lemonade. "And you think I care because...?"

"Oh Cara." Sandy shakes her head, giving up on the conversation.

"Thank you for letting us stay here, Cara. We really appreciate it. I told your mom not to worry about us. We'd have no problem finding a shelter or a park or something, but she insisted." Sarah's tone is comical.

"Ya right," Cara mutters.

I put down my sandwich. I've had enough of this girl. "She's not joking." I snap. "We live outside. Every day. We sleep on the streets, rummage through dumpsters, wash in polluted rivers. I know you have this chip on your shoulder about us being here, and I'm sorry. But we're really grateful to your parents for letting us stay here for a few days." My words hang in the air for a minute. I put my head down, feeling bad for lashing out. "I promise we'll stay out of your way," I add quietly.

Cara just stares at me, frozen in her seat. She opens her

mouth to say something, then slams down her cup and storms away from the table.

CHAPTER 35

We bought the marriage license! I take Sarah's hand as we walk down Common Street, following Sandy to a local cafe to celebrate. I let out a massive sigh of relief. Thank God she was there. We ran into problems with my ID. Sarah has her driver's license, but all I have is an old, ratty high school identification card. It's the only scrap of an identity I have left. Thanks to Mrs. Starbuck, they were able to get in touch with the New Haven city clerk and track down my birth certificate. I don't think in normal circumstances that would be enough, but as luck would have it, Sandy knew the woman from church.

We walk into the café and find a table. The place is packed. It's small with bright paint and lots of brick. I've never been in a Mexican restaurant before, but I like it. The clientele is very diverse. Sarah and I don't stand out like sore thumbs here. Although, that probably has more to do with the fact we're cleaned up and wearing borrowed clothes.

Sandy looks over the menu and asks us what we want. We decide to stick to drinks and desserts since we just had lunch. After fifteen minutes of indecision, Sandy comes back to the table with three Mexican sodas and Helado Explosions, a Mexican ice cream dessert.

"So are you excited?" She asks, digging into her mound of whipped cream.

"There aren't even words," Sarah replies. "You're like an

angel," she murmurs with a mouthful of chocolate.

"I know how hard it is, young love. I can relate to your situation. Steve and I got married right out of high school. We were about your age," she adds.

"Really?"

"Yup. The heart wants what it wants. And there's no timetable on that."

"So it was hard to get married, even back then?" Sarah asks.

"Yes ma'am. Especially when our parents disapproved. Being with Steve was the easiest, and yet the hardest thing to do."

I know what she means. Loving Sarah is easy, but it brings with it a string of insecurities, expectations I can't fulfill, and this aching feeling that if I ever lost her, I wouldn't live through it.

"Why didn't you parents approve?" Sarah asks thoughtfully.

"Mine were Jewish and his were Protestant. My parents wanted me to marry a nice Jewish boy," she chuckles. "But I fell in love with Steve."

I think of my parents. Even though they're pure evil, I still find it hard it hard to believe they wouldn't approve of Sarah. If anything, they wouldn't approve of her marrying me.

"How did you do it?" I ask.

"We both found minimum wage jobs, saved our money. We scraped up just enough to have the church ceremony we wanted. We didn't have it in his father's church, of course, but we found a nice little chapel outside of town." She puts down her spoon and smiles. "I went off to college a married woman. Steve visited me when he could, but it was an hour away by train. That was expensive back then." She catches my expression and adds, "It still is today for that matter."

"How often did you see each other?" I ask. I can't imagine being an hour away from Sarah. I take comfort in the fact that she's sitting right here.

"A couple times a year. Those were the longest years of my life. But no different than dating someone in the military, I suppose." Sandy gets a faraway look on her face. "We told our parents four years later. They would have cancelled our schooling had they known." I watch her face as pain comes to the surface. "My mother cried for days," she says sadly. I look away, scraping the cream off the bottom of my dish.

"Can I ask you something?" Sandy says, turning her attention back to us.

"Anything," Sarah answers. I feel myself getting anxious. I don't like it when sentences start that way.

"I don't mean to pry but, surely there has to be someone out there that loves you, who would take care of you both? A friend, a family member, anybody?" Sandy pauses before saying, "They'll regret losing you, you know. I'm sure they already do."

"It's not like that for us." I explain. "We met on the streets. It's not our relationship that brought us here."

It takes her a minute to process this. "You mean the two of you don't have family *anywhere*?" She asks with disbelief. Sarah stays silent, and I shake my head

"My aunt's still alive." Sarah says in a small voice. My stomach drops. "But I don't want to burden her," she adds. "She has enough to deal with already."

"Oh sweetie, you wouldn't be a burden! She's family. She could help you two get on your feet." She leans forward and asks, "Does she even know where you are?"

Sarah hesitates before telling her no.

Sandy brings a hand to her heart. "Good heavens. Sweetheart, you have to call her. She must be worried sick about you. How long have you been living out here?"

Sarah does a mental calculation and replies guiltily, "Almost eight months."

Sandy puts her hand on top of Sarah's. "You have to call." Sarah hesitates, then nods in agreement.

I push my sundae away like it's an explosive. It slides off the table and the dish shatters on the floor. Everyone's staring at me. Sarah asks me if I'm all right. I shake my head and get up from the table. I need air. I'm suddenly suffocated by the reality of our situation. I'm not good enough. Sarah's going to leave. Without thinking about the consequences of my actions, I slam through the front door and start to run.

CHAPTER 36

Sarah won't speak to me. I'm sitting outside her bedroom, cross-legged on the floor, panicking. Cara passes by and nods. "Your dinner's cold," she mumbles, feigning indifference.

I don't care, I think to myself, but to her I mutter "thank you" and watch her walk away. She goes into her bedroom. To my surprise, she doesn't shut the door. I lift myself off the floor. "Cara?" I call out before entering the doorway. She's sitting on the edge of her bed. She pulls out her ear buds and turns to see who it is. Her cheeks redden when she sees me.

"I'm sorry to bother you, but I'm desperate. Sarah won't talk to me and I don't know what to do." I cross the threshold, and look at Cara with pleading eyes. "You're a girl. How do I fix it?"

Cara looks away from me and laughs. "Sorry, you look funny in my dad's clothes." I crack a half smile. She puts down her ipod and clears her throat. "So, like, what did you do?" She makes eye contact briefly, then looks away.

I lean against the doorframe and tell her, "I ran out of the restaurant."

"Why?" She asks like I'm a moron.

"She was talking about contacting her aunt, in Maine, and I was afraid of her moving back. Leaving me. I freaked out." I shrug my shoulders. "I run when I freak out." I stare at the floor, embarrassed about sharing this with a stranger.

"You're getting married in a few days," she reminds me.

"What are you freaking out about?" Her tone is harsh, but her eyes aren't angry anymore.

My answer's simple. "Everyone leaves."

Cara nods like she understands, although I don't imagine she does. She stands up and walks over to me. I have no idea what she's doing, until she reluctantly reaches out for me. She wraps her arms around my waist and leans her head against my chest. I rest my right hand on her back, unsure of what to do. She feels soft, bigger than Sarah, and a lot warmer. Cara squeezes me so hard I have no choice but to hug her back. I think she needs it. I don't know much about relationships, but I'm pretty sure hugging in a situation like this is ok.

Several seconds later she pulls away. She looks up at me fondly and I take a step back. "What? I thought you could use a hug," she snaps, "my bad."

"Maybe you needed one, too," I suggest, preparing to get slapped in the face.

"Maybe," she mumbles. "I've never hugged a guy before. And my dad doesn't count."

"May I?" I ask, pointing at the edge of the bed.

"Sure," she assents, taking a seat on the other side.

"I'm surprised by that," I respond in a barely audible voice.

"By what?"

"What you said. About guys."

"Why do you say that?" She asks.

"Because you're pretty," I state simply, "and because you seem like a nice girl. Maybe a little scary at first," I tease, "but not so bad."

"Yeah right," she says defensively. "I'm not pretty, I'm fat."

"Are you kidding? I would have done anything to date a girl like you in high school." She turns bright red. "And you're not fat. *I* was fat. I was close to three hundred pounds! So you can imagine how many girlfriends I had."

"Are you a virgin?" She asks bluntly.

"Yes."

Her eyes widen. "And you're how old?"

"Twenty-one."

"Wow." She ponders this for a minute. "Well, at least you've hooked up. I'm sixteen and I've never even kissed a guy."

"I didn't kiss anyone until I was twenty. Sarah was my first."

"What? How? You're, like, buff and everything. Girls at my school would love you." I laugh really hard at her comment. She stares back at me, confused. "Don't you know?"

"No way," I answer.

"Hmm." She wrinkles her forehead. "Can I take a picture of you?" She asks, going to her desk to fish out a digital camera.

"I don't know." I haven't had my picture taken since high school, and that never went well.

"Please?" She preps the camera to take the picture anyway. "You don't have to move, just look at me. You don't even have to smile."

"Fine," I agree reluctantly, casting my gaze toward the camera. Cara tells me I look like I want to fight someone, and I smile, just as she clicks the picture.

"There," she says, putting the camera away. "Now I have an even bigger favor to ask."

"Oh no."

"Nothing bad. I was just wondering, um, can I tell the kids at school we hooked up? Now that I have your picture and all, it gives it more credibility." I hesitate. "It would make me more popular," she explains. "Please?"

I wish I wasn't such a pushover with girls. "I guess," I cave, "but you better tell your parents your plot. I don't want them finding out from a teacher at school and tracking me down."

"No way! That's embarrassing. Besides, I don't tell them anything anyway."

"Then the deal's off." I say sternly.

"Fine!" She agrees angrily. "You're annoying."

I chuckle. I'm fine with that if it keeps me out of jail. "So why do you hate your parents so much? They seem nice.

They're a hell of a lot nicer than mine. Sorry."

"I've heard swear words before. And I don't hate my parents, I just...I was an accident. That's why they're so old. They didn't want to have kids. They didn't want me." She picks at a loose string on the comforter.

"But they love you now, so what's the big deal? My parents planned to have me, and they treated me like shit. You have it pretty good, trust me."

She shrugs her shoulders. "Were your parents really that bad?"

"Yes. My father beat me on a daily basis, almost killing me a couple times. They killed my dog. They threw me into a pool when I was a baby. Should I go on?"

"My parents put down our first dog," she says softly, knowing it's not the same thing.

"Was he sick?"

"Yeah, he had cancer. He was a million years old."

"Well mine wasn't. And I highly doubt your parents shot him in the head."

Cara shrinks back, cringing at my words. She looks at me and shakes her head slowly. "Why would they do that?" She asks in a childlike voice.

"They're bad people. That's the only explanation I've come up with. It took me a long time to come to terms with that, that it wasn't my fault."

Cara puts her hand on top of mine. "Thanks for telling me all that," she says as she slides closer to me on the bed, her face only inches away from mine. I can sense her vulnerability. "Will you kiss me, Charlie?" She whispers. Her hand is clammy on top of mine.

I sit there, stunned, until the message registers in my brain. When it does, I jump off the bed and make my way for the door. My mind's racing. If Sarah saw that, she'd...

"Wait!" Cara calls after me. I stop in the doorway. "Sorry. I'm sorry, that was wrong. Will you turn around, please?" I spin around with a scowl on my face. I'm too angry for words.

"I don't know what I was thinking. I'm a mutant next to Sarah. Why I thought you'd be interested in me is, well, it's stupid." Her eyes fill up with tears. "I'm so embarrassed," she utters as she covers her face. Black makeup leaks from her eyes.

"Stop crying," I tell her softly. "It's not a big deal."

"Not a big deal? It's a huge deal for me!" She screams as she picks up her ipod and throws it at the bookshelf with all her trinkets. Several of them crash to the ground.

Sarah comes running into the room. "Cara, what's wrong?" My heart stops when I see her. Despite the red eyes and runny nose, she's the most beautiful thing I've ever seen.

"Nothing," she growls, "leave me alone!"

Sarah looks at me. "Charlie, what did you do?"

"Nothing," I say weakly. I stare at her with apologetic eyes. She bites her bottom lip when it starts to tremble.

"My God Sarah, he worships the ground you walk on. Get over it!" Cara snaps resentfully.

Sarah turns to her like she has all the answers. "But he ran away," she says weakly. Her eyes are locked on Cara, needy and desperate. Cara gives in to her softer side.

"He needed air. Didn't he tell you why?" They both turn to me and I say nothing. "Jesus Charlie. What's wrong with you?" Cara scolds.

Sarah giggles and wipes her nose. "Tell me," she says softly, looking at me again.

"I was afraid you'd call your aunt and leave me. Find someone better."

"Charlie, I'm marrying you. I'm not going anywhere. You don't have to worry about stuff like that."

"I'm so sorry." I move in to kiss her.

"I'm outta here," Cara mutters as she blows past us.

"Wait," I plead, chasing after her. I take her arm and turn her around so she's facing me. "I'm sorry, that was rude. Let Sarah talk to you. Please? She had trouble dating, too."

"Yeah right."

"She did. Guys were afraid of her in high school. Maybe

it's the same thing with you."

"I doubt it."

"Just talk to her. I'll take back our deal," I threaten with a grin.

"Whatever." She makes a face and stomps back into her room.

~~~

Sarah walks into the bathroom while I'm brushing my teeth. "Is she ok?" I ask with a mouthful of toothpaste.

"Yeah." She yawns, looking drained. "She told me she tried to kiss you."

I spit. "I was going to tell you," I say honestly, rinsing off the toothbrush Sandy gave me earlier.

"I know. She said you jumped away like she was on fire," she adds with a chuckle.

"I didn't want you to get mad," I explain, feeling bad for hurting her feelings. I swish out my mouth with water and look at Sarah in the mirror.

"That's good."

"Are you ok?" I ask gently, touching her shoulder.

"Yeah," she replies.

I set down my toothbrush on the edge of the sink. "I'm sorry Sarah, about earlier. I freaked out."

She takes a step closer to me. "It's ok. I wasn't going to call her anyway. Even if I did, you have nothing to worry about. From here on out, it's you and me, no matter what. All right?" She squeezes my hand and I nod in agreement.

I wrap my arms around her and bury my face in her hair. I think of how lucky I am that she forgave me. Sarah's the only thing I like about myself. If I lost her I don't know what I'd do.

I straighten up when we hear a knock at the door. "Sweetheart, time to go back to your room," Sandy announces as she opens the door and pokes her head through. Sarah and I come out of the bathroom, looking startled. "Steve and I are going to bed so it's time for you two to part ways. You're not married yet," she adds with a wink.

Sarah turns to me and says goodnight. We kiss briefly and she goes to Mrs. Starbuck. "Thanks again for everything", she says sweetly as she follows her out of the room. She smiles at me one last time before she closes the door. "Sweet dreams," she whispers at the last second, making me want to run after her. I linger at the door until I decide against it. Then I crawl into my delectably comfortable bed and think of how empty it feels without her in it.

CHAPTER 37

I wake to the smells of pancake batter and butter, and sunshine pouring in sideways through the blinds. I glance at the digital clock. Eight thirty! I didn't realize it was so late. I get up to use the bathroom but stop mid-stride. There's someone tapping at the door. I open it to find Sarah standing on the other side.

"I missed you," I say quickly, feeling really happy to see her. She grins at me, then squeezes through the opening and heads straight for bed. She crawls underneath the covers.

"I missed you too," she adds a minute later. "That's why I couldn't wait."

"I'm glad." I say as I crawl into bed with her. Her skin's warm. It smells like soap and chlorine. I kiss her shoulder blade and rest my head beside hers, throwing my arm over her stomach.

"We're getting married today," she whispers, resting her hand on top of mine.

"I know," I murmur lazily. I can't believe it's here. I thought those three days would drag on forever.

"Should we go downstairs?" She asks a while later. If Sandy finds us up here together there's going to be hell to pay. Or at the very least a lecture. She made it very clear that the bride and groom aren't supposed to see each other before the wedding. I just shrug and yawn and kiss her wrist. I want to savor these moments because tonight we'll be on the streets again.

We spend another half hour tangled up in bed, before we eventually go downstairs. We enter the kitchen holding hands and Sandy gasps at our bold and ill-fated move. Mr. Starbuck's sitting at the kitchen table over a plate of pancakes. He looks up long enough to say good morning, then returns to the business section of his newspaper.

"We know it's supposed to be bad luck to see each other before the wedding, but we don't care," Sarah says looking at me. "I want to eat breakfast together on our last day."

"I don't see what the big deal is," Cara interjects, looking at her mother. Sandy wipes her hands on a dishtowel. She mulls it over.

"Ok," she finally responds. "The decision's yours."

"Thank you. We appreciate it. The last thing we want is you mad at us."

"Of course not," she says with a laugh. She refills her daughter's orange juice then pours us both a glass. "Pancakes?"

"Yes, please." I answer. Sarah nods. We take a seat at the kitchen table across from Cara and Steve. It looks like a beautiful day outside. The kitchen window's open and a cool breeze sweeps the room. You can hear the hum of a lawnmower, scenting the air with freshly cut grass. I wish grass tasted as good as it smells.

Sandy sets down our plates. Tubs of butter and maple syrup are sitting in the middle of the table. I'm already starting to salivate. "Aren't you going to eat with us?" Sarah asks.

"I'll be there in a minute, sweetie. I'm waiting for the coffee to finish brewing," she says as the coffee maker clicks off and starts beeping. "There we go", she says as she pours the oily black liquid into coffee cups. "Coffee?" She asks, and we both decline politely. She settles in with her steaming mug and sets the other one in front of Steve.

"You drink coffee?" I ask. For some reason this surprises me.

"The elixir of life," he replies with a chuckle as he adds swirls of cream and sugar to his cup. I watch the coffee turn a caramel color. The smell's intoxicating. He lifts his cup and tips it toward Sarah and me. "To marriage," he says jovially, turning his gaze to Sandy.

"To marriage," she echoes with a loving wink.

~~~

Sarah gets up from the table and brings her dishes to the sink. I finish my second helping of buttermilk pancakes and drain the OJ before joining her. We load the dishwasher together while Sandy cleans the counter and Steve finishes the morning paper. Cara's still sitting at the table, punching something into her iPod. I'm suddenly overwhelmed with grief. The whole scene depresses me. My mind wanders to our pitiable nomadic existence. I'd love to give her this life.

"All right, time to get ready, you two." Sandy announces as she ushers us out of the kitchen. "The church is going to be ready at eleven so you have to get your butts moving."

"See you later," Sarah says wistfully, grinning from ear to ear in the doorway.

"See ya," I mutter, kissing her goodbye. Her lips still taste like maple syrup. I savor it as she walks away with Cara and Sandy.

"Ready?" Steve asks awkwardly, folding his paper in half and tossing it in the recycling bin.

"More than you know."

"Well, uh, don't be nervous. I'll walk you through what you have to do."

"Ok," I respond, suddenly feeling nervous.

"There's a shower down here if you want to wash up. I'll bring you some clothes."

"Thank you. You're a nice family." I tell him stiffly. He clears his throat and nods. He's a happy man, you can see it in his eyes.

I take a long, scalding hot shower and scrub off a few layers of skin. I crank the spout to cold at the end so I can put on my suit without sweating. Sandy already told me I have to wear one. I guess Steve has an old one that's too tight. The one he wore to their wedding, in fact.

A few seconds later there's a knock at the door and Mr. Starbuck's handing me the starched black slacks and suit coat. He hands me another hanger with a white shirt and black bow tie looped over the hook. My heart beats fast. I've never worn anything like this before.

"I can help with the tie if you'd like."

"Thanks."

"And I apologize in advance."

"For what?" I ask.

"The church isn't air conditioned."

I figured as much. Air conditioning is a luxury I occasionally get on the train, but seldom ever expect.

I hear Sarah and Sandy giggling upstairs. A similar sound comes from Cara, and that makes me smile. I can picture them up there fussing over Sarah, fixing her dress and her hair and making her feel pretty. I remember the first time I saw her on Christmas Eve. She was standing there with the kids, her head tipped back with laughter, the sun hitting her just right...

"How are you doing in there?" Steve interrupts.

"Good," I reply. The memory dissipates as I button the minister's suit coat, still smiling. The familiar laughter overhead is replaced by heavy heels clomping down the stairs.

"Sandy's driving the girls to church," Steve adds with an edge of urgency. I examine myself in the mirror, not entirely recognizing the man on the other side. In the black suit I look sophisticated. I look...good. Before I can tell Steve I'm ready, I hear shuffling outside the door. "Wait, sweetie, you can't go in there!" Steve blurts out in a panic. I brace myself for Sarah's entrance, feeling butterflies fill in my chest. But it's not Sarah that comes blasting in like a madman. It's Cara. She's carrying a tube of hair gel.

"It's an emergency, Dad!" She yells to appease her father. When she sees me she whistles. "Dang boy, you clean up nice." I laugh easily. Cara and I have become friends over the past couple days. I feel more comfortable around her now.

"You too," I respond, eying her up and down for effect. And she does. She's wearing a strapless teal sundress with a white sash and little heels. She has makeup on, too. Subtle makeup that makes her look feminine.

Her face reddens as she tells me, "I had to. I'm the maid of honor," she states proudly. I nod, feeling pleased that Sarah thought to ask, and confused because I'm not entirely sure what a maid of honor is, or does, at a wedding.

"So I assume your visit has something to do with my hair?" I ask, pointing at the dark blue gel.

"Cha," she utters. "We can't have you going out there like that, with your hair all askew."

"Of course not," I reply mockingly.

"May I?" She asks as she lifts a handful of gunk to my wet locks.

"Sure."

I watch in the mirror as she does her thing. My hair is a little long, I guess. It barely covers my ears so it's not terrible. It's nothing like the mop I had when Liam and I first met. My heart aches at the memory of my best friend. I've been thinking of him off and on all day. He would have liked it here. There's no doubt in my mind he would have been my best man.

"There. That'll do it," Cara exclaims, standing back, looking pleased with herself.

"Nice work. You wanna take a picture, show your friends?" I tease.

"Watch yourself Chas. I have pull with the bride."

"I don't know about that."

"Girls, you ready in there or what?" Steve urges from outside the door.

"Yes, Dad. We're ready." Cara swings open the door, says "ta-da", and points at me. I feel silly.

"Wow. You look sharp," Steve says, patting me on the back as I walk by. "Maybe a little too sharp. I don't think I looked that good in the suit."

Cara laughs at her father's joke. "I can't picture you and

Mom getting married."

"It was a long time ago."

"Can I see pictures sometime?" She asks.

"Sure you can, sweetheart." He looks pleased. He puts his arm around her and walks her out the front door.

We pile into the car and make our way to the church. Per Cara's request, Steve keeps the windows up and cranks the AC so none of us ruin our hair. I feel myself trembling with nerves. Cara puts her hand on mine and tells me to breathe.

"She absolutely *adores* you. You have nothing to be nervous about." I smile back, saying it all with my eyes.

We pull into the parking lot next to Sandy's empty SUV. "I gotta go, but you're gonna do great," Cara says as she scrambles out of the car and runs inside.

"Must be maid of honor duties," I tell Steve, feeling even more nervous now that she's gone.

We get out of the car and walk toward the entrance, a big heavy door decorated with stained glass. Steve turns to me apologetically and tells me to wait outside. "I have to go inside and put on my robe, but I'll send Sandy out here to tell you what to do."

"Ok."

"Remember Charlie, it's just you and Sarah. No one else." He pats me on the back and shakes my hand. Then he slips inside, leaving me alone on the front steps.

A few minutes later, Sandy's by my side running through the proceedings. We already signed the wedding license with a witness and a notary, so the major legal hurdle is over. She tells me my job today is to walk to the front of the church when she tells me to. Steve will be up there already and he'll tell me where to stand. After that, I just listen to Steve and repeat after him when told.

Sandy glances at her watch. "It's time," she says grinning. I take a deep breath. I feel nauseous. On par with Steve's advice I think of Sarah, and suddenly the urge to lose my pancakes goes away.

Sandy opens the front door and I obediently walk down the

aisle. I'm not sure where to put my arms so I keep fiddling with the buttons on my suit. I look up. Steve's smiling at me, but I can't bring myself to make eye contact. I feel nauseous again. *Pull yourself together*, I demand, looking around the empty church. *Nobody's here. Just you and Sarah*, I repeat, over and over, until I find my place beside Steve.

The front door opens again. I hold my breath until I see Cara on the other side. She comes towards me, smiling awkwardly, and looking around. When she gets closer she sticks out her tongue. I laugh and return the gesture, happy she's here. She doesn't stay long. Instead, she nods at her father and proceeds to the grand piano in the back corner of the room.

"Count to twenty-five," Sandy murmurs as she slips in the front door. She scurries down the aisle and takes a seat in the front row. She exchanges a look with Steve. A brief moment later, Cara starts playing. She's really good. She's playing Greensleeves. Liam played it for me once on his harmonica.

The front door opens. The music gets louder. My nerves run rampant until the moment she appears. When I see her, my jaw drops to the floor. She's wearing a white and yellow sundress and her hair's piled high on her head in a mass of curls. She's wearing makeup and jewelry and heels she can't walk in. She's absolutely stunning.

Sarah stops and covers her mouth when she sees me. "Keep walking, sweetie," Sandy whispers. Sarah ignores her request. Instead, she drops her hand and smiles at me, standing in the middle of the aisle.

"You look so good," she says brokenly. Tears are rolling down her cheeks.

I go to her. I tell her she's beautiful and take her hand. Sarah hangs on to it for dear life. "You ok?" I ask.

"I'm just so happy," she replies. "This is perfect."

"Every girl's dream wedding," I say sarcastically.

She laughs, then says seriously, "It is to me. I'm marrying my best friend."

I touch her cheek. "I'm so lucky," I say, dabbing at my

eyes. Sarah brushes the tears off her cheeks.

We walk to the front of the church together and stop in front of the minister. I look up, still holding Sarah's hand. The music slowly fades. Steve smiles warmly and begins to speak.

"Please turn and face each other." We square off our feet and I take her other hand. There aren't even words to describe the feeling in my heart as I stand there, staring at her.

Steve looks out at the two people in the audience. "Dearly Beloved, we are gathered here today to join Charlie Hope and Sara Angelo in holy matrimony. Into this holy estate these two persons present now come to be joined as one. If any person can show just cause why they may not be joined together, let them speak now or forever hold their peace." The room is quiet.

"Very good." He flips through the Bible in front of him until he gets to an earmarked page. "I'd like to do a brief reading from First Corinthians 13, verses 1-13." He clears his throat and takes a drink of water. Everyone listens intently.

"Love is patient, love is kind. It does not envy, it does not boast, it is not proud. It is not rude, it is not self-seeking, it is not easily angered, it keeps no record of wrongs. Love does not delight in evil but rejoices with the truth. It always protects, always trusts, always hopes, always perseveres."

Sarah sniffles and takes a breath. When Steve is done he closes one book and opens another. We sing *How Great Thou Art* from our hymnals while Cara follows along on the piano. Sarah overshadows everyone, and I'm as spell-bound as I was the first time I heard her sing. When the song finishes, everyone turns to her in awe. Steve says something about having her join the church choir and his wife concurs. I get the sense they're serious.

Cara returns to her seat and the Reverend proceeds with the ceremony. He lifts a loose sheet of notebook paper off the podium. He looks at Sarah, then me, and reads, "Marriage is a sacred union between two people who are deeply in love. The solemn vow you are about to make is one of the most beautiful acts of human love one can express. You are creating a new life together. A life of acceptance, compromise, and everlasting love. A marriage." He says with finality, reaching for his water. He wipes the sweat from his brow and continues.

"Charlie, do you take Sarah to be your lawfully wedded wife, to have and to hold from this day forward, for better or for worse, for richer, for poorer, in sickness and in health, to love and to cherish until death do you part?"

I lock eyes with Sarah as I say, "I do."

"Sarah, do you take Charlie, to be your lawfully wedded husband, to have and to hold from this day forward, for better or for worse, for richer, for poorer, in sickness and in health, to love and to cherish until death do you part?"

"I do," she says, with tears flowing freely from her eyes. I lift my hand to wipe them. She smiles and leans into my palm.

Sandy claps in the front row. I steal a glance at Cara, who hoots loudly and makes a face. Steve gives us a minute to calm the emotions. After the hoopla dies down, he tells everyone it's time to present the rings.

"We don't have any," Sarah replies quickly.

"You don't have any rings?" Sandy asks, standing up in her pew. She looks at our blank faces and adds, "Of course you don't. My apologies." She sits back down, red-faced, and folds her hands in her lap.

"Ok. We'll just skip that part," Steve mutters, trying to make light of the situation. "Onto a prayer—"

"Wait!" Cara interrupts. She scurries up to the front of the church and examines our hands. She looks down at her own, covered in inexpensive bling, and extracts two silver rings from her pinkie and thumb. "Try these on," she demands.

I stare at her in disbelief. There's more waterworks from Sarah. "Really?" I ask when I realize Sarah can't.

She snaps her gum. "Yes. You need wedding rings and I have a million of them. They were like, 5 for 5 at Claire's anyway, not a big deal."

I don't know what the Claire part means, but I thank Cara

and we try them on. Close enough. Sarah gives her a hug and tells her she's amazing. After several bloated seconds of emotional embrace, Cara sits down and Steve asks us to repeat after him.

"I, Charlie, give you Sarah, this ring as an eternal symbol of my love and commitment to you," I repeat, sliding the plastic ring onto her left hand.

"I, Sarah, give you Charlie, this ring as an eternal symbol of my love and commitment to you." She puts on my ring and doesn't let go.

Steve shuffles some paper at the podium, and addresses the audience. "By the power vested in me by the State of Massachusetts, I now pronounce you husband and wife!" He declares loudly. My stomach does a flip. "You may now kiss the bride," he instructs as he steps away, giving us our space. I look at Sarah. I'm *so happy*. I lift her off the ground and kiss her, spinning her around for everyone to see.

"I present to you Mr. and Mrs. Angelo!" Steve announces as the Starbuck family stands to applaud.

We exit the church, hand in hand, with big toothy smiles. Sarah and I look at each other in disbelief. "Mr. Angelo," she says with a breathless laugh.

"My wife," I say softly, realizing for the first time in a long time I'm not afraid. I'm not afraid of losing Sarah because we're in this together now. She's the family I've been looking for my entire life.

CHAPTER 38

We drive back to the Starbucks house, where they throw us an impromptu reception. Sandy pulls out chips, cheese and crackers, and veggies with dip. Sarah and I change into shorts and hang out by the pool. I help her brush out her hair, still crunchy with leftover hairspray, while Cara rehashes the ceremony from a spectator's point of view.

Sandy puts together a cake and marinates steaks for lunch. While we swim, Steve cooks them on the grill and Sandy reads leisurely by the pool. I squint into the sun, taking in the scene like a Norman Rockwell painting. The laughing, the love, the happy family we've been imposing on for the last few days. My mind slips to my mother and father. The family I'm no longer associated with by name. The screaming, the poverty, the smoky haze of anger and abuse. The contrast is extreme. I watch Steve bring his wife an iced tea and gingerly kiss her forehead. This isn't normal either, right? No one deserves to be this happy.

"So, what's your plan?" Sandy asks while cutting her steak.

I look to Sarah, then back at Sandy. "Well, I was kind of thinking about taking Sarah somewhere for our honeymoon. I mean, if you could drive us there that would be great."

"Sure I can, sweetie." She pauses long enough to swallow her food. "But what about after that? Do you have somewhere to go?"

"We'll be all right," I answer, cringing at the sound of my

own knife and fork scraping the plate when I press down too hard.

"Well, the three of us have been talking," she says looking around at her family, "and we'd love to keep you here a little longer. Put you in touch with someone, get you back on your feet." She sees the shell-shocked expression on my face. "There's no pressure. It's just something to think about." She says as she starts collecting empty plates. "I'll be back with dessert," she announces before going inside.

I feel anxious. A plethora of thoughts bounce around my head. I don't know anything but the streets. The thought of losing my security blanket, my homelessness, it makes me sick. We won't have our freedom here. And I'm not good with people. What if I can't get a job? What if Sarah does something with her life and I don't? At least on the streets I can protect her, keep her safe. I make sure she has warm blankets and food to eat. It gives me purpose. It makes me worthy of her love. She won't need that here.

Maybe Sarah will agree. She doesn't like to impose on people, right? Although, judging by the way she's looking at me with those big Bambi eyes, I'm not so sure.

I swallow the lump in my throat and try not to think about it. Sandy's here with the cake. Cara's grinning, holding up a bottle of champagne.

"I convinced my parents," she says slyly.

"I suppose a glass of champagne won't do any harm." Sandy agrees.

"Exactly! And it's a special occasion," Cara adds. Steve sits across from us, tight-lipped. You can see how he feels about the situation.

"That's very sweet, but we don't drink," Sarah explains.

"I don't either, dummy. I'm sixteen." She starts filling our glasses anyway. "It's your wedding. You need champagne. It's like, required or something."

"That's enough," Steve says when Cara gets to the halfway point.

"Fine," she says, moving to her own glass.

Meanwhile, Sandy slices the cake. It's beautiful. Sarah tells her this over and over again. It's frosted white with all of these peach and yellow flowers. In icing across the top it says 'Congratulations Mr. And Mrs. Angelo'. It tastes as delicious as it looks.

Cara puts down her fork and stands up with her glass of champagne. "As the maid of honor, I'd like to raise a toast to the new couple," she says looking at us. She pauses to clear her throat. "When I first met you, I thought you'd be stuck up and stupid and I read into things. But I was wrong, and you opened my eyes to that. You were nice to me even though I was a complete bitch." Her father bites his tongue while everyone else laughs. "So, for that, I thank you and wish you luck with your new life together. Cheers!" She exclaims, raising her glass.

Everyone drinks and Sarah and I lift our glasses tentatively. The champagne looks like ginger ale. How bad can it be? I take a quick sip and bubbles fill my nose. It's fizzy and sour-sweet. It kind of has a bite to it. I cringe at the taste and put down my glass. Cara's already drained hers.

"I like it," Sarah says matter-of-factly, surprising us all. "It's like drinking the stars."

I give it another try. My face scrunches into a frown. I gulp it down to get it over with. It leaves a weird after taste in my mouth and I conclude it's not for me. I can't, for the life of me, figure out why my father drank so much of this stuff.

I get the answer to my question a few minutes later. My head feels fuzzy and light, and the uneasiness in my belly goes away. Everything is right with the world. I can't help but smile. Sarah feels it too, I can tell. She's giggling at everything I say.

A few hours later, after the dishes have been cleared and the buzz has worn off, Sandy reminds us of her earlier proposition. Sarah looks to me for an answer.

"That's very generous of you, but I think we'll be ok." I look at Sarah, waiting for her reaction. She sighs, and slumps in her seat, and I know I've said the wrong thing.

CHAPTER 39

We say our thank-yous and our goodbyes at the front door. Before we leave, Sandy loads us up with dry food, clean clothes, and a calling card with their number hand-written on the back. She demands I trade my torn sneakers for a pair of Steve's.

"You've done too much already," I protest when she makes me try them on.

"Don't be silly. He has an extra pair. Besides, he's a pack rat, it's excessive. I wish you'd take a few more shorts and shirts."

"We would, but our bags are pretty full. It's amazing how even a newspaper feels heavy when you're carrying it around all day."

"Oh sweetie, I can imagine."

"But we appreciate it," Sarah chimes in. "I hope you know that."

"Of course I do." Sandy pulls her in for another hug. Her eyes are glassy when she steps away. "All right," she says with a sigh. "Let's get on with it then."

We leave in the shorts and t-shirts we're wearing, and Sandy drives us to Newton. Sarah doesn't know where we're going because I want it to be a surprise. Based on memory, I think she's going to like it.

Liam introduced me to Hemlock Gorge a few years ago. Both of us had an itch to get out of the city one day, and someone told Liam it was worth visiting if you like waterfalls. What had us sold is the fact it's free. And right on the green line.

We pass a sign that says Charles River Reservation. Sandy drops us off at one of the entrances and our coach turns into a pumpkin. Back to coexisting with rats, I ponder. Just like in the Disney movie. Although rodents here don't make you clothes or fight off evil stepmothers. I feel a stab of regret as she drives away, wondering if I did the right thing.

"What is this place?" Sarah asks as we enter the park, hand in hand. "It's beautiful."

"Hemlock Gorge. They call it mini Niagara Falls, I guess. Liam and I came here once a while back and it seemed pretty cool. I thought you'd like it."

"I do," she says, looking around with wonder.

We take the narrow entrance from Chestnut Street, and enter the park by a set of stairs near Echo Bridge. You can see the falls in the distance, Hemlock Curve and Silk Mill Dam gushing water into the steep gorge. The sky's painted blue and it stretches as far as the eye can see. Sarah points out lupine and wild iris growing near the water, among other things. She picks up a snapdragon and presses on either side of the bright pink and yellow bulb with her fingers. "Oop," she says giggling as it startles her with a popping noise. "I forgot how much I like these things."

The sun's slightly off center, making its descent toward the horizon. Sarah tilts her head back and closes her eyes. "This is the best day," she murmurs dreamily, stepping backwards toward the falls. She does a half-spin and grabs my hand. "Let's go!" She commands, opening her eyes and pulling me with her toward the gorge. I laugh at her energy as she drags me along behind. *This is the best day*, I think to myself with a smile.

~~~

We eventually make our way back to the snapdragons,

where we eat the food Sandy packed for us and continue to act like newlyweds. We're sitting on our elbows near the river, watching a brilliant tangerine sunset, when a park ranger in uniform approaches. He's a bigger man, with odd features. His face is weathered like a prune.

"Pahk closes at dusk," he announces, chewing on a toothpick.

I panic. This wasn't part of the plan.

Sarah puts out her arm to stop me from talking. "Thank you," she responds sweetly. Then she turns to me with an impish grin. I'm confused.

The man nods. "Have a good one," he calls jovially, mashing the wooden stick between his teeth. He tips his hat and continues walking upstream toward the dam.

"I'm sorry, Sarah, I didn't—" She shakes her head until I stop talking. Then she holds out her hand to me in an unexpected gesture. Without pause I take it.

Sarah drags me to the platform under Echo Bridge and starts kissing me. "You think he'll find us here?" She whispers against my lips. Her words echo off the bridge, sending a ripple of noise across the park. I cover her mouth but it's too late. The laughter escapes. The echo this time is even louder. So loud, in fact, that the ranger in the distance turns around.

"Crap. Come on!" Sarah starts running and I follow her lead. She's headed for the woods. The sky's darker now so it's hard to navigate through all the branches. She keeps running, taking me deeper into a mess of trees. I can't tell if she's actually scared or not. I'm inclined to think not because there's a spring to her step that suggests she's just playing with me. Eventually we reach a small clearing surrounded by Hemlocks. This is where she stops.

I bend down with my hands on my knees, trying to catch my breath. Luckily there's a cross-breeze to keep the bugs away, or else we'd be eaten alive here. I straighten up in an attempt to hide my fatigue. Sarah's cheeks are flushed but she doesn't look tired. I eye her with amusement. "So, what does the fugitive suggest we do now?" I ask, laughing at my own joke.

She takes a step toward me but says nothing. She has that look again. The one she gets when it rains. My breathing accelerates, waiting for her to say something. It's hard to concentrate when she looks at me like this.

"I'm ready," she says softly, taking out her clip. Her hair falls down her back in wet curls.

"What?" I ask numbly. I need a minute to absorb the implications of this.

Sarah takes off her shirt and drops it at her feet. "I'm ready now."

I swallow loudly. "You are?"

"I am," she answers confidently, slipping off her shorts. She's wearing the underwear Cara bought as a wedding gift. *Wow.* I mouth the words because I don't have to ability to actually say them. Sarah smiles at my dumbfounded expression and walks over to me, closing the gap between us. She touches my chest with an open palm, then grabs my shirt. She reaches for the back of my neck with her free hand. Her fingers tighten in my hair, pulling my face to hers. She kisses me slowly, methodically. My heart rate quickens.

I take off my shirt and spread it out at the base of a tree. Sarah runs her hands over my stomach, looking at me like I'm desirable. She unbuttons my shorts and helps me out of them. We both look down at the embarrassing display of my affection.

"I like it," she says shyly.

I look at her. She's painfully beautiful. And sweet. It takes everything in me not to rush this. I tuck a loose strand of hair behind her ear. I kiss her cheek, her neck, her shoulders. She closes her eyes and lets out a breathless sigh. I keep going. Her joy has an actual texture. I feel it radiating off her skin.

"I love you," I tell her as I kiss her lips again.

"I love you too," she says hurriedly, pulling me to the ground. Her kisses are more urgent now, like we're running out of time. I wrap my arms around her and lay her on her back. My desire is all-consuming. I can't think of anything else. I trace her stomach with my finger, kissing the soft white skin as I move south. My hand grazes her hip then curves slowly around her leg. She starts panting.

"Is this ok?" I ask, breathless. Sarah looks at me and nods. "Are you comfortable?"

"I'm good, trust me."

"I can get on top. Am I crushing you?"

She puts her finger to my mouth. "Shhh." She grazes my bottom lip with her thumb. I open my mouth slightly but she silences me again. She strokes my cheek with the back of her palm, then pulls my face to hers.

I close my eyes. There's heat behind my eyelids. My heart beats quickly as I kiss her, waiting for the inevitable. I can't keep my focus. We grab at each other until our impatience gets the best of us.

The emotion coursing through my veins is unlike anything I've ever felt before. It's too powerful for words. "Wait," I plead, racing through a plethora of math problems in my head. "Give me a second," I add weakly when she doesn't stop. I don't want it to be over too quickly.

It's extremely difficult to regain control of my body. Nearly impossible. When Sarah keeps going so do I. She touches me and whispers my name, and it's all over. My toes curl below me. In my mind I'm ten years old again. Riding the Hellivator at Six Flags, suspended two hundred feet in the air, waiting in anticipation for the free-fall. My stomach's in my throat but in a wonderful, adrenaline-rush sort of way. Then, before I know it, I'm falling. The fall's so fast and so intense that in the blink of an eye it's over. I'm left sitting at the bottom wanting to do it again.

I flop down beside Sarah, panting and gasping like a dog in July. My body's drenched in sweat but I feel amazing. Sarah climbs on top of me with a dreamy expression on her face. "Are you ok?" She asks.

I reach up and hold her face in my hands, trembling. "I should be the one asking you that. Did I hurt you?"

"I'm good," she says raising her eyebrows. She looks tired.

And hot. She wipes her forehead with the back of her hand. Then she kisses my lips again. I'm struggling just to keep my eyes open but Sarah keeps touching me. She strokes my cheek, then my chest. She laces her fingers with mine. If I didn't know any better I'd think she wanted to go for round two.

I feel the weight of her on my chest, the heat of her skin on mine, the quickened beat of her heart. I comb the hair out of her face and kiss her. When she kisses me back I have my answer.

It's not as hard this time. In fact, there's very little thinking involved at all. Our first time was a comedy of errors, no doubt. But our second time is perfect.

CHAPTER 40

Time flies when you're married. Or at least it seems that way for us. The calendar's pushing October and Sarah and I have very little to show for it.

I'm lying in bed at one of the overnight shelters in Cambridge, waiting for our clothes to dry. My mind drifts in and out of sleep. Between lapses I think about Sarah. She said she'd be right back. I try to blink away the exhaustion, to lift my head and go look for her. But it's too heavy, the room's too warm.

"Charlie?"

I slowly open my eyes. I see Sarah standing in the doorway with a manila folder. Her eyes are watery like she's been crying. "Whasswrong?" I ask, rubbing my eyes and trying to get my bearings. I'm gripping the sheets so hard, my left hand is white. "What time issit?"

"Four o'clock," she answers quickly. She joins me on the edge of the bed and I place my hand on top of hers. She stares at me with a distant look in her eyes.

"Are you ok? What's wrong?" I ask again. "What's in the folder?"

She sighs loudly. "I was looking at a Maine paper online, while I waited for our laundry."

"Online? I didn't even know they have computers here." I scratch my head and sit up. "And?"

"And I saw the missing persons report. I saw *my* picture,

Charlie. My aunt's looking for me." She bites her bottom lip.

Of all the emotions I expected to feel at this moment, jealousy was not one of them. But I am jealous. I've been here four years and no one has reported me missing. My parents won the lottery losing me from their lives.

"Charlie, did you hear me? What should I do?" She's bouncing around on her feet. It looks like she already has an answer.

"Maybe you should call," I suggest softly, not sure I mean it.

"Maybe." She says it like this was her plan all along.

My body tenses. "What about being a burden?" I ask, trying to consider all the angles. She hands me the folder.

"The woman that works here gave me this. It has all kinds of information on schools, and the military, and programs they have to help us. She was telling me about an online GED program she could get us into. We can get our degrees and get out of here, start our life together. We don't have to live like this anymore."

I recoil as if she slapped me in the face. *I never realized this wasn't good enough for you.* The words sit like hard caramel in my mouth, until I finally say them aloud.

"That's not what I'm saying, Charlie," she explains with a mixture of love and annoyance. "I'm just saying we can get out of here. Don't you want that?" I say nothing. "I'm in love with *you*, Charlie, not the shelters and free food in downtown Boston."

Ouch.

"But this is me!" I tell her. "This is my life. You knew that when you married me."

"But it doesn't have to be, is all I'm saying. Heather said there's an Air force base in Bangor, near my aunt's house. You can fly like you've always wanted to, and I can go to college for social work."

"You know I'm not smart enough for the Air force." My voice is flat.

"That's not true!" She growls in frustration. "Why are you

so hard on yourself all the time? You can do anything you want." She gets up and paces around the room. "All I'm saying is that we're not going anywhere like this. Don't you want a family someday? A home? Can you honestly tell me the Starbucks' lifestyle doesn't appeal to you?"

I'm a ticking time bomb ready to explode. I take slow and easy breaths, trying to suppress the anger and hurt I feel.

"What? Say something." She prods gently. "Think of how happy we were—"

"Stop! Dammit Sarah, stop! I can't give you that. I'll never be able to give you the mansion and the inground pool. I thought you knew that." She starts to say something then stops. "Maybe you married the wrong guy," I say between clenched teeth, fighting back tears. "Or, if you need all that stuff, then maybe I..." My voice trails off, as I know better than to finish that sentence.

Her bottom lip trembles. I can tell I hurt her, but in the heat of the moment I don't care. I feel my father's temper boiling inside me. I turn around and punch the wall.

Sarah backs into the doorway. She looks scared. I want to take it back, but the damage is done. "Sarah, wait." She ignores me and keeps going. I watch her barrel through the front door. Against my better judgment, I let her go.

CHAPTER 41

Regret sinks deeper in my chest. I sit on the bed with my elbows on my knees and my hands in my hair. *What did I do?*

It doesn't take long for me to come to my senses. This isn't an area I want her roaming around alone, especially at night. I grab our bags and shoot out the door like a bullet. I have this overwhelming need to find her, to apologize and make things better. I look around frantically but she's not there. She doesn't know Cambridge. I head for the closest bridge back to the city.

A car zips by me on the left. Fiery red leaves scuttle across the road, curling like Cape Cod chips. The sun's starting to set so it will be dark within an hour or so. I have to find her soon.

I push through pedestrians on the bridge, racking my brain. Unfortunately, Cara's not here to help this time. *Tell me how to fix this*, I plead, but nothing comes to mind. *Think, think.* I inhale the smell of decaying leaves that's so inherently fall. *Think.* Without warning, my mind flashes to one of our earlier encounters in the park. She went there to talk to her mom. I know where she is.

I take a few steps and stop. There's another shadow lurking in that memory. It's the jealous psychopath that has been following us around since the wedding, showing up and making threats. I'll never forget the look on his face when he found out we were married. If I didn't know any better, I'd

231

think he was in love with Sarah. But I do know better. You need to have a heart to be in love.

My chest seizes. Thump. Thump. *Take deep breaths, Charlie*. Thump thump thump thump. *There's no time for an anxiety attack right now*. My heart beats louder in my ears. *Go!* The voice of reason screams inside me. I picture Kain, with her.

I drop our bags and start to run.

~~~

I make it to Storrow Drive in less than ten minutes. A cool wind sweeps through, sending leaves spinning in vortex patterns down the street. I cross the foot bridge to the Esplanade, still jogging and searching for Sarah. There's a smashed pumpkin by the road. Other than that, the place is empty. Quiet. It's too quiet. I venture over to the water, hoping my prediction is right. To my overwhelming relief it is. I find her there, sitting on the end of the dock, dangling her legs off the edge.

I imagine she doesn't want to talk to me right now but I don't care. I have to make things right. I crunch through a layer of dead leaves, kicking them out of my path as I head for the dock. Sarah turns around when she hears me, looking startled by the noise. "Charlie." She grabs her chest and exhales. I've never seen her look more relieved.

"I'm sorry." I apologize quickly. "For all of it." My eyes are soft, repentant.

Sarah jumps to her feet. "I'm sorry, too. I don't care where we are, as long as we're together." She hugs me tighter than usual. I wrap by arms around her and bury my nose in her hair. Calm feelings flood my body.

I stroke the back of her head, wondering how long we'll make it before the topic comes up again. My next apology may not be so well received. I grab Sarah's face with both hands and kiss her. I guess it doesn't matter, as long as we're ok now.

CHAPTER 42

It's a crisp, breezy autumn night. You'd see a million stars if you were anywhere other than the city. Sarah and I sit hand in hand on the dock, watching the wind whip across the black water.

"I guess we lost our room," Sarah says solemnly.

"And our bags," I add, remembering this for the first time.

"What?"

I hear a twig snap in the woods. I hold up a finger. "Did you hear that?"

She presses her body into mine. "Yeah."

Cigarette smoke wafts in our direction and I get a sick feeling in my chest. This guy is really starting to get on my nerves.

Kain appears out of nowhere. He says, "We gotta stop meeting like this," and laughs.

"What do you want?" I bark, slowly getting to my feet.

"Nice to see you, too." He replies cryptically, flicking his cigarette butt on the ground. There's someone else with him. He's mammoth in size and covered in tattoos. He makes Kain look like the rat that he is.

"Who's this guy?" I ask pointedly.

"Spike wanted to meet the girl I keep talkin' about," Kain answers in a raspy voice.

I pull Sarah behind my back protectively. "I'd get out of here if I were you," I threaten. "We both remember what happened last time."

"Yeah, somethin' tells me we ain't gonna have a repeat performance of that." A piece of metal flashes by his side. There's a gun dangling from his right hand.

I feel Sarah shrink into me. She grabs a fistful of my shirt and whispers, "Be careful, Charlie."

I flip my palm upward and curl my fingers twice, inviting Kain forward. In response he cocks his gun. His bodyguard inches forward. *Don't worry, I have a plan.*

"Charlie, he has a gun," Sarah squeaks behind me, pointing out the obvious.

"I'd listen to her, tough guy. Hand her over and no one gets hurt."

"Fuck off," I spit angrily. "You're not getting anywhere near her."

He laughs. "Well I got a bullet here that says otherwise. One blow to the head and she's mine."

Sarah starts to cry. I want to turn around and hug her, tell her it's going to be ok, but I can't. I have a gun pointed at my head. This wasn't exactly part of the plan.

"I'll go with him, Charlie." She turns to Kain. "I'll go with you, as long as you don't hurt him," Sarah says in hysterics, looking at him from around my back.

"No you won't!" I snap. I reach behind me and grab her hand. "If anything happens to me, you run, do you understand me?"

"I love you," she says between sobs.

"Promise me, Sarah." I say more forcefully. But she doesn't listen. Instead, she pushes past me and starts running toward the enemy. Kain looks disgustingly happy. He lowers his gun and I see my opportunity.

Kain reaches for Sarah. While he's distracted, I grab his arm and kick him in the knee as hard as I can. The crack that follows is unnatural to say the least. Kain keels over and I elbow him in the back, dropping him to the ground like a rag doll. I scramble to get the gun but Kain's number two is closing in on me, so instead I grab Sarah and we run.

We head south down the river, trying to make it to the next footbridge as quickly as we can. I twist my neck to see what's going on behind us. I'm shocked and disheartened to see Kain back on his feet. He limps a few steps, before his limp turns into a trot and then a crooked run. "Catch them!" He screams through clenched teeth. Luckily the big guy's about as fast as his impeded friend. Kain curses him out for being so fat. Then he does something I wasn't expecting. He lifts his unsteady hand and pulls the trigger.

"Shit!" I exclaim, guiding Sarah to the left, and then the right. "Zigzag patterns," I instruct, as he peppers our ankles with shots. *It's slowing us down, and they're gaining ground*, I think anxiously. I look to the road for an escape, but it's too dark for cars to see us. If we dart into the street we'll end up getting ourselves killed. Even on the sidewalk, Kain could shoot us from the cover of the trees and never get caught. He intends to shoot somebody tonight. I could see that in his eyes.

"Charlie, I'm getting tired," Sarah mumbles, wheezing and panting with exhaustion. She trips and falls and I help her up. I'm sympathetic to the fact untrained legs can only sprint so far. Even mine are burning with fire at this point.

Ahead, the foot path veers around a fenced-in jungle gym. The bridge is too far. I could carry her, but that would slow me down even more. I turn around. Kain's no longer shooting at us, either to save bullets or because he's out. I'm not willing to bet on the latter. He stumbles, taking large strides with his left leg, quick to shift the weight off his right. I cringe when I see the hideous curve in his leg. He screams with every step. He's tougher than I gave him credit for.

I turn back to the playground. It may be our only chance. I tell Sarah I have an idea. "Do you have enough steam to sprint to the end of the straightaway, down to the playground there?"

"I don't know," she says with tears in her eyes, now moving at a jogger's pace beside me.

"Can you try for me?" I ask desperately.

"Ok," she says weakly.

"Ok. We're going to run down there as fast as we can, veer right towards the river, then get on our knees. I want you to crawl toward the playground, and go in the back entrance. We're going to hide under the jungle gym. Can you do that?"

She nods. I pray this plan works. Visibility is poor, especially the further away we get from them, and the fence around the playground provides additional cover. I grab Sarah's hand and start running. She follows my lead and we sprint the one hundred meters like our life depends on it. We do everything according to plan, and before we know it we're crawling on our bellies in a bed of crushed rock. We wedge ourselves against the far side of the fort and wait. I tell Sarah to take deep breaths and relax. I don't want our heavy breathing to give us away.

The screaming gets louder as Kain approaches. He grumbles something to his cohort, presumably about our whereabouts. *Keep walking.* Sarah clasps her hands in prayer. Then, for a moment, everything is still.

The next thing I hear is a limp leg dragging through gravel. He sees us. I grab Sarah around the waist and scramble out the other side, fighting for footing in the rocks. When I finally catch my balance, I put her on my back and run, away from the shooter, toward the back gate. My legs plead with me to stop. Before I get anywhere, Spike steps out of the shadows and trips me. I fall and Sarah tumbles off my back.

He rolls me over and digs a foot into my chest. Sarah cries out, asking him to stop. I struggle but I don't have the strength to get out of it. He's too heavy. He holds me there until Kain has time to get to us. I stare up at the sky, listening to his shallow breathing, watching the dismal situation unfold. It's getting harder to breathe. *This is going to end badly*, I finally admit to myself.

Kain's ugly mug glares down at me. He smiles wickedly through the pain. A second later I feel a searing pain in my side when he kicks me. It's accompanied by a blood curdling scream as he shifts his weight back to the good leg.

"Finish him, you fool!" Kain yells irritably.

"No!" Sarah shouts in dispute. She looks at me with weepy eyes, clutching her chest. They're asking me what she can do.

"Nothing. Just stay where you are," I instruct in a barely audible voice. I look from her to the man towering over me with my life in his hands. *Just get on with it*, I plead silently. Lift your foot and make a move. Give me a chance to fight. As if he heard my thoughts, he releases me. I cough and fight for breath but before I have a chance to catch it, the first blow comes. It's an easy kick to the ribs and it renders me useless.

Before I get my head straight he does it again, this time rolling me over with the force of the kick. I curl into fetal position, then struggle to get to my knees, gasping and spitting out blood. I fight to get to my feet. Suddenly I realize I've underestimated his strength, and overestimated my own. It has been a while since I've had a good fight. I'm out of practice.

Spike knocks my feet out from under me. The next series of kicks come so fast I don't have time to register the pain of one before he comes at me with another. In the midst of the abuse, I look up at the man beating me senseless. It's my father. I blink away the hallucination but my mind's overwhelmed with flashbacks. I close my eyes and I'm the fat, scared, lonely boy, trying to look tough but crying on the inside. *I can shut it off*, I think hazily. Like I did back then. Go to that place in my head and escape. Peter's and my place. Already I feel it happening. I feel myself slipping into unconsciousness. Everything feels fuzzy. No more pain...

"Stop, you're killing him!" A throaty cry rips through the haze. I don't know where it's coming from but it rocks me to my core. I'm not alone with my father. Someone else is here. It's a female voice. "Don't leave me," she pleads. She's telling me to fight. It can't be my mother, I think sadly, wishing it were. I'm confused. The voice tells me she loves me. You do? I want to ask, but nothing comes out. I'm having a hard time focusing on the words. I think I love her, too. It takes a minute then I see her. A beautiful angel surrounded by white light. It's Sarah. Suddenly I remember what I'm leaving behind. Who I'm leaving behind. And what they'll do to her when I'm gone.

I open my eyes. Sarah cries with relief. *I'm still here*, I mouth to her slowly. Everything hurts. I'm in unbearable pain and I can't make the shaking stop. I force my muscles to move me, to get me to my feet. It's my one and only thought. Kain watches me with amusement, and Spike looks to him for direction.

"He ain't gonna do nothin'," Kain says in a nasty voice.

Spike watches me like a child, learning to walk. I imagine I look a lot like one, stumbling around like I am. It's hard to see beyond my nose. All I need is one moment of clarity. When it finally comes I line up my arm. It's gone in an instant, but I fight through the foggy feeling in my head. I try not to let it take over. Spike turns his head to laugh at my expense and I throw a punch. It hits him square in the jaw. I stagger backwards.

It doesn't take him long to shake it off. He comes at me with a swing of his own and I go down hard. Through my squinty right eye I see Sarah come up behind him and grab his arm, pleading with him to stop. He jerks his arm and throws her back ten feet. The anger bubbles up inside me and I use that anger to get up again, to get to my knees.

Spike hits me again. And again. But I don't back down – at least not right away. I take it for quite a while, until I feel my body slowly reaching its breaking point. Things are starting to get quiet in my head and I'm seeing things in slow motion. I stay on the ground for longer this time. I see Spike coming near me from the corner of my one good eye and I know this is it. He's ready to kill me. I watch him gear up for the final blow, thinking how sorry I am that I couldn't save her. I feel a tear leak out of my closed left eye. But before Spike issues the blow to put me under, Kain tells him to stop.

"Wait. Don't kill him, you idiot. I want him to be conscious for this." Kain says wickedly. "Besides, I want to do it myself." Kain jams a dirty finger in Sarah's face. "You, over there, on your knees, now."

Sarah rushes over to me, as I'm kneeling where he wants us to be. She hugs me, sending a searing pain up and down my chest, as I attempt to hug her back. "I love you," she tells me through the tears.

"I love you, too," I mumble softly.

Kain positions himself in front of us and Sarah looks him square in the eye. "I don't think you'll do it." She says loudly.

"Excuse me?" He spits in our direction.

"I don't think you'll do it because deep down there's a good person in there. It doesn't have to end like this. There's still hope for you, Kain." Her words curdle in my stomach like sour milk. Unlike my naïve saint of a wife, I know just how hopeless he is.

Kain laughs. "Little girl, you don't know me one bit do you?"

"I think I do," she says meekly.

"Well you don't!" He growls, lifting his gun. "You never gave me the time of day. I tried to get to know you but you stood by and watched your guy here smash me up." Kain aims the gun like there's a bull's eye on my forehead.

"Wait, please!" She cries.

"I've waited long enough!" He screams in fury. "Now," he says in a softer tone, "I'm gonna count to three and you're gonna watch me kill your husband," he says sourly.

Sarah looks at him helplessly, pleading for my life. Her attempts are useless. When she finally realizes this, she addresses me with heartbreaking sadness. "Charlie?" Her eyes are wet with tears. "What are we going to do?"

I don't know what to say. I tried to protect her and failed. I fought back and lost. I racked my brain for a way out and came up short. I have nothing left.

"Three..."

In my final moments of life, I think back to my days on the train, reading and luxuriating in the warmth of the heater on my feet. I was a different person back then. Life didn't really start for me until Sarah came into it. I reach for her hand and squeeze. "Promise me you'll run," I whisper so low I can barely hear it myself. "You have to fight."

"Two..."

She squeezes back and I take comfort in that. I smile sadly

into the barrel of the gun pointed at my face. I wonder if Liam's waiting for me. My mind flashes to the train again, and the book in my hand. *The Jungle.* Something about the cover holds me, like there's a message in it, waiting to be found. What's that famous quote after Jurgis attacks Connor?

"They put him in a place where the snow could not beat in, where the cold could not eat through his bones; they brought him food and drink—why, in the name of heaven, if they must punish him, did they not put his family in jail and leave him outside?"

Suddenly it all makes sense. It's not me he's going to shoot. He wants me conscious so I can watch her die.

"One." He snaps his wrist and points the gun at Sarah. I lunge in front of the bullet and push her to the ground. I turn my head and watch the pellet as it comes at me, spiraling, in slow motion, and I know it's going to hit. It whizzes past the back of my head as I fall but I know I can't escape it. I prepare for the collision of shrapnel and skin. An instant before it rips through my back, I realize I could die; and my entire life flashes before my eyes.

I could write a two-hundred page book on everything I saw in that fraction of a second. Mixed in among the slideshow of images, I see myself as a child, playing with spare car parts and bugs, and Peter. I see us flying in a field with not a care in the world. I see my grandfather, and Fenway Park, and my dog Pepper. I see Liam, smiling with an intensity so bright I almost don't recognize him. I see Sam, Luiz and even Ethel, standing together on the Common holding hands. And of course I see Sarah. She's everywhere. Where we first met, the day I saved her, the day she saved me, our first kiss...

The crack of the shot rings in my ears. Sarah's cry is a universe away. There are no more flashbacks, only darkness. Yet, somehow, I know I'm still alive.

The pain is intolerable. It feels like someone's holding a blow torch to my back. I grip the grass around me and throw up. Everything hurts.

"Shh, it's ok." Sarah's leaning over me, trying to stop the bleeding with a cloth. Her voice is muffled. My eyes are like slits, but I can see her. She's not wearing a shirt and she's covered in blood. I lift my head slightly, trying to find Kain and his side-kick. I want to kill them both. But after a brief surveillance I see that we're alone. *What a coward.* My head drops to the ground with a thud.

"Charlie, stay here ok? And stay awake. Promise me you'll stay awake. I'm going to get you some help," she says through clenched teeth. She's in hysterics, shaking uncontrollably and looking terrified.

"Are you ok?" I slur. She shakes her head.

"I'll be right back." She kisses me gently, then gets up and runs to the road. As I watch her run away I wonder if this is real. I try to keep my eyes on her but my eyesight keeps blurring. It's hard to stay awake. She waves her arms frantically, standing there in her bra on the edge of Storrow Drive. I don't like this. I try out my voice but it's a whisper at best. I want to tell her to come back. It's not safe.

I slide myself forward an inch at a time, until a sharp pain forces me to stop. It's a lightning bolt under the skin that keeps spreading. I clutch my chest and realize my shirt's soaked through with blood. *Help.* I try to call out but the words harden in my mouth. The pain intensifies and I find myself fighting for breath. I roll onto my side and struggle, not knowing what to do.

Out of the corner of my eye I see Sarah running at me with an older couple. *I'm in God's hands now,* I think to myself calmly as my body stops seizing and I start to slip. I watch them come at me in slow motion as the image fades, one person at a time, until I find myself hurling into black velvet darkness. While I'm falling I listen for her voice, soft and soothing as she tries to bring me back to life. Soon enough, that too, starts to fade. I know it's not looking good for me.

"He's not breathing," is the last thing I remember before everything goes still.

CHAPTER 43

My insides feel like molasses. *Where am I?* Voices float around me in the dark, talking in whispers. *Am I alive, or am I dead?* I can't tell. I hear a door open and close in the distance. More voices. I slowly come out of my morphine-laced sleep.

I lift my head and realize just how awful I feel. Everything hurts. I'm achy, and nauseous, and very much alive. I squint into the florescent light. Sarah's sleeping by my bed, unscathed and clutching my hand. When I see her I feel euphoric. I don't know how we made it, but we did.

An IV drips beside me and nurses flutter around fussing over monitors and tubes and beeping machines. "How do you feel?" One of them asks. She hands me apple juice and I shake my head. My throat feels too raw to drink.

She injects something into my arm and my head swims with whatever drug cocktail she's giving me. "Like I've been shot," I answer, taking in the room. "Where am I?" I ask. There's a plate of saran-wrapped food next to the bed and a TV hanging in front of me. I've been washed and wrapped in bandages, and I'm surrounded by pillows and soft white linens. Both Sarah and I are wearing blue scrubs. For a second I wonder if I'm in heaven.

"You're on the emergency ward at Mass General," she says softly, unwrapping my food. "Do you think you can eat something? It's been a while and you need your strength." I ignore her question and look at Sarah. "Is she ok?"

"She's fine," she whispers, "just tired. She's been worried about you."

The nurse checks my vitals, pushes the food at me and leaves. Maybe it's the drugs, or the trauma my body's been through, but I'm not the least bit hungry. Instead, I lie there staring at Sarah. I watch her eyelids flutter and her chest rise and fall until I can't take it any longer. Her expression is so sad. I stroke her cheek and she stirs beside me, blinking until she registers my face.

She snaps upright and gasps. She puts her hand over her mouth, then throws her arms around me and starts to cry. I'm touched by her reaction.

She kisses me over and over again, too happy to know the pain she's causing by pressing on me like this. I hold my breath and kiss her back, pulling her as close as I can without triggering the heart monitor. It feels so good to know she's safe. I drop my head to her shoulder and breathe her in. I try to articulate how happy I am to see her, but I can't. I'm too choked up for words.

"I'm sorry to interrupt." A middle-aged nurse with a red ponytail and white sneakers pokes her head in the door. Her nametag says Mindy. "We need you to try to eat something, hun. We want to make sure you can keep it down." She comes into the room and Sarah slips off the bed and returns to her chair. "The sooner we clear you for recovery, the sooner we can get you out of here," she says with feigned concern. I know the translation: if you're not a paying customer, you have to leave.

"You're going to send him out there like this?" Sarah asks in a panic.

"If he can eat he should be fine," the nurse reassures. "His vitals look good, he's been all stitched up—"

"He's hooked up to a catheter for crying out loud," Sarah argues. I lift the blanket and look down. Yikes. Now that I'm aware, I feel the pain.

"I'm sorry, darling, but it's not my policy. The hospital says if you're conscious and stable you have to go. Unless you have a way to pay for the room?" No one says anything.

"Speaking of that, how are we supposed to pay for the costs we've incurred already?" I ask sheepishly.

"Generally what happens is we send you a bill and you pay as you have the money. Many low-income patients pay in the fifty dollar a month range." I look from Sarah to the nurse. We don't have fifty dollars a month, let alone an address to mail the bill to. "You pay what you can," Mindy says in a gentle tone.

"Thank you."

"You're welcome."

"And, uh, thank you for saving my life." I add.

"You're welcome, hun. That's my job." She says with a wink. "We thought we'd lost you for a minute there. You coded twice." My head swims with the implications of this new information.

"Can I use the bathroom?" I ask desperately, thinking I'm going to be sick.

"Of course you can," Mindy replies. In haste, I shimmy myself to the side of the bed until a painful snag reminds me I'm connected to a catheter. "Oh, hold on sweetie." I grit my teeth while she takes out the catheter and unhooks a few tubes. "This one you'll want to wheel around with you," she says, pointing to a bag of clear fluid. "At least for now."

Sarah helps me step down. When my feet hit the cool linoleum, I'm overcome with nausea. The room spins around me. I close my eyes and take deep breaths, until the dizziness goes away. I wrap one arm around Sarah and grab the pole of fluids with the other. I feel incredibly weak, almost too weak to stand.

"Do you need my help?" Mindy volunteers.

"No, I'm good," I answer through clenched teeth. Every step is agony.

"I'll be back with more morphine," she mutters as she hurries out of the room. *Thank you.*

Sarah stabilizes me from behind while I do my business. Next to nothing comes out. It's still incredibly raw from the tubes. After huffing and swearing my way through, I turn to the mirror over the sink to wash my hands. I gasp when I catch my reflection.

My face is a battlefield, covered in welts and cuts. The skin's purple from all the bruises, and swollen, particularly around the eyes. There's a missing patch of hair over my left ear where they had to stitch me up. I touch the band of gauze, wrapping from the bullet hole in my back to my breastbone. I'm unrecognizable.

The image morphs into the ten year old version of me, coming home from the hospital after I "fell down the stairs". *How did I let this happen again?* I think to myself sadly. I swore I'd protect you.

Sarah sees my haunted expression and tells me it will be ok. She touches my wrist and urges me to go on. I turn on the water and let it run. She talks about shelters taking us in and giving me medication, and about how quickly everything will heal. I tune it all out. All I hear is water, white noise in my ears as it rushes down the drain.

I make it safely back to bed, where Mindy ups my morphine, checks my temperature, and urges me yet again to eat. I move the fork from the plate to my mouth, but I don't taste any of it. Mindy looks pleased and brings me seconds. I give them to Sarah but she isn't hungry either.

Not before long, the morphine kicks in. I roll my head to the side and smile at Sarah. She's fretting about the hospital kicking me out before I'm ready.

"It doesn't matter," I say jovially. "You're going home."

"What?"

"I want you to call your aunt. It's not safe here. I should have known that before yesterday and I'm sorry."

Her dazed expression turns into a goofy grin. "Charlie, you're talking nonsense. It must be the drugs."

"No, it's not. I'm thinking clearly for the first time in a while. I want you to call her." I touch her hand and she pulls it away.

"You said *I'm* going home. You're coming with me, right?"

She asks reluctantly. I take a deep breath and sigh. Sarah looks furious. "No, no, no. You can't do that. You're my husband. You can't just send me away. If you're going to stay here and get yourself killed, then I am too." She says defiantly.

I feel sick, wondering if I'm doing the right thing. "I want you to be safe, to have a good life. I can't give you that here."

"I'm not going to leave you, Charlie. I'm only calling if you're coming with me." Her arms are crossed, and she won't look at me. A few minutes pass in silence, until she finally asks, "Don't you want to be with me?"

"Of course I do."

"Then why won't you come to Maine with me?" She asks.

"Because I—"

"Don't you dare say you'll hold me back because you won't. I'll make sure of that." She snaps.

I play my other angle. "What about your aunt? She can take in one of us, not two. Even you said yourself you don't want to be a burden."

"I did. But that's up to her to decide. She has a missing ad out there, for crying out loud." She takes a sip of my water. "And who knows, maybe we could help with Daniel? Or call that sweet old woman from Shaw's if we have to. She said she has a basement apartment we could use until we get on our feet. It will be ok. We'll figure it out, I promise."

I lie there and think about it. Life with Sarah, outside of these city lines. Through the haze I process it slowly. With my defense mechanisms down, I actually hear what she's saying. For the first time I consider, *maybe she's right.*

"You're willing to fix me?" I ask. It's more of a plea than a question. "Because I don't think very highly of myself. And I'm going to need that if you want me to do anything with the real world."

"I'll spend every day trying," she says with a grin. It's nice to see her smile. "Besides, this *is* the real world. It's just a harsher version of it. And you did just fine here."

"Yeah. Look at me," I reply with a chuckle, examining my scars. Sarah laughs too.

"Sorry to interrupt!" Mindy exclaims as she breezes into the room with a bag of laundered clothes. Our clothes. I guess it's that time. "How are you feeling?" She asks, examining my chart.

"Can we make a phone call?" I ask, ignoring her question.

She looks at us and furrows her brow. "Sure." She points at the phone beside Sarah on the wall. "Just be sure to dial a nine first."

Sarah stares at it like it's on fire. She chews her bottom lip.

"Do you know the number?" I ask, touching her arm.

"Yes." She answers with a guilty expression. They must have been close.

"Let me give you two some privacy. I'll be back in a minute with your release forms." Mindy says as she leaves the room.

I slide over to make room for Sarah. She climbs into bed with me and leans her head on my shoulder. "Are you sure you're ready for this?" She asks. "This will change everything you know."

I put my arm around her and kiss the top of her head. "You better call before I change my mind."

She takes a deep breath and picks up the receiver. "I love you," she says as she dials the number, holding her breath. After the second ring I hear a woman pick up. She says hello three times and I watch the color drain from Sarah's face. I squeeze her hand for moral support.

"Aunt Nancy?" She says, shaking. There's a long pause, and then the woman on the other end starts to cry.

EPILOGUE

I'm cruising down the Maine Turnpike, drumming the steering wheel and belting out the words to the song on the radio. The sun's still out, the windows are down, and I'm loving life. I crank up the volume and punch the gas pedal.

I pull off the highway on my normal route home. Shortly after the first turn, I spot a broken down Buick on the side of road. I slow down to make sure everything's all right, and as I get closer I notice the license plate says GODSWORK. I pull in behind the gold car and slowly approach the white-haired woman in the driver's seat. She's fishing for something in the glove box.

"Ma'am?" I tap the window. "Ma'am, are you all right?"

She turns to face me and I freeze. It's Eleanor, the old woman that paid for our picnic lunch a lifetime ago. She doesn't recognize me.

"Are you ok?" I ask again. She rolls down her window and smiles.

"Well aren't you nice. You look an awful lot like my grandson," she says before turning back to her glove box.

"Can I help you with something?" I offer, keeping my distance.

"I'm trying to find my cellular. My daughter bought me a cellular a few Christmases ago, for emergencies, and I can't seem to find it in all this mess."

I can't help but smile. "Well I don't have a phone," I

explain, "but I can give you a ride somewhere if you need it. It's no trouble."

Eleanor accepts my proposition with a heartfelt thank you. I help her out of the Buick and into my rusty blue Corolla. She asks me to drive her to her daughter's place, a duplex near the university. On an impulse, I ask, "How's your husband doing?"

Her milky blue eyes soften as she asks, "You knew Ed?" She pulls a lace handkerchief out of her pocket and holds it in her lap.

"I met him once," I reply carefully, wishing I could take it back. "I'm sorry for your loss."

"Me too, dear." She blows her nose noisily. "Me too."

~~~

I finish my commute home in silence. It's funny how life has a way of circling back. Sarah calls these things ripples, when someone does something nice for you and in turn you do something nice for someone else. We've seen a number of them over the years. It's amazing how one life can affect so many others that way.

Seeing Eleanor again reminded me of how much time has passed. I'm a different person than I was back then. We left Boston almost five years ago, and my only regret is not knowing what happened to Sam. We went to see him before we left but he was gone. His stuff was gone, Sasha was gone. We asked the local police if they'd seen him, or moved him, but they said no. There wasn't even a print on the pavement. It was like he vanished into thin air.

A lot has happened since then. Sarah and I went to live with her aunt, uncle and cousin in Maine. We got our GEDs and ironically enough, helped Daniel, her autistic cousin, apply for jobs. Sarah applied to college. She took a few classes at the University of Maine, which eventually turned into a full-time push to get her degree in social work. It was a good day when we found out Nancy was appointed Sarah's legal guardian in the will. Since she works for the University, Sarah gets to go for free.

The inheritance was another nice surprise. Sarah's mom left her some money when she died. It wasn't enough to cover books and clothes and food for a year, but it helped. To cover the rest of our expenses I got a job. With much pushing and reassuring from Sarah, I applied for a position at the Bangor Air Force base. I found out at the interview you need a college degree to be a pilot, but they have tuition assistance and scholarships, so with any luck I'll get to fly someday. In the meantime, they had an opening in air traffic control, which still sounded pretty cool.

Two months later they sent me away to basic military training. By the time I returned, I had enough money for first and last month's rent on a little apartment down the road from Nancy and John. We let Daniel live in the other bedroom, and kept an eye on him, but in my opinion he didn't need us. He has a severe case of OCD, and his mind functions differently than mine, but he gets along just fine on his own. It took breaking away from his parents to learn that.

They say success is a product of hard work. In our case, it was a product of luck, or divine intervention, or whatever you want to call it. The hard work followed after that. My luck changed the day I met Sarah. I was drowning, and she taught me how to swim. She taught me to believe in myself, and in others, and the power of forgiveness. I eventually forgave my parents; although I still haven't spoken to them. I called them once and got a message that the telephone line had been disconnected. I don't even know if they live there anymore.

I tried to forgive Kain, I really did; but watching him get arrested on national TV was how I found my peace. Two years ago he assaulted a BU student with a big-time lawyer father. They found him guilty on trial, but deemed him criminally insane. Now he's living in a mental hospital somewhere in Massachusetts. That one really threw me for a loop.

I think of how different our lives turned out as I pull into the driveway. I approach the modest blue house with the peeling paint and crooked front porch. We can just barely afford this place on my military salary. It's a starter home, sitting on a lot the size of a postage-stamp, with popcorn ceilings and shag carpets. But I love it. I love everything about it. The creaky floors, the smells, the crayon on the walls. It's home. We moved here a little over a year ago. Daniel got a job at a local grocery store and took over the apartment. It was okay for three people, but it was just too small for four.

I turn off the engine. As I've come to expect, Kimmy, the old mutt we rescued from the shelter, comes barreling out the front door to greet me. I scrub her neck and ears, and listen to the cicadas hum in the yard. Kimmy's some sort of Labrador-mix. Poor girl has a bum wheel, but it doesn't stop her from running around like a maniac most of the time.

A short minute later I go inside the house. I put my hat on the counter and unlace my shoes. Kimmy jams her nose in my eye. Whatever's bubbling on the stove smells delicious.

Sarah rounds the corner with our little man in tow. He's chattering about diapers and big boy pants. She shakes her head and laughs. Potty training isn't going so well.

"Daddy!" My son runs at me, unsteady on his fat little legs. He holds out his arms to be picked up.

"Hey buddy," I say as I kiss him and scoop him off the ground. I ask about his day, which always gets him babbling since he's two, and loves to hear himself talk. Sarah towels off her hands.

"Hi Daddy," she says as she does a half spin and kisses me. My heart skips a beat.

"Hi." The sight of her still stops me in my tracks. She puts her hand on my chest and smiles. I usually can't wait to get out of this starchy uniform, but for some reason Sarah can't keep her hands off me when I'm in it.

"Are you hungry?" She asks, returning to the sink. She starts cutting up tomatoes and throwing them in a pot. I watch her move around the kitchen, mesmerized. Her hair's pulled back in a loose twist and she's wearing my favorite jeans.

You'd never know she just had a baby. Well, six months ago now I guess.

"Where's the peanut?" I ask, putting Liam down. I unbutton the top two buttons of my uniform.

"Sleeping. She was fussy when I picked them up at John's." Nancy's husband John watches the kids while we're at work. He's on disability for Lyme disease, but he's good with children. He's had twenty-two years of practice with Daniel.

"I'll go check on her," I volunteer.

"Are you going to see Hope?" Liam asks anxiously. "Can I come?"

"Not this time, little man. She's sleeping. But when she wakes up you can see her, ok?"

"Otay."

I walk down the hall and into the baby's room. There's a small desk fan in the window, cranking out air. I tiptoe over to the crib. Hope's lying on her back with her eyes open. Her mouth's parted slightly and her tongue's sticking out. Against my better judgment, I move closer.

She kicks and waves her fists in the air when she sees me. She's wearing the pink and yellow onesie that Aunt Nancy picked out. I reach down to touch her belly and she latches onto my finger. Her hands are so tiny. They remind me of a little frog.

"My beautiful girl," I whisper as I swaddle her in a blanket and lift her out of the crib. She's so soft, and warm. I kiss her forehead and breathe in her delicious baby smell. She's not even one and already she owns me.

We go to the corner of the room and sit in the rocking chair. It's nice and quiet in here, which is something I'm not used to these days. I look down and Hope's plump pink lips stretch into a yawn. She's tired. She must have missed her nap today.

I hum to her and rub her back, rocking her until she falls asleep. After I place her back in her crib I stare at her for a while. She looks like an angel, with her ice-blonde hair and porcelain skin. She's a mini version of her mom. Liam, on the other hand, got the short end of the stick. He's my son through and through. My complexion, my eyes, my stubborn ways. And everything Daddy does, he wants to do. Sarah bought us matching Red Sox caps for Christmas.

I shut the door quietly behind me and head toward the commotion in the living room. I find Sarah on the floor tickling Liam. He lets out a high pitched squeal that makes me laugh. "She was up?" Sarah asks with a lazy smile, rolling onto her elbows. I forgot that the baby monitor was on.

"Yeah, but she's out now. I rocked her back to sleep," I say as I lean down to kiss her. Liam climbs on his mom's stomach and wedges his way between us.

"Hope's a baby," he announces smugly. "I'm not a baby anymore."

"No, you're not," I agree, kissing him on the head.

The timer goes off in the kitchen and Sarah gets up. I set the table while Sarah dishes out the food. Liam grabs Kimmy's tail and follows her around the room, loving life. Kimmy looks at me with those big brown eyes.

"Liam Samuel Angelo, leave the dog alone and go wash up for dinner." Sarah scolds.

Liam drops her tail and races unsteadily down the hall toward the bathroom. "Come on Daddy!" He calls behind him.

We wash up and I place him in his highchair, where he manages to get chili all over his face the second Sarah puts it down. "Are you getting any of that in your mouth?" I tease. He chomps on his food like a chipmunk, ignoring me completely. Sarah winks.

"So Liam, are you excited about next weekend?" She asks.

"Ya," he replies, with his cheeks full of food.

"We're going to Boston, remember? To see the Red Sox play. And to go on a Duck Tour. You get to see where Mommy and Daddy met."

His eyes perk up. "Will Papi be dere?" He asks with his mouth full. David Ortiz is Liam's favorite player.

"Yeah, he'll be there, buddy."

"Is Hope coming?"

"No, sweetheart. She's going to stay with Aunt Nancy and Uncle John. She's too little to go to the game."

"Oh," he says with disappointment. He loves his sister, despite his jealousy when she's around. "Can I be a besboll plair like Papi?" He asks.

"Son, you can be anything you want." I tell him proudly. I really believe that, too. He's very smart for his age.

Liam nods and slaps his tray, sending chili flying across the room. "All right little man, you're done," Sarah says as she takes the dish away.

"I think the high chair got more of this than you did," I remark, cleaning off his hands. He smiles.

"Time to scrub you down! Kiss Daddy first," Sarah says with a mischievous grin as she lifts him out of the chair. He plants a wet one on my cheek. I wipe off the chili and lick my fingers.

"Payback, Sarah!" I call after her. She just laughs.

They disappear into the bathroom and I mop chili off the seat. Five minutes later, Liam comes out, followed by my wife, wearing nothing but a pair of Spiderman bottoms and a puffy diaper. He yells something excitedly, and races into the living room.

"Hold your horses mister. We have to brush those baby teeth," Sarah says as she follows him with a toothbrush and a shirt.

"I'm not a baby!" He trills with a smile, launching himself onto the love seat.

~~~

We do our usual routine: dinner, thirty minutes of cartoons, then a story before bed. At Liam's request, I read 'When you give a mouse a cookie', for the hundredth time. I could recite that one in my sleep.

"Daddy, I want a mouse," he says sleepily as he pops his thumb in his mouth.

"I don't know if Mommy would go for that one."

"Then I want kitty," he says reaching for it with his fingers. I hand him his stuffed animal. It's an orange tiger I won for him at the carnival.

He clutches it in his arms and says slowly, "Kitty has a fever, Daddy." He blinks a couple times. "Maybe he should stay home with Hope when we go to the besboll game."

"That's a great idea, buddy," I respond, kissing him on the nose. "I'm sure Hope would like that."

"I know." He says closing his eyes.

I pull the covers up around his chin and sit there until he falls asleep. He has the longest eyelashes I've ever seen. I brush his hair to one side and watch his belly rise and fall rhythmically as he breathes. My parents must have been wired wrong. I'd never do *anything* to hurt him.

I crack open the window before I leave. It's a hot summer night and without air conditioning, it can get pretty sticky around here. As I walk back to the door, Liam makes a sucking noise and rolls over with kitty. "I Love you, Daddy," he says in a barely audible voice. My heart melts.

"I love you too, son," I say with my hand on the doorknob. "Goodnight."

~~~

I find Sarah in the kitchen studying for her exams. She's singing along to the radio and tapping a pencil on her book. When she sees me she gets up and walks around the table. I open my arms for her and she nestles against my chest. "Did you have a good day?" I mumble into her hair, now long around her shoulders. It smells like a mix of jasmine and lavender.

"I did. I found out I have another internship in a couple weeks." She leans back to see my reaction. Every time Sarah does an internship she ends up bringing kids home. It's usually for a week or two, to keep them away from their families until the trial.

"What?" I ask with a chuckle. "Once you're full-time it's only going to get worse, so I might as well get used to it now." I take her hand and kiss it. "Besides, I wish I had someone like you to protect me from my parents. I can't take that away from them."

"I love you," she says getting on her tiptoes to kiss me on the lips.

"I love you, too."

I fill the sink with soapy water and start to do the dishes. Instead of studying, Sarah helps me dry. We work in companionable silence for several minutes. As crazy as it sounds, I actually look forward to this mundane activity. It means there's food on the table. And it's a few minutes of peace and quiet that Sarah and I get to spend together. I hand her another plate. She takes it and dances around the room with it, spinning and swaying and moving her hips. I drop my sponge and watch her, suddenly ready for bed. She laughs self-consciously and puts the plate away.

Halfway through the stack a slow song comes on the radio. I look at the dishes, then Sarah, and smile. "Dance with me." I say, turning off the water.

"What?"

"Come on," I urge, pulling her away from the sink. I twirl her a couple times, then tug her back to me.

"When did you learn to dance?" She asks playfully.

"I was born with these skills," I say, obviously joking. I touch my nose to her neck and breathe in her perfume. Her body feels so warm and safe. I straighten up to kiss her.

"Can I ask you something?" She says.

"Depends." I brush the hair off her shoulders and kiss her neck. Sarah takes a deep breath. "I thought you had a question?" I ask impishly. When she doesn't respond, I tilt her chin so I can see her face. She looks very serious.

"Is everything ok?" She nods. Then, without warning, she grabs my face and pulls it toward hers. We start kissing like teenagers. I tangle my hands in her hair and she pulls at my shirt until eventually it comes off. Before I know what's happening, Sarah backs me into the wall and pins me up against the cupboard. I spin her around and lift her onto the counter. The salt and pepper shakers tumble to the floor and both of us pause. Sarah giggles, with a finger pressed to her lips. Kimmy snores loudly in the other room.

"We should probably go to the bedroom," she whispers. She grabs my belt loops and pulls me closer.

"Good idea," I agree, kissing her again. She kisses me back while she fumbles with my belt. It's hard to remember what I'm supposed to do.

"Bedroom," she reminds me as she hooks her legs around my waist.

"Right." I pick her up and run with her to the bedroom.

How did I get so lucky? I wonder, as I lay her down on the bed. I think of my life before Sarah. I was the guy on the CharlieCard, stuck on the train, trying to find my way home. Sarah kisses me. None of that matters anymore. Somehow, I found my way here.

READING GROUP GUIDE

Discussion Questions

1. Why is it such a big deal when Charlie's water falls on the floor in the first chapter?

2. After reading Liam's journal, Charlie admits that deep down he knew Liam was gay. Were there any indications of this in the first few chapters?

3. Early on in the book, Charlie is jealous of the fictional man on the front of Boston's subway pass (the "CharlieCard") based on a story from his grandfather. By the end, he compares himself to this man. Why do you think his perception changes, and what does his analogy mean?

4. Charlie refers to himself as damaged and broken. He bases his friendship with Liam on the fact they have this is common. Do you think he considers Sarah broken after he learns more about her?

5. Charlie doesn't see himself the way others do. What is the significance of the scene where he catches himself smiling in the mirror?

6. Charlie's favorite book, *The Jungle*, is mentioned several times throughout the novel. Why do you think Charlie feels such a strong connection to Jurgis, the main character in the story?

7. This novel explores the contrast between kindness and cruelty. Charlie encounters both during his time on the streets. Why do you think some people feel such a disgust for Charlie, while others want to take him in?

8. Throughout the book, Charlie likens himself to animals. Animals he meets seem to feel comfortable around him. Why does Charlie feel a stronger connection to animals than he does to people?

9. During their time in Lawrence, Charlie is envious of the people they encounter because of their lifestyles. If this is the case, why does he turn down so many opportunities to finally leave his life on the streets?

10. Why does Charlie drop his surname, Hope, and take on Sarah's? In the epilogue, what is the significance of naming his daughter Hope?

11. A theme in the book is that outward appearances can be deceiving. Everyone has a story and things aren't always as straight forward as they seem. Can you name a few examples of this in *Charlie Card*?

12. What do you think happens to Sam and Sasha at the end of the book? What is their role in the story?

13. There is a significant shift in Charlie's religious beliefs over the course of the book. What events foster this transformation, and what does he believe at the end?

14. Despite their circumstances, Charlie and Sarah do a lot of good for other people, and things work out for them in the end. Do you believe in "ripples"?

15. *Charlie Card* gives a voice to the faceless people of the streets. They live in a world where time stands still, anxiety is common, and poor people can't get married. Do Charlie's perceptions make you think about homelessness differently? Do they make you think about your life differently?

Jen,
Thank you so much
for supporting my book!
You're such a sweet person
& I'm really glad
Denise introduced us.
I think we're due for
another play-date
soon!!
♡ -Tara
Howe ☺

Made in the USA
Lexington, KY
24 April 2013